OTHER-WORLDLY LOVE

"If you will remove your clothing," she said softly, with just the faintest blush beginning to stain her delicate features, "I will put more of this salve on that wound at your waist. It has bled onto your garment."

He caught another whiff of that heavenly perfume she wore. He wanted to kiss the hand on his shoulder. He wanted to draw her around to face him and hold her in his arms and lie with her on the thick, springy moss. "I don't know your name," he said.

"I am Janina Tamat. Let me anoint your wound." She leaned forward and began to apply the creamy stuff to his left side.

Reid's arms closed around her so that her head rested on his chest. He felt her sigh, and shudder a little, and then melt against him. She belonged where she was, in his arms. This lovely, delicate, unknown creature was the other half of himself. They had to join together, had to become one. It was predestined.

Other Leisure Books by Flora Speer:

VENUS RISING
BY HONOR BOUND
MUCH ADO ABOUT LOVE

Destiny's Lovers

FLORA SPEER

LEISURE BOOKS NEW YORK CITY

*For my brother Pat,
my "technical advisor"
on the art of sailing,
with love and thanks
for the help and advice.*

A LEISURE BOOK®

AUGUST 1990

Published by

Dorchester Publishing Co., Inc.
276 Fifth Avenue
New York, NY 10001

Printed in the United States of America.

Destiny's Lovers

CHAPTER 1

The sun was still below the horizon when Janina and Tamat approached the shore. Though the ceremonial road from the village was smooth and level, it was a long walk for the elderly priestess. Janina slowed her steps to ease the strain on the woman who had been her great-grandmother's older sister.

Tamat was in her ninety-eighth year. For more than sixty years she had been known only by her family name and by the designation of High Priestess and Co-Ruler of Ruthlen. Her spine remained unbent by advanced age and she wore her elaborate white-and-gold headdress with easy dignity, yet there was about Tamat an air of fragility. Everyone in Ruthlen knew that Tamat was near to the end of a life devoted to her people and their Chosen Way. Only Tamat did not speak of her approaching death or of what would happen after it.

Except to Janina.

"You are the only one left," she had said three days before this day, "the only descendant of our line. You must succeed me, Janina. You must keep the line unbroken for a little longer."

"How can I?" Janina asked. "If I attempted to take your place, I'd only shame you, and our ancestors. No matter how hard I try, I'm not a telepath and never will be."

"It is possible," Tamat said, "that you do not try hard enough. I have seen you looking at the young men on festival days."

"Do you think I'm reluctant because I'd have to remain a virgin for the rest of my life?" Janina exclaimed with a bitter laugh. "I'll remain a virgin whether I'm a priestess or not, because I lack the one quality necessary to an adequate mating. I'm not a telepath. No man would want me. And the looking you speak of has shown me that there is not a man in all of Ruthlen that I would want."

"Perhaps," Tamat said, "there is something I can do to help, if you are willing to take the risk. You have completed all of the necessary theoretical training. You know how to contain and control the Gift when it is released to you. It only remains locked in your mind. We must open the door of your mind and set it free. There are ways. Trust me, Janina, and I'll see you High Priestess Designate before I die, for I cannot believe that anyone born of my grandmother's blood is not a telepath. Your Gift *must* be released! If it is not, then Sidra will be High Priestess when I am gone, and though she is acceptable in every other way, she fails the first test—she is not a Tamat."

Here, for just a moment, an ancient hand rested gently upon Janina's.

"I am aware, dear child, that Sidra loves you not. If she becomes High Priestess, your life will be an unhappy one."

"I trust you, Tamat." Janina looked directly into her great-great-aunt's silver-blue eyes and wished with her entire heart that she could make contact with all the knowledge contained within Tamat's mind. That was the way a High Priestess was made, by a complete mind-linking with her predecessor. If Tamat said there was a way for her to do that, there *was* a way, and Janina would attempt it. "Tell me what to do."

And so now Janina walked beside Tamat on the ceremonial road to the sea, her body and mind relaxed by the potent herbal mixture Tamat had prepared and made her drink just before leaving the temple. Janina had fasted for the last three days, and had slept not at all during the previous night. She felt neither hunger nor weariness, but only a weightlessness in her body, as though she were too light for her bare feet to touch the ground.

Behind the High Priestess and Janina walked Sidra, Tamat's assistant priestess for more than twenty years. Beside Sidra was Osiyar, the High Priest and Co-Ruler of the village, a blue-eyed, golden-haired man, handsome beyond all belief, who lived deep within himself and loved neither man nor woman. After them came the other priestesses and priests and most of the villagers. Janina could feel the disapproval of the villagers like the cold hand of an enemy against her back.

For as long as she could remember, the people of Ruthlen had looked down upon Janina with disgust, scorning her company and occasionally declaring that she ought to be banished because she was different. She lacked the Gift all the others had, the ability to meet mind with mind. During her childhood, she had often been pelted with stones and spat upon by the other children. In her teens, she had been laughed at and mocked by her contemporaries. Never had her parents tried to stop this treatment, for they felt shamed and humiliated by her lack of a quality everyone else possessed.

Now that she was twenty and a woman grown, the villagers ignored her most of the time. She had no friends and, since the deaths of her parents, no other relatives except for Tamat, who had loved her and accepted her as a scholar priestess when no one else wanted her. But she had repaid Tamat with an inability to do the one thing the kind-hearted woman had ever asked of her. She would probably be unable to do it today, too. Once again she would fail Tamat. Were it not for the euphoria induced by the mixture she had drunk, Janina would have wept before the entire company, disgracing herself and Tamat forever.

They had reached the shore. The procession of villagers and temple folk fanned out into a ragged line two or three deep at the place where the road ended. There they stayed, among the dunes and rough grasses at the edge of the beach.

Janina, Tamat, Sidra, and Osiyar walked across the beach. The steadily growing daylight revealed a wide stretch of fine white sand bounded on both left and right by tall, rocky headlands. The sand was perfectly clean, bearing no trace of marine life or human activity.

Halfway across the beach Tamat stopped, the others pausing with her. The sky was now an opalescent rose with a faint tinge of gold along the horizon. On this day there was no morning mist. Janina wondered if Tamat had commanded it away.

"It is time," Tamat said.

Leaving Tamat standing between Osiyar and Sidra, Janina walked forward to the water's edge. She stood there a moment, feeling the moist sand between her toes. A tiny wave foamed cool salt water around her feet. When the breeze blew her sheer, sleeveless white robe against her slender form and lifted a few strands of silver-gold hair, Janina felt a chill along her upper arms. Another wave swept across her feet, splashing her ankles and the hem of her robe.

The tide had turned and was coming in. The wind was from the sea, the twin moons had set, the sun was about to rise. The moment of testing had arrived.

Janina took a deep breath and lifted her arms. An instant later, the uppermost rim of the sun showed above the edge of the world. Janina cupped her hands, holding them out toward the rising sun, willing the Power to come to her, to fill her hands with light, to unlock itself from the deep recesses of her mind.

Tamat could do it. Janina had seen the aged priestess standing in this same spot with her feet in the sea and glistening light spilling out of her hands into the air around her until Tamat was encased in sparkling silver.

Janina focused all her strength and all her will upon the rising sun. Her eyes swam with tears from the glory of it as the huge, orange-gold disk swelled until it rested exactly upon the horizon.

Now. Janina opened her mind and lifted her arms above her head.

A shadow skimmed across the face of the sun and rested there. Janina ignored the sudden murmuring behind her, for in the shadow she saw a face. As it became more distinct, she realized that it was a man's face, though it was like no man she had ever seen before, dark and ugly, and yet—and yet, known and beloved. Black hair, thick black brows, dark eyes.

"He comes . . . to change everything." Janina's voice was a high-pitched moan, foreign to her own ears. "New people on this world. I can feel them. A man comes. Beloved . . . He will change . . . change . . ."

Sudden blackness enveloped her. She collapsed toward the sea now swirling about her knees and knew nothing more.

CHAPTER 2

Reid was lost. He had become separated from the others as they fought their way through an unnaturally dense forest. At first it had been pleasant to be out of the reach of Herne's sour remarks about their expedition and Alla's constant lectures to him on the plants and trees they were passing.

He raised one hand, drawing his fingers through dark, curly hair, thinking how upset Alla would be if he wasn't there to order around and try to protect. Alla's mother and his had been sisters, Reid and Alla had grown up together, and while she was only two years older than Reid, Alla had always treated him as if she were his mother. She had even joined Tarik's colony when she learned Reid had signed up for it. She was entirely too protective of him. He loved her, but a man needed room to breathe and make his own life.

He wished one of the other women from the colony had come along on this trek instead of Alla, someone with whom he could have bedded down at night for a little uncomplicated entertainment before sleep. Herne wouldn't have minded. Herne didn't care about anything but medicine and complaining.

Where in the star-blasted universe were his companions? Looking about him, it was easy to see how they had disappeared so quickly. There was something mysterious, even eerie, about the thick, silent forest, the warm, humid air, the gently drizzling rain. He couldn't move without brushing against damp leaves, and the foliage muffled sound most effectively.

Soon after the voices of the others had faded, he tried to use his pocket communicator to contact them again, only to discover it wasn't working. That made him angry. He was the communications officer on this expedition. If there were something wrong with his equipment, he should have known about it and made the necessary repairs. But there had been nothing wrong with the communicator until now. Nothing at all.

He pulled the cover off the offending communicator for the third time. He checked it once more, but could find no reason for the malfunction. Slamming the cover back into place, he shouted, but there was no answering call.

"Beloved . . ."

At first he thought it was the leaves rustling, or the buzzing of insects. When he heard the sound again, he peered through the trees, wondering if Alla or Herne might be playing a trick on him, though it would be out of character for either of them.

"Beloved . . ."

"Where are you?" he called, spinning around, then around again, the action causing a miniature rainstorm as moisture showered off every leaf he touched. He was surrounded by green. He had never seen so many shades of one color. The moss at his feet was a rich gold-green, the underbrush pale green which turned paler still when some movement of his revealed the silvery undersides of the leaves. Over his head, green vines looped back and forth between the trees, and far above the vines, the tops of the trees were the deepest green of all. He could not see the sky. It was screened from view by thick layers of leaves.

Even the air was green, soft and moist and scented by a hundred varieties of leaves and by the tiny purple flowers that grew wherever the trees left them room enough.

"Come, beloved . . ."

Oddly, he was not afraid after hearing that tantalizing whisper. Nothing about Dulan's Planet frightened him. He had felt at home on it as soon as his feet touched its soil. That was why he had volunteered to join the exploration team. He was going to spend the rest of his life on this world, so he wanted to know all of it.

He had willingly joined the colonists who set out to establish a secret listening post on Dulan's Planet, to observe any Cetan activity that might be construed as warlike and report it directly to the Leader of the Jurisdiction. The Cetans and the Jurisdiction had only recently signed a peace treaty after space-centuries of war, and Leader Almaric was not completely certain the Cetans could be trusted.

Heading the ten colonists was Almaric's younger son, Tarik, with Tarik's wife, Narisa, as second in command. They had made their headquarters upon an island in a large lake, where there was a shelter built more than six centuries before by a vanished race. Once their communications equipment was working well, they had begun to explore the planet. The first group to set out had chosen the southern area of the continent they had landed on, and had relayed massive amounts of information back to headquarters before returning eight days later.

Reid had volunteered for the second expedition, toward the east. Of course Alla had then said she wanted to go, too, and Herne had grumbled that he might as well go along on this trip, because the third expedition was scheduled to explore the rocky northernmost region of the continent and he hated cold weather and certainly did not want to be assigned to that group.

The three of them had been ferried by shuttlecraft for an entire day across a barren, stony desert before they were set down at the edge of a prairie. They planned to trek to the cliffs which their scanning instruments told them rimmed the sea. When they reached the cliffs, they would signal for pickup by the shuttle.

Two of the Chon had gone with them. The friendly, telepathic birds indigenous to Dulan's Planet were seldom far away from the colonists.

Reid, Alla, and Herne had tramped across the prairie for three days, finding nothing more interesting to report back to headquarters than a wide variety of grasses and small mammals, and a remarkable number of stinging insects.

The forest had been a relief from the unbroken glare of the orange-gold sun, but as they moved into the trees, they lost their winged companions, who apparently did not frequent this part of the planet. Reid missed them. Still, he could understand why they did not come into a forest so impenetrable. Among the closely packed trees and draped vines there would be no space for the large birds to spread their wings and fly. When they were gone he felt a peculiar sense of loss, almost of foreboding, as though the Chon were trying to warn him of something. He mentioned his feeling to the others. They said they had noticed nothing strange.

"Beloved . . ."

Reid stuffed his nonfunctional communicator back into the waist pocket of his high-visibility orange treksuit and looked upward, to see if the owner of the mysterious voice was hiding there, but he could discern nothing except the thick canopy of leaves. He decided there was no point in staying where he was.

"We are supposed to be exploring," he said aloud to the disembodied voice. "I will explore, then. Perhaps I'll find you, or at least find the others." He moved forward.

"You have fostered a prophetess!" Osiyar stared at Tamat across Janina's limp figure. He had snatched her from the surf just in time to keep her from being swept out to sea. She lay across his arms, her long wet hair dragging in the sand, her eyes closed. On her otherwise peaceful face there was the faintest hint of a line between her brows. Whether it was a line of pain, or of bewilderment at what had happened to her, no one could tell. Osiyar kept his eyes fixed upon the High Priestess. "Did you know of this before?"

"I did not know, I only suspected," Tamat replied. "Because she is of my grandmother's blood, some portion of the Gift must be hers. I tried repeatedly to touch it and could not. I thought it was locked within her because she witnessed the horror of her parents' death. But I never dreamed the Test would result in prophecy."

"You should have told me what you planned, dear Tamat." Sidra spoke in a low-pitched voice, sweet as the nectar of the reddest flowers of the khata plant. "I might have helped you. With our minds joined we might have reached her, and there would have been no need for this terrible Test."

"Sidra, you do not love Janina," Tamat replied. "You have always been afraid of her, as most of the village is afraid of her. Now we know why."

"Since she is not a true telepath, she can never be High Priestess," Osiyar said.

"No," Tamat agreed, and with an aching heart she watched the tiny flare of triumph in Sidra's blue eyes.

"Will you banish her?" Osiyar asked.

"Never." Tamat's voice cracked on the word. Banishment meant certain death, for there was nothing beyond the narrow strip of land that was Ruthlen, only empty desolation and danger.

"What will you tell them?" Osiyar inclined his head toward the villagers still waiting at the far edge of the beach.

"The truth," Tamat replied.

"They will kill her with demands that she take the potion again and again so they can know the future," Sidra objected. "Tamat, I may not love Janina, but I do love you, who have been my teacher all my life. I would not see you bowed down with grief at Janina's death, which will happen if she must drink that strong brew too often. Tell the villagers only a part of the truth. Say that she has a portion of the Gift, but it is inadequate to qualify her to be High Priestess. Then let Janina remain with us, as a lesser priestess. She will be well cared for all of her life."

And her Gift well-used by you, Tamat thought. She knew Sidra heart and soul, knew her need for power and her frustrated lust for Osiyar. Once Tamat was dead, Sidra would have no compunction about feeding the potion to Janina so she could use the girl to gain knowledge of the future in order to improve and consolidate her own position. And though Sidra might never break her Sacred Vow to remain a virgin, she would probably find a way to use Osiyar to satisfy her desire for him in some other manner. Tamat suddenly felt the weight of every one of her ninety-eight years crushing her.

"Tamat? Are you ill? I knew the walk was too long for you." Sidra reached out a hand to steady her, but Tamat drew herself up, brushing aside her assistant's concern.

"I am not ill. You are right, Sidra. Janina must remain with us as a lesser priestess. It shall be as you say." Tamat silently promised herself she would think of something else for the future. Tomorrow, after she had rested, she would think of another plan. "Osiyar, can you carry her to the temple?"

"Easily," the priest replied. "She is a small weight."

Tamat turned and began to walk toward the villagers. Behind her back, Sidra and Osiyar shared a long, silent look.

"Beloved, come to me. I need you . . . help me . . ."

Reid jerked himself awake, uncertain if it was

day or night. He had been walking for so long that he had lost all sense of time. He imagined that days must have passed because he was so tired. His food packets were gone. He must have eaten them, which further convinced him he had been in the forest for a long time.

He had given up hope of finding Herne and Alla. Poor Alla was probably frantic with worry over him. He was sorry about that, yet he remained confident they would all be found soon. If he did not send periodic reports back to the headquarters building on the lake, Tarik would begin a search for them. But how could anyone find him in this strangely luxuriant forest when his instruments would not work to guide rescuers to him?

His instruments. Reid felt for his communicator. He found it in the waist pocket where it was supposed to be, but the packet of other communications equipment he usually carried slung over his left shoulder was gone. He could not recall having dropped it. He decided he had most likely removed it the last time he slept, and then had forgotten to pick it up again when he moved on. He turned around, half determined to retrace his steps to try to find it, before he realized that he had no idea which way to go to backtrack. At that moment, he wasn't even certain in which direction he had been going when he had heard the voice. With all the greenery pressing around him, he had no means of orientation. Shaking his head at the dense lushness of trees and undergrowth and hoping to get a better perspective on his location, he stepped backward a couple of paces. He stepped off the ground into empty air.

With well-trained reflexes immediately alert, he caught at a bush to stop his fall. To his horror, the bush began to pull out of the ground. Grunting with the effort it took, he heaved himself upward to catch at another bush. This one was sturdier than the first, with deeper roots. It held while Reid slowly, painfully pulled himself back to solid ground. He lay on his belly, his legs dangling into emptiness, unable to move any further until his heart had stopped its thunderous pounding and he could breathe normally again. Then he pulled himself all the way up, rolled over, and looked down into the abyss into which he had almost fallen.

It was a deep, narrow ravine. The thick foliage had screened it from his view, and he was so tired and confused that he had not noticed the brighter quality of light where the ground suddenly fell away and the trees ended.

He stared across the tops of tall trees to a rock wall on the opposite side which towered so far above him that its uppermost heights were lost in clouds and mist. The only interruption in the solid, gold-brown rock was the narrow veil of white water cascading down its length to lose itself in the green far below. On either side of him, the ravine extended as far as he could see.

"Beloved . . . please . . ."

"Stop tormenting me!" he yelled. "Star-blast

you for a coward—whoever you are, show yourself!"

"Please . . ."

"Leave me alone!" Jumping to his feet, Reid formed his hands into fists, ready to fight the possessor of that ghostly voice, but nothing materialized. "I can't help you if I don't know who or what or where you are. Damnation! Either stand where I can see you or go away!"

The response to this furious outburst was silence. Temporarily relieved of the annoyance of the voice, Reid considered his situation. He knew there had been no ravine on the computer model of this area that he had studied so carefully back at headquarters. Remembering that model, he felt a prickling at the nape of his neck, accompanied by a sense of something eerily wrong, something far beyond his experience. He knew deep in his soul that he had wandered into a place where he should not be.

He thought later that he must have been mad or delirious to be so indifferent to danger or common sense, but the longer he stared at the bare rock escarpment confronting him, the more strongly it beckoned to him. He thought that if he could get down into the ravine, cross it, and somehow climb far enough up the cliff face, he would surely be permanently free of the irritating voice that was either inside his head or whispering into his ear, he couldn't tell which. He believed if he could just get above the smothering leaves, his communicator might work again. If it did, he would be able to contact Alla and Herne, or, failing that, to reach Tarik at headquarters and ask for help.

The first thing he did was to make certain the communicator was securely fastened inside his pocket. Then he grabbed at the dangling end of a long, thick vine, pulling at it until it unwound from the branches of the tree where it had been growing and tumbled to the ground beside him. He wrapped one end of the tough, fibrous vine around the trunk of a sapling. Once convinced that this makeshift rope was secure, he held onto it while he let himself down over the edge of the ravine. He slid almost to the end of the vine, which brought him within reach of a particularly tall tree. Kicking his feet against the rocky side of the ravine to swing himself outward, he reached for the topmost branches.

He was not to have a second chance. When he was at the outermost limit of his swing, the vine tore loose from the sapling. With a loud whoop of dismay, Reid fell into the treetop. Grabbing for anything that might stop his fall, he clutched at leaves, small branches, and round, yellow, sticky fruit. He fell through a tangle of branches, bumping and scraping his hands and face, until he caught a branch strong enough to support his weight. He thought his arms would be pulled out of their sockets by the jerk when he stopped falling, but he held on tightly to that lifesaving branch while around him the debris he had created fell away toward the ground.

Cautiously, Reid edged his way along the

branch to the tree trunk. Having reached it, he clutched it tightly and began to descend, using the branches as though they were the rungs of a ladder.

It was a long way down, and he paused on the lowest level of branches to look around. Here at the bottom of the ravine the still air was misty with moisture. The voice he had heard before was silent, perhaps because the roar of the waterfall was so overwhelming. If he followed that sound, he would come before long to the cliff wall. He dropped to the ground and, ignoring numerous bruises and cuts, began to walk again, pushing his way through ferns almost as tall as he was, slipping now and then on moisture-soaked mosses.

He was frequently distracted by swarms of brilliant blue butterflies or by small red-and-yellow birds with exceedingly long tail feathers. The waterfall blotted out any sounds the birds made. By the time he reached the cliff, Reid's head was reverberating with the noise.

He did not waste time looking for the pool into which the water fell. The sound of it had guided him as he had intended, but he knew he would have to get away from the roaring of that relentless cascade or he would be unable to use his communicator. Turning left, he made his way along the base of the cliff, brushing aside the undergrowth, trampling delicate flowers without thought in his eagerness to find a place where he could climb.

The waterfall was a muted rumbling in the

background before he located what he sought, a section of rock face rough enough to offer foot and hand holds. It offered even more, for as he tilted his head back to look upward, he saw a narrow gap in the rock, a shelf backed by a cleft that looked just big enough for a man to fit into. He could climb to it, use his communicator to call for help, and then take shelter in the cleft until the shuttlecraft arrived.

He began to climb. It was hard work. The sun was high overhead and mercilessly hot. Reid was worn out by the lack of food and sleep, and his hands were already torn and bleeding from his descent into the ravine. Drugged by fatigue, he grew careless. He slipped, scraped his cheek against the rock, and tore two fingernails to the quick. Worse, he tore his treksuit. The strong fabric saved his life when a waist pocket caught on a jutting rock and stopped him from an almost certain fall, but he heard the fabric rip. A moment later, as he scrambled to get better hand and footholds, he heard something bounce against stone, then strike a second time and shatter before falling earthward.

He did not have to check to know what it was. The communicator, his last hope of summoning help, was gone. He clung to the cliff in despair, spread out upon the rocks like some bizarre human sacrifice clad in fluorescent orange. He was too weak by now to curse or weep.

He knew he had only two choices. He could release his grip on the slippery rocks, lean backward just a little, and follow his communicator into the green denseness below and be done with it. Or he could pull himself together, continue to climb, and try to reach the niche he had seen from below. Once there he could rest and think what to do next.

Reid pondered those two choices for long, agonizing moments. The eerie quality of the last few days impressed itself upon him again, along with the recognition of how strange and unnatural it was that he, a man in vigorous, reasonably happy youth, should think with pleasure and relief about dying. He knew something was wrong, something was happening to his mind, yet during those few moments when he clutched at the slippery surface of the cliff, he, who loved life, almost succumbed to the temptation to give up, to end everything. He was so incredibly tired, and it would be so easy . . . so easy . . . The lure was seductive beyond all resistance.

"Beloved."

Just as Reid began to allow the fingers of one hand to loosen their hold on the rock, a familiar soft voice sounded in his ear. Then, softer still, and now a murmuring inside his head, the voice came again. "Beloved . . . come to me . . . I will help . . . come."

Somehow, he knew not how, the choice of living or dying had been made for him, and in some deep recess of his mind he gave thanks to the possessor of that gentle, insistent voice. He did not really want to die, not before he had discovered what lay ahead once he was off that star-blasted cliff and far away from the abnormally dense forest. He wanted to find the owner of the voice that had saved him.

Gathering his last reserves of strength, he began to climb again. He went upward so slowly, so painfully, that when he finally reached the cleft in the rock, he had to crawl into the cool shade and lie down for a while before he fully realized where he was.

He found himself face down on crumbled dead leaves in what was not a niche at all, but a tunnel leading back into the cliff. There was air blowing through it, sending the dead leaves scurrying along the stone floor, a breeze that echoed a woman's whisper.

"Beloved . . . come . . ."

He saw a dim light far ahead. Wearily, Reid dragged himself to his knees and began to crawl deeper into the tunnel.

Janina lay on her bed in her room in the temple, staring at the ceiling and trying to recall what she had just dreamed. She remembered a face, dark and filled with pain, seen for the second time. She had tried to touch him, to tell him not to worry, that she would help him. She thought she had asked him to help her, too, but she could not remember now what she had wanted him to do for her. When she tried to think about it, the dream faded away completely. Her feeling of loss was so strong that she wanted to cry. She told herself her depression was one of the after-effects of Tamat's herbal potion, which had probably also caused her strange dream.

After her Test, she had slept for most of the day. When she wakened near evening, Tamat told her all that had happened and the decision that had been made about her position at the temple. Sidra would rule after Tamat—Sidra who disliked Janina—together with Osiyar, who loved no one. Her life would be in their hands. Janina did not really care about not being High Priestess. She had never wanted that burden. What distressed her was the knowledge that she had failed Tamat.

She told no one, not even Tamat, that she remembered everything. She did not quite know why she kept silence, except for a desire not to hurt Tamat any more than she already had. She knew that a true priestess would not have remembered what happened while she was in a potion-induced trance.

She thought again about the man she had seen. She could not get his unusual face out of her mind. She felt as though she had known that stranger for all of her life, and yet she had never met anyone who looked the least bit like him. No one in Ruthlen had dark, curly hair or a large, slightly hooked nose. Nor had she ever wanted to put her arms around any man who lived in the village or the surrounding farmlands.

Sighing over all the unanswered questions that troubled her, Janina rolled out of her low bed and went to the bathing room to perform her morning ablutions. Then, dressed in the loose, untrimmed white robe of a scholar priestess, she entered Tamat's audience chamber.

Sidra and Osiyar were there before her, both of them facing Tamat. Their words to the elderly High Priestess sounded to Janina like an attack.

"What are we to do about her prophecy?" Osiyar demanded. "We all know it must be true, though we followed your command and did not touch her mind during the Test. We could have helped her, you know. It is allowed."

"You surprise me, Osiyar," Tamat replied with a touch of dry humor in her voice. "I did not know you cared about Janina's welfare. She had to do it alone. It was the only way to make the Test a true one."

"What of this dark man she saw?" Sidra asked, shivering. "Is he a Cetan? Does the prophecy mean they will attack us again?"

"He's not a Cetan," Janina answered her, advancing into the room. Her intent in speaking had been to reassure Tamat, but when Sidra and Osiyar swung toward her with puzzled faces, she realized her error. She wasn't supposed to remember what she had seen. "From what Tamat has described to me of my prophecy, it was not violence I foresaw. Therefore, the man cannot be Cetan."

"Just so." Tamat looked relieved. "We can't know if the man is friend or foe until he comes here."

"But if he will change everything," Sidra insisted, "then we ought to prevent him from coming. We need to strengthen the blanking shield. Let us join our power, Tamat, you and Osiyar and I. We will search for his mind, too. Once we hold him in thrall, we can destroy him or send him elsewhere."

"Later. I will speak with Janina now." Tamat dismissed Sidra and Osiyar with a slight gesture of one hand.

"Dear Janina," Sidra reminded in her khata-sweet voice, "when Tamat has finished with you, remember it is your turn today to visit the pool in the mountain and bring us the Water. I know you won't mind, as you are so fond of the grove." She went out with a smile in Tamat's direction.

"I sometimes wish," Tamat said, "that we were not bound so tightly by the laws our ancestors laid down for telepaths, to control the Gift and preserve the privacy of each person. I would dearly love to steal deep into the minds of those two."

"They would know at once what you were doing," Janina said, more than a little shocked at Tamat's suggestion. Prying into the minds of fellow telepaths was strictly forbidden except in dire emergencies.

"I think that in her heart of hearts," Tamat went on, "Sidra is not so chaste as she would have us believe."

"She would never break her vow," Janina whispered, horrified at the idea.

"She would not," Tamat agreed. "Not since my great-grandmother's day has any priestess willingly surrendered her body to a man. You will recall from your studies that the High Priestess Sanala was soon discovered in her lustful perfidy. When the time came for the Sacred Mind-Linking, she could not hide what she had done, so she was overthrown and set adrift. That was when my great-grandmother's older sister became High Priestess, and the honor has remained in our family ever since."

"Until this day." Janina spoke the last words of the story, knowing them by heart. She had heard the tale many times.

"The honor would have ended with you in any case," Tamat said, making light of a sorrow Janina knew hurt her deeply. "Since your parents left no younger daughter to marry and bear future priestesses, you would have been the last Tamat to hold the position. Sidra will be no worse than many High Priestesses we have had in the last six hundred years.

"My child, are you well today?" Tamat changed the subject abruptly. "The potion you drank can have unpleasant aftereffects, but it was necessary to give it to you."

"I'm so sorry I failed you." Janina's silver-blue eyes were filled with tears. "I wish I could be everything you wanted me to be."

"Hush. I love you no matter what you are, or are not." Tamat's frail hands cupped Janina's face. "You have never failed in love or respect toward me. We cannot change what is. You can still live a safe and useful life here in the temple compound."

They both knew that was true only so long as

Tamat lived. No one could foretell what would happen afterward, under Sidra and Osiyar's rule.

"Go," Tamat said, kissing Janina on the cheek in a rare gesture of affection. "Bring us this day's Water for the rituals."

She looked after the departing girl with a secret, knowing smile.

Reid thought he must be dreaming, or possibly he had gone completely insane. With growing incredulity he had stumbled through the last few space-feet of the smooth-walled tunnel, toward the astonishing vista opening just ahead of him. Now there was moss beneath his feet once more, and trees and bushes growing everywhere, but this was not the overgrown thickness of the forest. This looked like a garden. He knew it could not be a garden, because he was in the middle of the mountain. He could see on every side the sheer gold-brown of solid rock rising upwards for thousands of space-feet until the rock ended and the cloudless, purple-blue sky began.

Some cataclysmic force long ago must have torn the center out of the mountain and allowed this open area to form. He saw a pair of the long-tailed, red-and-yellow birds he had noticed before in the ravine, and thought it was possible that birds had deposited the seeds necessary to make the area look as it did. But there was no easy explanation for what else he saw when he moved forward.

A round pavilion, a small white structure surrounded by columns, sat beside a quiet pool which reflected the building in its limpid surface. The pavilion was a miniature version of the ancient structure Expedition Leaders Tarik and Narisa had discovered on their previous visit to this planet, and which now served as their headquarters.

Reid blinked several times, trying to clear his sight, but the little building stayed where it was. It was an illusion. It had to be.

Abruptly, Reid was aware of something, some *presence*—and he knew he was in a sacred place. He told himself it was ridiculous to feel this way, with a chill running up his spine and his hair standing on end. His training was in science and mathematics, which ought to have made him immune to the kind of superstitious reaction he was experiencing. Yet he knew in some deep inner part of himself that the presence existed. He knew when it—whatever it was—accepted him. He felt giddy with relief and exhaustion.

He staggered across the soft moss, catching at tree trunks to maintain his balance. He nearly fell into the pool, but righted himself and continued his erratic course along the edge of the water until he reached the pavilion. It had three steps all around it, made of polished white stone. The columns were stone, too, as was the domed roof. There was a clear substance set into the center of the dome, to let in the light. The effect of openness and the concentrated light in this peculiar place within the mountain made the building seem to glow against the green background.

Reid's legs gave way. He sat on the topmost step, leaning his back against a column, trying to think. His mind was clearer now, with the unknown presence gone from his consciousness. The pavilion was immaculately clean, the garden—for that was how he thought of it, that was what it must be—was carefully tended. Someone had to do that regularly. Someone intelligent. Possibly someone who would help him find Alla and Herne and help them all get back to headquarters.

But there wasn't supposed to be intelligent life on Dulan's Planet. The telepaths who had once colonized it had all been killed in a Cetan raid six hundred space-years before, except for the Dulan for whom the planet had been named and a few friends, who had escaped to that larger white building on the lake, where they had left a record of their history. Was it possible that others had escaped, too, and, unknown to Dulan, had built this structure?

They would be telepaths. Reid found that idea intriguing. Centuries ago, the Jurisdiction had banished all telepaths, which was why a colony of them had settled on this planet in the Empty Sector, so far away from Jurisdiction territory. Reid had never met a telepath, but he saw no reason why normal humans could not exist on friendly terms with them. It was just such dangerous open-mindedness which had earned him a place in Tarik's expedition to this world.

Reid heard a sound behind his back. He turned, instantly on guard. *Footsteps*. He had not noticed the stone path on the opposite side of the pavilion. It curved away through the trees, toward the gold-brown wall of the mountain. Someone was coming along the pathway. He hesitated only a moment, and only because he was completely unarmed, before he realized that if this was a telepath coming, there was little he could do to defend himself. He stood up, moved to the center of the pavilion, and waited.

CHAPTER 3

Janina was always glad when it was her turn to fetch the Water for the priestess's rituals, and particularly so today. She wanted to get away from the temple complex, to be alone for a while without the responsibility for her usual duties. She would use this precious time to convince herself to accept as gracefully as possible the terrible fact of her failure the day before, and her inevitable fate as a lesser priestess under the rule of Sidra and Osiyar. She did not mind the hot, dusty walk from the village, nor the climb up the pathway which only a priestess might use, to the entrance into the mountainside. She loved the cool, shady quiet of the sacred grove. It was so different from the brilliant sunlight of the village and the everpresent glare from the sea.

It seldom rained in Ruthlen. Fog was not

unknown in the time each year just before cold weather arrived, but the usual condition was sunshine tempered by dry land breezes. Water was supplied by streams flowing from the mountains behind the village. The soil between mountains and sea was fertile and responded well to irrigation; the sea gave up fish and edible vegetation. Famine was unknown.

A few farmers gathering the early harvest glanced up as Janina passed them, the water jar strapped to her back. No one spoke to her. She did not expect it. She was used to being ignored. No one threw stones at her any more, not since Tamat had taken her into the temple, and that was all that mattered to her in her relations with folk who were not priestesses.

Janina went on her way so deep in thought that she scarcely noticed when she finally emerged into the grove inside the mountain. She had taken only two steps along the stone path before she was jolted out of her concentration by the sense that something was different. She felt the man's presence before she saw him. She knew at once who it was.

"You have come," she breathed. "Just as I foresaw."

He was huge and dark and ugly, yet she felt no fear of him at all. He was dear to her; in some strange way he was part of her, though they had never met before except in her brief prophetic trance and in her dream. As she drew nearer, she saw that he was younger than she had imagined. He could not be more than a few years older than she was.

He stood in the exact center of the little pavilion, watching her. He wore a suit the color of the blazing orange-gold sun. He was so magnificent it hurt her eyes to look at him, until she noticed that his suit was torn and dirty. Beneath the stubble of a dark beard his face was scraped raw on one cheek and swollen here and there where insects had bitten him. The hands he held out to her were torn and bleeding and very dirty. And his eyes, which she had not seen clearly before, were a dark and stormy grey, set deep beneath thick black brows.

"Please," he said, "I'm lost. I need to contact headquarters. There are two others, friends of mine, back there somewhere in the forest." He made a gesture, vaguely indicating the area behind him.

"You are not a god," she said, her heart swelling with joy at his presence. "A god would not be dirty and tired."

"It was you."

Her accent was strange. She spoke in a space-centuries-old dialect of the standard Jurisdiction language, yet Reid had no trouble understanding her or recognizing her voice. Tense grey eyes met gentle silver-blue ones, met and held while between them passed a spark of recognition beyond any ordinary meeting.

"You spoke to me before," he mused, half to himself. "It was your voice I heard. You called me 'beloved.' You saved my life. I—whoever you are, thank you." In that moment he knew deep gratitude combined with wonder and a sense of delight that he had been spared to meet her.

"I knew you would come," she said, then, "Reid. Your name is Reid. How odd that I only know it now, not before. Perhaps I had to see you to know it."

Reid hadn't the faintest idea what she was talking about, but it didn't matter. She was the most exquisite creature he had ever seen. She was small and slender, her figure perfectly proportioned. Straight, silver-gold hair flowed across her shoulders and down her back to below her waist. Her silver-blue eyes were the shade of the morning mist over the sea, touched here and there with flecks of pale, delicate purple. Her nose was straight and short, her skin had a faint golden sheen to it as though it was flushed by the sun, and her soft mouth was like a sweet, rosy flower.

Reid felt like an alien brute beside her. His tall, hard-muscled figure loomed over her shorter form. He thought sadly that one so delicately made, so clean and fresh, must find him repulsive. He ran a hand across his face, trying to remember the last time he had taken a pill to keep his beard from growing, or the date of his last bath. He winced when he reached the scrape on his right cheek.

"You are injured," the lovely apparition said. "If you will sit down so I can reach your face, I'll clean your cheek and put a salve on it. Over there, on the moss, away from the pavilion."

Reid thought his legs probably wouldn't hold him up much longer anyway. He went where she told him to go. He stood swaying awkwardly, watching as she lifted one of the stones in the floor of the pavilion and took out a box.

"Sit down, please," she ordered again, opening the box to remove something from it. He dropped to the moss a few space-feet away from the edge of the pool.

She was on her knees beside him, her slender, rosy-tipped fingers annointing his injured cheek with a creamy ointment she scooped out of a translucent blue container. She smelled wonderful, like all the flowers of the universe mingled into one perfume. Her skin was flawless, her hair like liquid silver. The soft pink tip of her tongue protruded just a little, caught between white teeth while she concentrated on what she was doing. She appeared to be totally unaware of the effect she was having on him.

Reid felt a wave of warmth suffuse his tired body, re-energizing him. It was not lust, nor even lust's sweeter, gentler cousin, desire, but something more, something richer and deeper. There was an eternal quality pervading his feelings toward the young woman kneeling next to him, though he did not know how he could react in such a way toward a complete stranger. And yet, she was no stranger to him at all. He felt as if he had always known her.

She finished with his cheek. She looked into his eyes, smiling, and Reid was lost, body and soul, heart and mind.

"If you will remove your clothing," she said softly, with just the faintest blush beginning to stain her delicate features, "I will put more of this salve on that wound at your waist. It has bled onto your garment."

"I hadn't noticed." He paused with one hand on the pressure-sensitive opening of his treksuit, the strangeness of his situation threatening to overwhelm him. He sensed again that there was a mysterious, more-than-human presence in the hidden garden. For all he knew, his lovely companion might be that presence. With an effort, he rejected that idea. He desperately wanted the silver-haired woman to be as human as he was. Attempting to reduce an unexplainable experience to what he could see or hear or touch, he decided that the best way to deal with circumstances he could not understand was by concentrating on practical matters. That included physical comfort. "What I really need, before any more medical treatment, is a bath. Is it permitted to use the pool?"

"No. The pool is sacred." She solved his problem quickly, however, and the crease that had appeared between her brows smoothed away. "There is another spring, near the entrance to the grove, which we use to cleanse ourselves and the water jars before taking the Water from the pool. I can bring you some of that. Have you touched the Water in the pool?"

The frown was back, just for an instant, but it disappeared at his honest answer.

"I only arrived here a few moments before you appeared. I did not touch the pool. All I did was walk across the moss and sit on the pavilion steps. I hope that's not forbidden?"

"It can be forgiven, as can your presence here, since you were in obvious need of help." There was a twinkle in the depths of her soft, pale eyes. "I often sit on the steps myself. It's a good place to think. How did you find the grove?"

As he explained, he kept his eyes on her, partly because he feared she would vanish if he looked away, partly because looking at her gave him such pleasure.

"How brave you are," she whispered, then added, "I have always been told there is no one living in the world on the other side of the ravine."

"That is no longer true," he told her. "There are ten of us. Or, rather, there were ten of us. I'm not sure Alla and Herne are still alive." He stopped, thinking about the possibility of Alla's death, and of Herne's. He hoped it wasn't so. He hoped they had been found and rescued by now. As for himself . . .

"Where are so many strangers living?" she asked in amazement, interrupting his thoughts.

"Except for the two who were with me, my friends are at least a quarter of this world away from here," Reid replied.

"How fortunate you are to have friends."

Reid gazed at her lovely face, thinking that

those she lived with had no judgment at all if she were friendless.

"We never go across the ravine," she told him. "We only go into it occasionally to gather special plants to use for medicines. Like this." She indicated the blue salve container she still held, then set it into the box beside other containers in several shapes and colors.

"I'll get your bath water while you undress." She picked up the water jar and walked away down the curving stone path, leaving Reid to strip off his boots and treksuit in privacy.

When she returned he stood barefoot on the moss, wearing only his skimpy, skin-tight lower undergarment. She set down the full water jar and pulled a clean cloth and a square green container out of the box that held the ointment.

"Use this," she said. "I must pour out the water for you, to make certain it flows away from the pool and not into it. We may not contaminate the pool."

The green container, made of polished stone with a hinged lid, held a semi-liquid cleansing agent, and the water from the jar was warm. Reid decided he didn't care if she was watching him or not; he wanted and needed a bath.

"Are there hot springs here?" he asked, lathering his shoulders and arms.

"Yes," she replied, busying herself with rearranging the contents of the box and not looking at his nearly naked body. "Sometimes the mountains smoke. Tamat says it is all part of the same system, which gives us fertile land and clear streams with all the water we want. Only this mountain does not smoke. Its heart is open to us, and the sacred pool is here."

"Volcanoes," Reid said, scrubbing his legs. "This one probably blew out its core centuries ago." He paused to look at her again, wondering why they were carrying on this geological discussion when he wanted to know everything about her.

"I do not understand 'volcanoes,'" she told him. "I only know what our High Priestess Tamat has told me—that once, long ago, the mountains spread fire and destruction across Ruthlen, but they have slept for many years now. Never in living memory have they caused devastation. They are the guardians of our good fortune. So long as we live in harmony with them, the mountains will not fail us."

Reid nodded, only half listening to this retelling of what he assumed was a local legend. Most of his attention was on the young woman's beautiful face.

"If you will kneel once more," she said, "I will wash your back. There are pieces of leaves and other more unpleasant things stuck on it, and it is scratched in places."

Reid went down on his knees. She took the cloth and the cleanser from him and began to rub at his back, resting one hand on his shoulder as she leaned forward. He caught another whiff of that heavenly perfume she wore. He wanted to kiss the hand on his shoulder. He wanted to draw her around to face him and hold her in his arms and lie with her on the thick, springy moss.

Suddenly he remembered that she must be a telepath. She probably knew what he was thinking. She had known his name. But she had asked questions of him as though she was unaware of anything outside her own small portion of Dulan's Planet. If she were a telepath she should have known without asking—unless she was trying to trick him for some purpose of her own. Reid thought about that while she finished with his back, then washed his neck and ears and lathered his hair.

"How dark you are," she murmured. "How large and strong."

That soft voice, those caressing hands, were too much for any man to bear. Reid felt himself becoming aroused. He also felt great embarrassment about it. She must know. She must be playing with him.

"Stay where you are and I'll get more water to rinse you," she commanded. He remained on his knees until she returned, afraid that if he stood she would see what he could not control.

She upended the water jar over his head. The contents of this second jar were icy cold. With a shout, Reid stood, shaking off the deluge. She calmly handed him a small, dry cloth, only adequate to mop his face and stop the worst of the runoff from his hair.

She took up the blue salve container again and moved away from him to sit on dryer ground a little farther along the perimeter of the pool, beside a bush heavily abloom with large, six-petaled red flowers. Reid dried himself as best he could, then joined her, sitting on the moss beside her. The crimson blossoms emitted a sweet scent that in his exhausted and unfed state made him feel dizzy. Or perhaps it was just the presence of a lovely young woman that affected him.

"I don't know your name," he said.

"I am Janina Tamat. Let me anoint your wound." She leaned forward and began to apply the creamy stuff to his left side.

Reid's arms closed around her so that her head rested on his chest. He felt her sigh, and shudder a little, and then melt against him. She belonged where she was, in his arms. Reid knew it with an absolute certainty that shook him to the depths of his being. This lovely, delicate, unknown creature was the other half of himself. They had to join together, had to become one. It was predestined.

"Janina," he murmured, his mouth on her hair. He lay back against the moss, still holding her. The red flowers drooped above them, the languorous effect of their fragrance relaxing and arousing him at the same time. She lifted her head to look down at him, her pale hair spilling across her shoulders and his bare chest.

"Reid, I must tell you something important," she began, the frown line reappearing between her brows.

"Later," he whispered harshly, pulling her face down to his. Later she could tell him she was a telepath who knew everything he was thinking, who understood why suddenly he was burning with a molten fire that could only be quenched by her pale coolness. She had beguiled and enticed him, washing him, tending to his wounds, tempting him as she did so, and all because she knew, as he did, that they were fated to come together like this, in this beautiful grove. When their lips met, a white-hot passion erupted in him, beyond control, beyond anything he had ever felt before.

Janina moaned as Reid's mouth touched hers. She knew she should not allow this to happen. She was forbidden to men. But—oh, his mouth was warm, and sweet, and tender. Just for a moment she would let herself feel what it was like to be held and kissed by a man. Only for a moment, perhaps two. After that, she would tell him he must stop.

But the kiss went on and on, and his arms tightened around her even more, and she knew she did not want him to stop. She wanted to stay in his arms forever. For all eternity.

Reid rolled over, pining her beneath him on the moss. She felt his weight pressing down on her, from his broad, heavily muscled chest crushing her young breasts, to his strong arms across her back, to his long, taut legs which held her own firmly between them. She could feel the wonderful hardness of him pushing at her, burning through her robe. How marvelous, how incredibly beautiful it was. How absolutely right.

His mouth moved against hers, encouraging

her to open her lips. When she did, his tongue slid into her mouth, found her tongue, and began to play with it, teasing her into a pulsating panic of new awareness.

His hands were on her small, firm breasts, caressing the sensitive mounds until they ached. And still his tongue, still his lips, drove her wild, until he left her mouth and began kissing her throat, pushing the wide neck of her robe aside, trying to reach her bare breasts beneath it. The neckline wasn't quite wide enough, so he lowered one hand to lift the hem of her robe.

"Take this off," he urged. "Please, Janina."

She sat up to do his bidding, turning her head aside as she moved, so she could catch her breath. Thus she breathed deeply of air not scented by the red khâta flowers, and her whirling senses cleared enough for her to remember who and what she was. She looked at the man reclining beside her and thought her heart would break.

He pulled her robe upward, trying to help her remove it, his hand caressing along her leg to the inside of her thigh. Janina put her hand on top of his, stopping him.

"Reid, I understand what you want, but I cannot do it," she said. "I am a priestess sworn to eternal virginity."

Something beautiful and precious went out of his expression. His face hardened. The look in his grey eyes was terrifying. She thought he might strike her, or throw her back onto the ground and take what he wanted by force.

"I'm sorry," she said. Innocently trying to comfort him, she put out one hand to touch the rigid manhood straining upward beneath his undergarment. "I tried to tell you before you kissed me the first time."

"No!" He pushed aside her hand. With sudden explosive energy, he sprang to his feet and raced to the edge of the pool where he stood with his back toward her, breathing hard. Around them the sound of his angry cry echoed and re-echoed against the rock walls of the grove.

"At first I did not understand what we were doing, because no man has ever kissed me, or touched me in that way. I have always been kept apart from men," Janina explained, thinking she knew how he must feel, because she had not wanted to stop, either. She had felt an emotion while in his embrace, an opening to a kindred spirit, which she had never experienced with anyone else, not even when Tamat occasionally touched her thoughts. What she felt for Reid was so strong, and so important, that it had immediately broken down any barriers of strangeness between them. But her emotions could not overcome the boundary set about her by her sacred vows. She had to make him understand that. If the look on his face when she ended his lovemaking was any indication of his feelings, understanding would be difficult for him.

"It is forbidden to touch a priestess in that way," she said quietly. "I should have stopped you at once, I know, but it was so lovely. Your mouth was so sweet. I wish I could do what you want. I ache because I cannot. Now that you have held me in your arms I think I will ache for you all of my life. But I cannot break my vows. Please try to understand. Please don't hate me."

"I cannot rape a priestess of any religion. I will not touch you again." The words were hard and cold, like stones from an icy stream. He turned to face her suddenly, and she saw that passion had not gone from him completely, though it was controlled now. "What I do not understand is why you chose to torment me in this way. As a telepath you must have known everything I was feeling, how much I wanted you, and believed it was meant to be. You encouraged me. You made a fool of me."

She was on her feet now, too, to face him bravely, though she was much smaller than he was and trembled at the thought of his anger unleashed against her.

"I am not a telepath," she said. "The others are, but I am not."

"What?" He looked hard at her, all passion gone. He was cold and tough, as he must ordinarily be, and she believed he was searching her face for evidence that she was lying.

"I am not a telepath, which is why at my advanced age I remain only a scholar priestess in a simple robe," she informed him.

"But even so, you are still sworn to virginity." He said it as though it rankled him, and no doubt it did, after the last hour. Janina realized that she had hurt him badly, and, as he had complained, she had made him feel like a fool.

"All priestesses take the same vows," she said in a gentle voice, so she would not anger him further.

"I don't see any point to that." He sounded sullen, his anger unappeased by her explanations.

"It is so the priestesses will be free to dedicate themselves to their work without the distraction of emotional entanglements with men," she told him.

"Exactly what is your work, Janina?"

Still that sullen tone. She did not blame him for it. She answered the rude question politely, though she oversimplified the facts.

"We lead the people of Ruthlen in their worship of the lifegiving sun and the twin moons. We keep the yearly records so the farmers will know when to plant and when to harvest their crops before the heavy frosts come. We advise the fisherfolk about the phases of the moons and warn them when dangerous tides are due. We search the skies day and night, continually standing guard in case the Cetans come again to plunder and kill."

"Cetans?" He frowned and took a step toward her. "When were Cetans last here?"

"Six hundred years ago," she replied promptly and saw him relax at her answer. "We lived elsewhere then. The Cetans destroyed our original city and killed or enslaved all but a few of our ancestors, who later fled to safety here, far away from the old settlement."

"I see." She was fully aware of how carefully

he watched her as he put his next question. "The others are all telepaths?"

"I said so," she told him sadly. "I am the only one who lacks the Gift."

"Then how did you know my name?"

"I foresaw your coming," she said, apparently stunning him with the simplicity of her answer. "I saw your face."

She thought at first that he did not believe her, but then he nodded and asked, "Will you take me to the others?"

"Let me draw the Water first, and you may return to the temple with me," she promised. "Reid, please don't tell anyone what we did here."

"You needn't worry about that," he said. "I won't say a word. No man likes to be played with and then tossed aside."

"I suppose no woman does, either," she remarked coolly, stung by his words, and went to wash out the water jar before filling it with Water from the pool.

"Won't they all know anyway?" Reid asked, watching her strap the brimming jar into a harness and settle it on her back. He did not offer to help, not wanting to touch her and chance awakening feelings he ought not to have.

"There are laws governing use of the Gift," she said, starting down the stone path. "No one will invade your mind without your permission. Only Tamat is permitted free access. She does not use it often. She is old, so the strain of accepting another person's thoughts and emotions is exhausting to her. Step carefully here until your eyes grow accustomed to the dark."

They entered a tunnel similar to the one Reid had used to find the grove, except this tunnel slanted downward and had steps carved into it at several spots along the way. It seemed to him that they walked a long distance before they came out onto a stone terrace located halfway up the mountainside. He stood blinking in the blindingly bright sunshine, letting his eyes adjust to it. Janina waited patiently while he looked around.

"What in the name of all the stars—?" Reid exclaimed. "There is nothing even remotely like this on our computer model of the continent. Where are we?"

"This is Ruthlen," Janina replied.

"It shouldn't be here," Reid insisted. "It *can't* be here."

But it was, and it was perfectly real. A curved range of six mountains isolated the crescent-shaped lowland from the interior of the continent. As Janina had told him, five of the mountains bore wisps of smoke or steam clouds at their peaks, evidence of volcanic activity. From the mountains to the edge of the sea, the narrow area of inhabited land sloped sharply downward. Most of it was divided into terraced fields which were dotted here and there with farmhouses. It was near the end of the growing season, so the fields were gold with grain, or in some places, a rusty orange shade. Thanks to Alla's constant lectures, Reid recognized the rusty color as one of the most ancient of grains, Demarian oats. He could see men working among the crops, their backs bent to a rich harvest.

The village, so small a place it was hardly worthy of the name, was nestled into the northern point of the crescent, in a location well protected from winter gales. Tiny, thatch-roofed houses in soft shades of blue, yellow, or pale orange clustered together along two streets that crossed at right angles. Reid saw boats moored against a wharf which extended far out into the sea. He wondered at the length of it before he recalled the twin moons and realized that because of their gravitational pull, the tides on Dulan's Planet varied widely, and a boat tied up near shore at high tide could be stranded on land during low tide.

"Where do you live?" he asked Janina.

"In the temple complex." She pointed, and Reid stared.

It was so different from the rest of the village. It stood just to the north of the houses, on a flat space that he was certain had been carved out of the solid rock. The complex was round, with a low, white stone wall along the perimeter and the temple itself in the center. The shape and style of the temple duplicated both the little pavilion in the grove and the building which was now Commander Tarik's headquarters. It had twelve pillars forming a colonade around its outside, and a domed roof set with translucent material to gather light for the interior. Six smaller buildings of identical design were spaced at intervals around the main building. All were white.

One of the village streets ran past the single entrance to the temple, then continued onward, suddenly becoming a wide, stone-paved road. A little beyond the temple complex, a high outcropping of rocks formed a wall extending into the sea. The road curved around the landward side of the rocks and disappeared.

Reid saw that Janina, apparently thinking he had looked long enough, had begun to descend the steps cut into the mountainside. He followed her, marveling that his feelings toward her were continually changing. Once they were well away from the unknown presence in the garden and the scent of those star-blasted red flowers, he had recovered his wits, and his clamorous, uncontrollable desire for her had subsided enough to allow him to wonder what in the name of all the stars he had been doing, trying to ravish an unknown girl.

He cast a quick glance at her, walking beside him in quiet calmness. She was lovely, but he had known beautiful women who left him untouched emotionally. Why had he felt such certainty that he and Janina were meant to be together? He had felt that way even before he had gotten close to those red flowers. What was happening to him? Was it some cruel telepath's trick, to make him feel this deep bonding to a virgin priestess, a woman he could never have?

He did not know the answers to those questions, but he thought he would be well out of a very peculiar situation if he could convince Janina's people to help him get back to headquarters at once. Perhaps, if he were far away from her, he could forget her and begin to feel free again. He quickened his steps. He was eager to meet this Tamat of whom Janina had spoken. He had quite a few questions for her.

CHAPTER 4

To get to the temple, Reid and Janina had to take the road into the center of the village, then turn left on the street leading northward out of it. But first they had to pass the terraced, stone-walled fields. A farmer looked up at them, dropped the armload of grain he had been tying into sheaves, and ran after them, calling loudly to his neighbors to come along.

"A stranger!" he yelled. "A giant has been in the sacred grove—and with a priestess, too."

"What is he saying?" Reid demanded. "I only understood part of it. Have I committed some sin by setting foot in the grove?"

"It doesn't matter what they think," responded Janina. "Anyone or anything that is different is a scandal to them. Tamat will silence them quickly enough."

Reid gave her a sharp look but said nothing more.

By the time they reached the village, at least a dozen people had left their work in the fields to trail after Reid and Janina—men, women, and a few children. The villagers joined the parade, murmuring their surprise at the sight of a newcomer, and their horror at where he had been. When Reid saw two boys sprinting ahead of them, he knew the High Priestess would promptly be informed of his arrival.

As an outsider coming into an isolated community, he had expected to be the object of much curiosity, and possibly of hostility. What he had not expected was his own sense of amazement. He thought he must appear to them as a dark, hairy, frightening alien, for these people were all alike. Everyone he saw was small in stature. Even the men seemed to be at least six space-inches shorter than he was, and they all had blond hair and blue eyes. There were minor variations. Janina's silver-gold hair was the lightest, but the darker shades ranged only to a soft golden brown. The eyes, now fixed upon him in astonishment and outrage, varied from the palest silver-blue to a deep shade that almost matched the sky. He saw a few heavy-set, middle-aged men, but most of the people were slender.

In his mind, Janina stood out from them all. Her hair was the palest, her eyes were the softest, and her quiet, dignified bearing amid the growing clamor set her apart from farmers and villagers alike. She answered none of the rude questions now being called out to her, but walked silently through the village and turned onto the road toward the temple. When the crowd began to jostle both of them, Reid moved closer to her, in case she should need protection.

"He's a Cetan!" someone cried in a voice full of fear.

"Or a Jurisdiction officer!" screamed someone else with no less concern.

"He has desecrated the grove and the Water!"

"And the priestess!"

"She's not really a priestess. Without the Gift, she's not one of us. She's only allowed in the temple because of Tamat. She ought to have been banished years ago. Just wait until Sidra becomes High Priestess. Janina won't last long then."

A stone hit Reid between his shoulders. He whirled around to search for the thrower, and the tormentors nearest him fell back a little.

Janina had not paused in her steady steps. Reid hurried to catch up with her. He could feel the villagers closing in behind them once more.

"Can't you walk faster?" he said, not because he was afraid but because he was suddenly concerned for her safety. He did not want to see her harmed.

"It wouldn't help," she replied calmly. "If we try to run away, they will overpower us and it will be worse. They might hurt you badly." Without breaking stride she gave Reid a quick look from mist-blue eyes. "Ignore them. We will be inside the temple complex soon. Tamat will send them away."

After they had left the village behind them and were approaching the graceful temple, the hostile crowd trailing them fell silent, drawing back a little. Reid thought perhaps they were in awe of the man who stood at the opening in the low wall surrounding the temple complex.

The man was robed in darkest blue trimmed in silver, and he was the most handsome man Reid had ever seen. He was almost as tall as Reid and looked like some magnificent mutant among the shorter villagers. His jaw was square and his nose was perfect. Smooth, golden hair hung to just below his ears. Sparkling, sea-blue eyes looked directly into Reid's with cool assurance. On his brow, just above his eyes, the man bore a tattoo, a large blue dot between two blue crescents. Reid learned later that these signs represented the sun and the two moons. Along with the knotted, rope-shaped gold bracelets on each wrist, the tattoos were the identifying marks of those bound into full priesthood.

"This is Osiyar, our High Priest and Co-Ruler," Janina informed Reid, in a voice that told him she held the man in either reverence or fear. To the handsome man she said, "He was awaiting me in the pavilion. His name is Reid, and he is the man I saw in my Test. I thought it best to bring him here at once."

"I'm not certain that was wise." Osiyar looked past Reid, to the people still hovering nearby, who were obviously angry and frightened. Osiyar raised his voice to address them. "There is nothing to fear. The man is not a Cetan, nor are there Cetans coming to attack us. Tamat will examine him and will tell you later what will be done with him. Return to your homes until Tamat calls you together."

With numerous curious looks in Reid's direction, the crowd meekly dispersed. Osiyar spoke to Reid again.

"Come with me," he said.

Reid was struck by the deep coldness of the man. Osiyar had offered no word of greeting, much less of welcome or even curiosity, and his manner toward Janina was that of a person far superior to her. To his dismay, Janina left them as they reached the temple, hurrying along the colonnade and out of sight before Reid could call her back. Osiyar waited by the huge twin doors, watching him with cool eyes. Reid followed him inside.

It was just like the headquarters building at the lake, with an inner colonnade, twelve rooms arranged around the perimeter, and a large round central room. Unlike the other building, however, this central room held no computer. It was empty except for two women, but the strength and power of the older woman seemed to fill all the space. She was ancient, and so frail that she ought to have been laid low by the weight of her gold-and-white disk and crescent headdress. Her robe was white with gold designs on it of stars and fantastic symbols which Reid could not interpret. Blue eyes the exact shade of Janina's looked him up and down.

The other, younger woman was stunningly beautiful, with golden hair and a mature, well-rounded body. She wore pale blue trimmed in silver. Reid saw her eyes fix first upon Osiyar's handsome face before moving to his own face, then back to Osiyar again, as though looking for some clue from him.

Osiyar had just presented him to the priestesses when, to Reid's great relief, Janina reappeared, without the water jar.

"You are late," Sidra told her harshly. "You have delayed the midday ritual by your dallying."

"Never mind," Tamat said in a patient voice. "Janina has an excuse for keeping us waiting."

Then, at Tamat's order, Janina described how she had found Reid, while he wondered again that telepaths should use speech to communicate when there was no need.

"And there were others with you?" Tamat asked Reid.

"I don't know if they are dead or alive," he replied. "We mean you no harm, priestess, nor will we interfere in your lives in any way. The purpose of our small settlement on this planet is to watch the movements of Cetan warships and report them to the Jurisdiction. We would be happy to inform you of any possible danger to you from the Cetans."

"The Jurisdiction has banished all telepaths," Sidra said, her lovely face cold.

"Commander Tarik has a kinder view of those

who differ from Jurisdiction norms," Reid responded. Then, deciding there would be no better time, he made his important request of Tamat. "Priestess, I have lost my communicating equipment, so I have no way to contact my friends. Would you use your telepathic powers to reach our headquarters? I believe you would find Tarik open to such a message."

Sidra's indrawn breath sounded like the long hiss of a beautiful, dangerous reptile.

"How dare you?" she whispered. "The Gift may not be used for trivial matters."

"I have lost a cousin and a friend out there in the forest," Reid declared. "I want to help them. Tarik will send others to try to find us, and they may fall into danger, too. The safety of intelligent life forms is not a trivial matter."

"Well said." It was Tamat who answered him.

Reid had looked at Sidra as he spoke to her, but now he turned his attention back to Tamat. Their eyes met and held, and Reid felt the oddest sensation. It was as though gentle, invisible tentacles entered and caressed his mind, pressed delicately, and then withdrew.

Reid's jaw fell open. It had been so easy, so effortless, yet he was certain Tamat now knew all that was in his mind at the instant she had touched it. He knew something else, too. She had wanted him to be aware of what she was doing. If she had not wanted it, he never would have known.

Everything in his mind. That meant Tamat knew how intensely aware he was of Janina, now standing quietly beside Sidra, and she knew what they had almost done in the grove. He thought he saw astonishment, anger, and then understanding in Tamat's eyes, though the aged face did not change expression.

"He speaks true," Tamat said.

"Then you will help me?" Reid asked, so relieved he almost forgot his embarrassment about Janina, as well as his concern that his mind had been entered and explored so easily. "You will contact Commander Tarik and tell him where I am and about Herne and Alla?"

"I will consider it," Tamat replied.

"While you are considering, my companions may die." Reid reacted to Tamat's measured tones with impatience. "They need help now."

"You must understand," Tamat said, "that the safety and security of my people is my primary concern. I will try to devise a means of warning your Commander Tarik about your lost friends without divulging the presence of our village. But you, Reid, cannot be allowed to leave Ruthlen to report our location, to bring other outsiders here."

"I wouldn't do that," Reid began, but Osiyar interrupted him.

"You could not avoid it. You would have to explain where you were, and inevitably your friends would learn about the blanking shield," the priest said. "Tamat, will you allow him to live, or will you order him set adrift?"

"He will live, for now," she replied after a moment's deliberation. When both Osiyar and

Sidra looked ready to protest this decision, Tamat continued, "Think how useful he could be to us. Think of the knowledge his mind contains about the universe beyond Ruthlen. But Reid has something more important even than knowledge. He appears to be perfectly healthy, despite the ordeal of defeating the full force of our blanking shield in the forest and the ravine. In fact, he is filled with amazing vitality. A man so strong, a man brave enough to face unknown telepaths and keep his wits with him must be made of superior genetic material. After so many centuries of isolation, we here in the village are all too similar. Our gene pool has grown weak. It needs an infusion from an outsider.

"Yes," she went on, nodding to herself, "we will allow Reid to live, and in return he will lend himself to us. Reid will stay in the temple complex until he has learned our ways. Then, on the festival nights of the full moons and dark moons, he will mate with whichever women choose him."

"He is not a telepath. It will never be a true mating," Sidra objected before anyone else could say anything. "He will dilute the telepathic abilities of any children he begets."

"Consider Janina's situation and know that what you suggest is by no means certain," Tamat returned. "Janina's parents were both true telepaths, yet she is not. Therefore, it appears that variations in this inherited trait can occur. I believe it is possible that a non-telepath, mated to a telepath, can produce a child who is a true telepath. I am surprised you do not agree with me, Sidra. We have discussed this problem often enough—how sickly many of our people are, how they are born with defects that kill them at an early age. We know well the reason. It is because the same small group has interbred for centuries. Let us try this experiment. It cannot leave us in worse condition than we already are. It may help us."

"As you wish, Tamat." Sidra bowed her head in acquiescence.

"I have an obvious objection to this plan, and I'm surprised you haven't thought of it," Reid said, knowing he need not voice his true thoughts, for Tamat surely knew how he felt about Janina. He wanted to declare publicly that he would mate with no woman except Janina. He did not, because, recalling that she was sworn a virgin priestess, he feared that such a declaration would place her in jeopardy. Instead, he tried to make Tamat change her plans for him by raising a practical question. "Won't the men of the village be angry about the arrangement you propose, and resent me because I can make free with their womenfolk? Wouldn't that anger rebound upon you and the other priests and priestesses and thus create problems between temple and village?"

"Not at all," Tamat replied with smooth confidence. "The men are accustomed to sharing their women, and the women to sharing their men. The number of births among us is low, and freedom between men and women is one way to increase our population. Only a few couples prefer to keep exclusively to each other, and all of them live on farms well outside the village. Oddly enough, they usually produce four or five children, some of whom later come to live in the village, so we do not insist that those couples share themselves with others. Therefore, you will be required to lend yourself only to women of the village. You need not worry about angering anyone but me, Reid.

"Osiyar, I will see him housed with you," Tamat went on. "You are the one who has the most contact with the villagers. Begin by teaching Reid their ways. We will also accustom the villagers to his presence. By the time the moons are both full again, by the night of the next festival, there should be at least one or two women who will choose him, if only for the novelty he represents. If he is successful in impregnating them, there will be other willing women at later festivals."

It was then that Reid heard a sound from the previously silent Janina, just the beginning of a quickly smothered sob. Looking at her frozen face, gazing into her mist-blue eyes, he saw pain and knew with a stab of mingled guilt and joy that she was not indifferent to him even though she had refused his love-making. And he also knew that she believed there was nothing she, or he, could do to prevent the fate Tamat had just decreed for him.

* * *

In late evening, Osiyar joined Tamat in her small audience chamber for their daily discussion of events in Ruthlen. As always, no one else was present, not even Sidra.

"There is only one thing to talk about tonight," Osiyar observed, seating himself next to her, "and that is Reid. The man has an incredibly strong will to live if the urge to destroy himself could not overcome him in the forest or while he was ascending the cliff. That is our last defense against anyone who tries to penetrate the shield to enter Ruthlen. Reid should be dead by now, would be dead were he any other man. Which makes me wonder, Tamat—did you bring him here deliberately?"

"No," Tamat replied. "I was informed by Philian, who was on duty then maintaining the shield, that a man had entered the outermost defenses. I am as surprised as you are that he succeeded in reaching us, but now that he is here, it is only sensible to make use of him instead of destroying him."

"For the present," Osiyar agreed, watching her face closely for any change of expression. "And in the future?"

"Ah, who can foretell the future?" said Tamat with an odd inflection to her voice.

"Under certain circumstances, Janina can," Osiyar replied quietly, his eyes still on Tamat's face. If he saw anything there to indicate what Tamat's deepest thoughts might be, he gave no sign. After a pause he spoke again. "I would not disagree with you when anyone else was present, but Sidra's objection to allowing Reid to mate with the village women is a sound one. I can only conclude that you have some well-founded but unrevealed reason for your decision to use him in such a way."

"Osiyar, you have shared my growing despair at the decline in our population, and at the inherited ill health of so many of our people. You know my fear that within another generation or two, Ruthlen may cease to exist, for few will remain alive." Suddenly Tamat's eyes were shining with excitement. Her voice became that of a much younger woman, a woman with renewed purpose to her life. "Dear friend, share now my joy at the new hope we have been given, for Reid could well prove to be our salvation. I searched his mind thoroughly, and he has a portion of the Gift. He has never been trained, of course, having spent his life in the Jurisdiction where use of the Gift is strictly forbidden. He could not control his ability should it be set free in him, so we must take care never to rouse it, or he would go mad and be useless to us. But his children can inherit the Gift from him as well as from their mothers. Reid brings us not only new genetic material, but a fresh infusion of telepathic strength. He is exactly what Ruthlen needs."

"I knew you had some deeper purpose." Leaning back in his chair, Osiyar regarded her with respect and affection. "I am also certain you have some other plan for Reid besides this mating arrangement. You would never do anything so serious as allow a stranger to live here without several good reasons."

"I see certain possibilities," Tamat replied, not denying what Osiyar had said. "More than that I will not say just now."

"And Janina? What of her?"

"Janina has done nothing wrong," Tamat declared, a little too quickly. Osiyar's eyebrows went up, and he looked at his Co-Ruler with a slight smile.

"Nothing?" he asked in a tone weighted with meaning.

"Very little," Tamat amended. "Janina is a victim of her own innocence. She cannot be blamed for anyone else's transgressions."

"And you love her. That is enough for me to know. I am willing to drop the subject of Janina's actions."

"She will remain true to her vows, unless she is released from them," Tamat declared.

"Will you release her?"

"Not I. Not yet. But, dear Osiyar, there are greater powers than those of Tamat of Ruthlen," the High Priestess said with a soft laugh. "Even I cannot rule over the emotions of others, and emotions, as you and I know, are often unruly and have been known to spoil the best of plans."

CHAPTER 5

On *the morning after Reid arrived in Ruthlen,* Sidra summoned Janina as soon as it was daylight.

"On Tamat's command," Sidra said, "you and I will go to the sacred grove to make certain nothing has been disturbed by Reid's presence there."

"I told Tamat all was well," Janina answered. "Reid did not touch the Water."

"Nevertheless, you will come with me."

When Sidra used that tone, Janina knew there was no way to stop her. Obediently, she strapped the water jar to her back and walked beside the older priestess through the village, where Sidra was greeted with low bows of reverence and wishes for a pleasant day while Janina was pointedly ignored as if she were invisible.

The people of Ruthlen had never been an especially kind folk. Their constant fear of renewed attack from the Cetans and their precarious perch on a tiny crescent of land at the edge of a dangerous sea did not incline them toward the gentler virtues. But they had always been honest and hardworking, and usually fair toward one another. These were necessary qualities for a community that was so few in number.

Lately, however, Janina had been disturbed by signs of increasing dishonesty. In the distribution of fish on days when the catch was poor, in the settling of a boundary dispute between farmers, in the question of who would inherit a tiny cottage just outside the village, Sidra had recently begun to speak for the side that paid her the greater honor. Though Osiyar was the final judge of all such disputes, and though he prided himself on his unbiased fairness, he listened to Sidra's opinions when they were offered, as well as to Tamat's. Sidra had no hesitation about speaking her mind on these occasions, nor any apparent qualms about favoring those plaintiffs whom Janina had previously noticed currying her favor in anticipation of the day when she would become High Priestess. All was done so subtly, so delicately, that neither Tamat nor Osiyar could object to Sidra's careful reasoning.

Thinking how different Sidra was from Tamat, forcing to the bottom of her mind an uneasy sense of encroaching corruption, Janina heaved a deep sigh and turned with Sidra onto the road leading to the sacred grove. And there, when she lifted her eyes toward the tall peaks, her thoughts were distracted from Sidra's activities.

"The mountains are casting out more steam than usual," Janina observed.

"Perhaps they are displeased by the presence of a stranger among us," Sidra observed sourly.

Janina knew Sidra did not believe what she had just said. In fact, Janina doubted that Sidra believed in anything at all except the telepathic powers of her own mind and of the minds of the other priests and priestesses. And Tamat. Sidra's love and reverence for Tamat was deep and true. It was that fact, and that alone, which made Sidra tolerable to Janina.

When they entered the sacred grove, Sidra went directly to the pavilion, while Janina stood on the moss, looking into the pool. She felt the quiet presence that nearly always greeted her there. Whatever it was, it had not been disturbed or offended by Reid or by what they had done the day before. Glancing at the khata bush with its weight of crimson flowers, Janina drew a deep breath. She did not regret allowing Reid to embrace her, but she understood it was best never to let him touch her again. Remembering the strength of his arms around her and the warm pressure of his body on hers, she began to tremble. It would be difficult to stay away from him.

Sidra's cool voice recalled her to duty.

"Lift the stone," Sidra ordered. "Let me see if more medical supplies are needed. It is almost time to go into the ravine to gather the last herbs of the season, and we ought to be prepared in case someone is injured on the way."

Once convinced that the only result of Reid's unauthorized visit to the sacred grove was the need for a full pot of salve to replace the nearly empty one Janina had used on his wounds, Sidra appeared to relax.

"Before we return," she said with a last glance around the grove, "let us investigate the tunnel Reid used."

She led the way to the opposite side of the grove. She knew exactly where the tunnel was. It was no secret to the priestesses. Sidra pulled back a bush that had grown during the warm weather until it partially blocked the mouth of the tunnel. She entered it, Janina following her.

The ceiling was low enough to make them bend their heads while they walked through it to the opening in the face of the cliff. They stood together on the narrow rock shelf, looking across the ravine to the forest. Janina saw nothing but the green trees and the dome of the purple-blue sky above them. She knew Sidra, trained as she was and possessing telepathic powers second only to Tamat's, was able to see the shimmering boundaries of the blanking shield.

"Look here." Sidra moved to the very edge of the rock shelf, pointing downward. Janina stepped forward to stand beside her. "See how far Reid had to climb. What a determined man he is. I think he will prove difficult to overcome. I will need to strengthen myself against him. Lean over and look, Janina."

At the thought of that height, Janina's knees began to shake, but she made herself obey Sidra. Looking straight downward into the deep, deep ravine made her feel dizzy.

Sidra's hand came to rest on her shoulder, pressing a little too hard. Janina pulled away and stepped back into the tunnel.

"Why, Janina, do you imagine I'd push you?" Sidra smiled her lovely, false smile. "I'd never do anything that stupid. There would be too many questions to answer. I'd be known at once for the guilty one."

She put an arm across Janina's shoulders, drawing her back through the tunnel to the grove.

"Why should I want to destroy you when you can be so useful to me, Janina? Of course, your usefulness will not last long, and then . . ."

Sidra left the thought unfinished, but Janina knew what she meant. When Tamat was gone, when it was no longer necessary to please the aged High Priestess, when Sidra herself was High Priestess, and after she had forced Janina to swallow the herbal potion again and again until her mind was broken by prophesying, then Janina's usefulness would end. Then Sidra would find a reason to set Janina adrift, to face the terrors of the deep sea. And then she would find a way to destroy Reid, too.

Janina knew it as surely as if she were a

telepath and had entered Sidra's mind. Under the weight of Sidra's arm, Janina shivered, and watched Sidra smile at her again.

On the walk back to the temple, the Water for the priestesses' rituals safely sealed into the jar on her back, Janina's thoughts turned once more to Reid. How brave he was to scale that steep cliff! She would have been too frightened to attempt it. She was afraid of so many things—the great height from which she had just looked down, the vast rolling sea, the monsters that lived in its depths. The list of her fears seemed endless.

Until today, her worst fear of all had been the fear of losing Tamat. It was because she knew how precarious the old woman's health was that Janina had never revealed to Tamat any of the threats, veiled or open, which Sidra made about the time when Tamat would be gone and Janina would be helpless against the power of her successor.

Now Janina had a new and even greater fear—that something would happen to Reid, that Sidra would *make* something happen to him. It was worse than contemplating her own death. It rivaled the pain of knowing that Tamat could not live much longer. Janina wanted Reid safe and well. She would do anything to help him—anything that would not harm Tamat.

She ought not to feel that way about Reid. She had taken sacred vows that forbade her from thinking of men. But she *knew* him, in the deepest reaches of her soul he was part of her, and she would give her life, if necessary, to protect him.

"Will you take me to Tamat, please?" When Reid's deep grey eyes met hers, Janina looked away, knowing she ought not to respond to the warmth she had seen in his expression.

"You should be resting, Reid, and not out so early in the day. Tamat wanted you to have adequate time to recover from your ordeal in the wilderness," she said.

"I slept well last night and I feel perfectly healthy," Reid told her.

"Is your room comfortable?" she asked politely, to keep him there in the temple courtyard with her while she thought about his request. Tamat was in private conversation with Sidra and could not be disturbed. It would not do to have Reid bursting in on them. Both priestesses would be angry if that happened, and if Sidra learned that Janina had done nothing to prevent such an intrusion, she would find a way to punish Janina, and probably Reid, too.

"My room is delightful," Reid said with just a touch of impatience. "The two scholar-priests who live in the same building are charming young men. Osiyar is an agreeable and pleasant host. I want to see Tamat."

"If you have questions about Ruthlen, you should ask Osiyar," she said, growing nervous under his steady gaze. "Tamat has ordered him to explain the customs of Ruthlen to you, so you will not offend the villagers. Oh, I'm sorry. I shouldn't have said that. I'm certain you would never offend anyone."

"Except you. I have offended you. I've made you feel uneasy with me." He put out one hand as if to take her arm. Janina moved backward quickly to avoid him, afraid that if he touched her, she would do something she should not do. Such as touch him in return. Or melt into his arms and beg him to kiss her. She was certain he saw her fear, for he withdrew his hand. But then he moved a step closer, further disconcerting her by his nearness.

"Janina," he said in a hard, firm voice, "take me to Tamat. *Now.*"

"But she is with Sidra."

"Indeed she is not," said a sweet voice behind Janina, "for I am here. Good day to you, Reid. You wish to see Tamat? Could not I help you instead?"

"I prefer to speak with Tamat."

The faintest shadow of annoyance passed over Sidra's lovely face, then cleared.

"Janina, you should be ashamed of yourself for keeping our guest standing here in the hot midday sun. Take him inside at once. Offer him something cool to drink, and then ask Tamat if she will receive him. Do it now, girl! Don't dawdle so!" In a swirl of pale blue robe, Sidra left them and walked across the courtyard toward Osiyar's house.

"If you will follow me." Janina led the way into the temple.

"Is she always so sharp with you?" Reid asked.

"She's very busy," Janina said. "She has many duties, and I fear I am a poor help to her. I'm not very intelligent, you see, so I'm fortunate to be permitted to live in the temple complex at all. It is only Tamat's goodness that allows such a deviation from the requirements for a priestess —even a lesser priestess, as I shall be."

"Even if everything you've just said is true, which I doubt, that is still no excuse for rudeness," Reid declared.

"Sidra doesn't mean to be rude. It's just the way she is. Would you like cool water, or perhaps some fruit?" When Reid refused any refreshment, Janina left him in the central room while she went to speak to Tamat.

"She will see you," she said, returning a few moments later. "Reid, please be kind to her. We in Ruthlen frequently live to be well over one hundred years old, but Tamat's health is fragile and she has grown weaker in the last year. She has asked that I remain with her, in case she needs assistance. Will you mind that?"

"Not at all," Reid said, giving her a long, steady look that made her blush.

"Well, Reid," said Tamat as soon as he entered her chamber, "what do you want of me this day?"

"I want to leave Ruthlen. I want you to help my friend and my cousin."

"You are an impatient man, I fear." Tamat sat in a large armchair carved from white stone, which was softened by thick green cushions on the seat and back. She motioned to a similar chair next to hers. "I have not yet decided what I will do about your companions. You may not leave us. If there is anything else you would like to discuss, I will be happy to converse with you."

"I do have a few questions," Reid admitted, seating himself in the chair Tamat had indicated.

Janina saw he was hiding anger in an effort to be polite to Tamat. She thought she could understand how he must feel, being prevented from doing the one thing he wanted. But in time he would learn to accept his fate, as she was learning to accept hers. He would have to learn. There was nothing else he could do.

That morning was the first of many when Reid visited Tamat to ask her innumerable questions about the people who lived in Ruthlen. Janina came to love those visits. From her position behind Tamat's chair she could watch him without being obvious about it, and she could occasionally answer one of his questions herself under the guise of sparing Tamat the effort.

"You are more attentive than usual these days," Tamat said to her one morning just before Reid arrived. "Is it concern for my welfare, or interest in Reid that brings you to me when you need not be here?"

"I am always concerned about you, Tamat," she answered quietly, "but I must confess to a great interest in what we can learn from an outsider. You have always told me that knowledge ought to be my primary quest, that in time I might be able to use it as some poor compensation for my lack of telepathic ability. I know my wits are of inferior quality, but I try to exercise them as much as possible."

"There is nothing wrong with your wits, Janina," Tamat observed dryly. "Sometimes I suspect they are a bit too quick. Well, stay with me and learn what you can from Reid. I always enjoy your presence. Only, do not let Sidra grow annoyed with you, as she will if you neglect your other duties."

"Yes, Tamat." Janina told herself her desire to be in the same room with Reid was perfectly innocent. Daily she tested her resistance to the attraction she still felt toward him. She had to teach herself to be strong, to adhere scrupulously to the vows she had so nearly violated with Reid. She could never give herself to him, and she told herself that in time she would find joy in having sacrificed her selfish longings in order to better serve the temple and Ruthlen. She would not allow herself to deviate again from the Chosen Way.

That morning Tamat told Reid how their ancestors had survived the Cetan attack of six hundred years before. Janina had heard the story many times, yet still she listened with undiminished pride in the accomplishments of the founders of Ruthlen.

"There were just twenty of our people," Tamat said, "who were deep in a nearby forest cutting wood for charcoal, and some were gathering medicinal herbs. When they realized what was happening in the city, and knew they could not help, they fled still deeper into the forest where they found a cave and hid in it. At their bidding, the Chon drew the Cetans in another direction and thus saved our ancestors. After that day's terrible battle, all the telepaths in the settlement were dead and the Chon were lost to us forever."

"Not everyone was killed." Reid told Tamat about Dulan and the other survivors, and about the Chon who still lived at the lake.

"I am happy to learn that the great birds are not extinct," Tamat said. "They were once a vital part of our history. But I know of no one named Dulan. Our records were destroyed along with the beautiful city of Tathan and the farmlands surrounding it. All we have left of the time before the Cetan raid is memory. The few people who remained alive decided to flee far away from Tathan and hide themselves, hoping thereby to escape another Cetan intrusion. After a long and difficult journey, they arrived here and built this small village, where we live by fishing and farming."

"Did they also build the pavilion inside the mountain?" asked Reid.

"They made the pool a sacred spot, because the Water in it is clear and perfectly pure," Tamat replied. "You should not have been there. Even Osiyar may not go there. It is a place reserved for priestesses only. Do not return to it."

"I hope you will not punish Janina because I was there."

"No. Your presence in the grove was not her doing." Then, looking deep into his eyes, the

High Priestess added, "She is not meant for any man, Reid. Do not touch her again."

Tamat had never said a word to Janina about the day when she had found Reid, though Janina knew Tamat understood what they had almost done. Now, Janina felt herself blushing, and she saw Reid's face flush at Tamat's direct order, but he made no promise. Instead, he asked Tamat another question.

"Can you tell me why the computer model of the continent we have at our headquarters does not show the area around Ruthlen? According to our information, the forest extends to the very edge of steep cliffs, which fall off directly into the sea. We have no information about the ravine, or the mountain range, or the village."

"We use a blanking shield," Tamat replied. "All who are full priestesses, including myself, take turns maintaining it. The images you spoke of are exactly what outsiders are expected to see. It is our protection against a Cetan return, or against anyone else who would harm us. No one can enter the shield unless we wish it."

"I got through it," Reid pointed out.

"Yes," Tamat said, looking at him strangely.

"You maintain this shield with your minds?" Reid then asked.

"We do," Tamat answered. "We have strengthened it since you have come, Reid. You will not be able to breach it a second time." She smiled at him, but Reid understood the threat implicit in her words. He could not blame her. She had a right to protect her people in the way she believed was best. But he had a right, too—the right to seek his freedom.

"Reid, why are you pacing back and forth across the courtyard?" When he swung around to glare at her, Janina saw that his grey eyes were dark with anger. She faced him trembling, yet determined not to back down until she knew what was troubling him. She attempted a smile, though in his present mood he frightened her. Gathering what little courage she possessed, she tried again. "You look like a caged animal."

"Do I? Perhaps I look caged because that is what I am."

"Oh, no. Never that."

"Then what would you call it?" he demanded, frowning down at her.

"You are our guest," she said. "You are perfectly free to go wherever you want within the boundaries of Ruthlen, which is the same freedom the rest of us have."

"Janina, you know as well as I do that I am a prisoner here."

"Don't say that." She wanted to touch him, but she could not, not here in the open courtyard, where anyone could see them. "It hurts me to know you are so deeply unhappy."

"Does it hurt you enough that you'd help me escape?"

"Escape?" She stared at him, terrified by the idea. "Don't even think of such a thing."

"Why not?" His voice was harsh and filled with anger. Janina watched him trying to control his feelings until he spoke more calmly, yet still with strong emotion. "I am being kept here against my will. Therefore, I have the right to try to escape if I want. You people don't seem to understand that I have a life, and friends, and important work, beyond Ruthlen. I want to return to all that. I wish your High Priestess would believe I'd never bring others here if you want to remain isolated. Commander Tarik would respect Tamat's wishes, too. What about the sea? I'm a fairly good sailor."

"The sea?" He must think she was incredibly stupid if she could do nothing except echo his words, but the sudden question had surprised her. She answered him promptly and definitely. "You can't leave by the sea. Once you reached deep water the sea monsters would eat you. That's why the fisherfolk only go as far away from the shore as the near side of the swift current."

"Monsters?" He looked as though he would burst into laughter.

"Besides," she added quickly, seeing that he did not believe her about the monsters, "you could be observed from the village until you were far enough out at sea to be below the horizon. There is no place to hide out there."

"That kind of thinking I can understand," he said, nodding. "As for sea monsters—well, there may be something in the deep water that I don't know about. I'll accept that much of your sea monster story. I'll have to go by land then."

"Don't. Reid, please don't. You will only be

caught and brought back here. Then you truly will be a prisoner. Please accept your fate. It's the best thing for you. It's the safest thing."

"Janina, why are you loitering here with this man?" Sidra had come up to them so quietly that her question startled both of them. They had been standing close together, talking in low tones. Now they hastily moved apart. Sidra acted as though she had caught them in some forbidden activity, but her voice was silky-smooth. "Stay away from her, Reid. There are women enough in the village to assuage your lust, if that is what you want."

"We were only talking," Janina declared, feeling like a naughty child under Sidra's mocking gaze.

"Tamat needs you," Sidra said. "While you have been wasting the day with Reid, our High Priestess has been waiting patiently for her neglectful attendant. As for you, Reid, go to Osiyar and ask of him the questions you were asking Janina. I'm sure he can give you more intelligent answers than she ever will."

"We will talk again, Janina," Reid said.

"No," Sidra told him, "you will not, for if you do, I will see to it that Tamat punishes both of you."

"How?" snarled Reid. "By taking away my nonexistant freedom?"

"Ah, Reid," Sidra replied with a soft trill of laughter. "You have no idea what punishment means until you have been punished by a telepath."

"Reid," Janina said, trembling now in as much fear *for* him as she had earlier been afraid *of* him, "please obey Sidra. You must learn to follow our customs."

With Sidra close at her back, Janina hurried toward the temple.

"I'll be watching you," Sidra said.

"I know," Janina replied. "You always watch me, to catch me in any mistake."

"Insolence is not the proper way to deal with me," Sidra murmured as they went through the double doors and into the central room. "I require from you the respect due to my position."

"Yes, Sidra." It was useless to defy the woman. In any contest of wills between Janina and Sidra, Sidra had always won. Janina thought she always would.

"Dear Tamat." Sidra's voice was suddenly khata-sweet when they reached the door of Tamat's private chamber. "I have found our errant scholar priestess in the courtyard, exchanging mysterious confidences with Reid. You will have to ask her the subject of their talk, for she won't tell me."

Janina felt a stab of guilt at the frowning look Tamat bent on her, but she made no effort to defend herself. There was nothing she could say. Sidra was too clever for her and would twist anything she said to make an innocent conversation with Reid appear as something unbecoming to a scholar priestess.

In a way that Sidra apparently did not suspect,

that day's talk with Reid had not been innocent at all. Janina feared he might put himself into danger if he decided to attempt an escape. She could not let that happen. She wanted Reid safe, and, if possible, she wanted him happy. Later, when Sidra had gone, Janina dared to question Tamat's edict about Reid.

"Do you think it's wise to keep him here against his will?" she asked.

"There is nothing else I can do," Tamat answered. "His presence in Ruthlen is an accident. He has done nothing to warrant setting him adrift, and if I were to banish him into the wilderness, he would only find his friends again. Then they would all intrude upon us here, to destroy our peaceful life."

"He's terribly unhappy. He wants to leave. He's like some great sea bird beating its wings against a cage. Tamat, I'm certain he would swear never to reveal the location of Ruthlen, if only you would let him go. Tell him about the other passage through the mountain, the one we use when we go to gather herbs in the ravine, and let him leave that way." Janina gulped back a lump in her throat, for there was one thing she did not want, yet for Reid's sake she would suggest it and make herself accept it. She spoke quickly, before she could change her mind. "You could even block his memory so he can't remember anything about Ruthlen or anyone he has met while here. His friends would think he had been wandering around lost for all those days, and so would he."

"No," Tamat said emphatically, "I will not block his mind. I would not do that to Reid. It would destroy his latent—I'll not harm Reid's mind."

"You are harming him by keeping him here against his will," Janina cried. Then, seeing that Tamat was immovable on the subject of Reid, she asked, "If you will not let him go, will you at least save his cousin and his friend? Knowing they have been rescued will comfort him, I'm sure, and make him more content to stay with us. Part of his need to leave us is his concern for his kinswoman."

"That is well-reasoned," Tamat admitted. "Reid is so important to the future of Ruthlen that the effort I must expend to touch his commander's mind would be justified if it would result in his contentment. I will think seriously about your suggestion, Janina. Here, take this food away. I'll eat nothing until I decide what to do about Reid's lost companions. I want to rest now. Let no one disturb me."

Janina thought Tamat would grant her request. Everyone within the temple complex ate sparingly and, except at the twin moons festivals, drank no stronger brew than the herbal *dhia*, in order to keep their minds clear and their bodies healthy. They believed this regimen improved their telepathic powers, and always, before making some great telepathic effort, they fasted. Tamat's refusal of food was a sign that she was preparing to contact Reid's friend Tarik.

"Why are you so happy?" Sidra stood in her

way, looking at the untouched tray of food. "Is Tamat ill? Is that why she does not eat?"

"She wants to be alone, to rest." Janina knew even Sidra would not have the effrontery to intrude on Tamat.

"I hope she ordered an appropriate punishment for you, to teach you not to meet alone with men."

"Reid and I were in the courtyard, in plain view of anyone in the temple complex or on the road outside," Janina said quietly. "That could hardly be called meeting him alone. I told Tamat what he and I discussed, and she understood."

"Which means you will not be punished." Sidra's perfectly arched brows drew together in displeasure. "You will not always be treated so leniently, Janina. There will come a time when Tamat's favoritism toward you will cease, and you will be under my rule."

"Yes, Sidra." Janina bowed politely. "If you will excuse me, I will return Tamat's tray to the kitchen." She could feel Sidra's piercing blue gaze fastened on her back as she crossed the central room and entered the kitchen.

CHAPTER 6

"*I knew we would find you here,*" *Tarik said* triumphantly, helping Alla into the cargo bay of the hovering shuttlecraft and steadying her while she unfastened the rescue harness from the ropes.

"Where is Reid?" she snapped, not bothering to thank him.

Tarik did not answer. He was busy helping Herne through the open hatch in the deck. As soon as the physician was aboard, Tarik closed the hatch and moved forward into the main cabin.

"Well done," he said to his wife, who had been piloting the shuttlecraft while he lifted his lost colonists to safety. Narisa flashed him a bright smile, then relaxed, letting Tarik take the controls.

"Tarik, I asked you a question," Alla said, following him into the cabin. "Where is Reid?"

Narisa's smile vanished. She seemed to be giving all her attention to the navigational instruments as she laid in a course for headquarters. Nor did Tarik look up from the controls.

"Someone answer me," Alla demanded, her voice low and deadly calm.

"Sit down and fasten your safety harness," Herne advised, taking a seat himself. "We are going home to a hot meal and a comfortable bed. It's about time, if you ask me. What took you so long, Tarik?"

"We've been looking for you for days," Tarik said, "ever since we first lost contact with you. Why didn't you use your communicators?"

"Because they stopped working," Alla responded from between clenched teeth. "Tarik, *where is Reid*?"

"Please sit down, Alla." Narisa half-turned in her seat, and Alla saw the pity and concern in her expression. "We have looked everywhere for Reid, as well as for you. We've used the heat sensors, and the magnetic tracking gauge set for the frequency of your communicators. When neither of those instruments showed anything, we tried high-resolution image-screening to search literally every space-inch of territory between the desert and the sea. We found no trace of anyone down there."

"If that's so, how did you locate us?" Herne asked.

"It's an odd thing," Tarik said. "I woke up this morning convinced we would find you in just the spot where we did. I suppose it's possible the Chon were able to seek you out by some means known only to them, and then put your location into my mind. But it's strange, because I thought those birds stayed away from this part of the continent. Anyway, you were where I thought you would be, and I'm glad of that."

"Did you ask the Chon about Reid?" Alla persisted.

"Days ago," Narisa responded. "We asked them about all of you. They knew nothing."

"Are you sure you searched the entire forest?" Alla could not let it go. Her voice was tight, her eyes blurry with hot tears. "We have to find Reid."

"Narisa told you," Tarik said patiently. "We have checked any place he might be. There is not a space-inch of land we haven't searched. The forest grows right up to the edge of the cliffs, the cliffs drop off abruptly, and the sea begins. There is no beach, just the end of the land. And we've covered all the area back to the stony desert. There is no trace of him. I'm sorry, Alla, but we have been forced to conclude that he's dead. Narisa and I both firmly believe that."

"It's what I've been telling her for days," Herne said in an irritated voice. "She won't listen to me. She refuses to believe we won't find him."

"You are right about that," Alla said through

tight lips. "I'll never believe Reid is dead, not until I see his body. We will keep on searching, Tarik."

"Let it go, Alla," Herne urged. "It's a tragic loss and a miserable shame, but it can't be helped. This sort of thing happens occasionally to exploratory teams. It's part of the risk, and you ought to have been prepared for it when you signed on to come to Dulan's Planet. Reid was my friend. I will miss him, and I'll grieve for him, but he's gone and there is nothing we can do to change that fact. You will just have to accept it, as the rest of us will."

"I won't," she declared stubbornly.

"We cannot keep on looking," Tarik told her, using the commander's voice he seldom employed on this planet. "We have done everything reasonably possible to find Reid. I cannot afford to commit more personnel or supplies to a fruitless venture. Unless we discover some new and highly credible evidence to suggest he's still alive, the search for Reid is ended as of this moment. I will record that he is missing and presumed dead."

"He is not dead." But Alla sat down, pulling the safety harness around herself. She saw Tarik and Narisa exchange a glance of agreement and knew they would not listen to anything more she had to say on the subject. They knew how much she loved Reid. They would think that was why she couldn't believe he was dead, or accept Tarik's decision. But Alla knew in her heart that Reid was still alive. She vowed she would not allow herself to sink into despair or depression, because some day, something would happen, the new evidence Tarik insisted upon would appear. When it did, she would seize on it and use it to make him understand that he must resume the search for her cousin.

Hoping he would find information that would show him how to leave Ruthlen, Reid decided he would learn as much as he could about the isolated crescent of land that was protected by both natural barriers and the mental powers of Tamat's priestesses. He quickly discovered Tamat felt so secure behind the blanking shield, and so certain he would never find a way to breach it again, that she was willing to answer any questions he put to her. Thanks to Tamat's orders, Osiyar and Sidra were also valuable sources of information.

It did not take Reid long to understand the uncomplicated way of life led by most of the citizens of Ruthlen. Their ancestors had been ordinary people, not the leaders of the original city. Tamat had told Reid they were charcoal-makers and herb-gatherers, and now their descendants farmed, using only the simplest of machinery, or they fished. Because of the almost constant sunshine they were able to use solar power to heat their homes, for hot water, and for lighting units, but over the centuries they had apparently forgotten the more advanced technologies which the original telepaths had understood and which were so clearly displayed at

Dulan's old settlement where Tarik made his headquarters.

While their material existence was remarkable for its lack of complexity, their mental capabilities had not degenerated over the centuries and were far beyond Reid's comprehension. Within a few days of his arrival, he knew he would never be able to sort out all the laws, conventions, and etiquette surrounding the use of telepathy which ruled their lives.

Easily the most remarkable of the telepaths was the High Priestess, Tamat. Though Reid disagreed with her decision to keep him in Ruthlen, Tamat's devotion to her people and her obvious honesty soon earned her his deep respect. It was not hard to understand Janina's attachment to the elderly woman, nor the awe with which priestesses and villagers alike regarded her.

"Why," Reid asked her one day when they spoke alone, "do you people bother talking when you communicate with each other? Wouldn't telepathy be quicker, easier, and less subject to misunderstanding?"

"What you say is true, and there was a time when we always communicated in that way," Tamat answered. "But the Gift was too often misused, and at last it was used by those who possessed stronger abilities, to control others who were weaker. That was soon after this temple was built. Finally, after a period of terrible strife, there arose a great High Priestess who made the laws we still live by today. The first of those laws is that mind-to-mind contact must be by mutual consent, except in severe emergency. The exception is so we may help anyone who is too badly injured or ill to give consent. Whoever is High Priestess is granted right of free access to anyone's thoughts at her discretion, but the selection of a male Co-Ruler who is also High Priest has set additional limits upon the power of the High Priestess.

"This is our Chosen Way, Reid, which requires that the powers of all telepaths must be strictly controlled and properly used. No deviation from the Chosen Way is ever allowed. The penalty for those, particularly priests or priestesses, who break our laws is truly terrible."

"But what is the benefit in possessing telepathic ability that one is forbidden to use?" Reid objected.

"Use of the Gift is not forbidden," Tamat told him, "Only its misuse. The honest opening of one mind to another creates a strong bond in the intimate relations among family members or dear friends. True mating is impossible without it, for in the act of love, minds must join as well as bodies. In these private instances, the Gift is used freely, but by mutual consent, as the law decrees.

"The Gift is the most important part of our heritage and is essential to our identity as a people. Our ancestors were banished from the Jurisdiction because of their telepathic abilities, and our sense of ourselves as a special community was forged during the trials of a long wandering before they found this planet and settled on it. That history, that common heritage, keeps us bound together now, for as separate individuals we would be death-condemned outcasts in most of the galaxy."

"As Janina is an outcast in Ruthlen?" Reid asked softly.

"Janina, and a few others during our short time on this planet," Tamat agreed, with no obvious recognition of the irony in Reid's words or her own. "The fates of the non-telepaths among us have always been sad. I have tried to protect Janina by keeping her here at the temple. To the folk of Ruthlen she is an abomination who can never partake of our community. Were she not under my protection, she would be banished to die alone in the wilderness or on the sea."

"Janina is not an abomination!" Reid exclaimed, angered by this attitude.

"Not to me, Reid, but she is of my blood and I love her, and that makes all the difference," Tamat responded. "Others are not so kindly disposed toward her."

Tamat's words left Reid wondering what his own fate would be without her protection.

On another day, he learned from Tamat that one aspect of her position was the preserved memory of the original city of the telepaths and its culture, which was transferred to each High Priestess by her predecessor. This memory, added to Tamat's own inherent telepathic ability and the wisdom and knowledge she had acquired during nearly a century of life, provided the basis for her personal power. He also learned that Sidra and Tamat would soon link their minds, during which time Tamat would transfer the ancient memories to Sidra, so that Sidra could carry on the traditions after Tamat's death.

"Sidra has developed her telepathic Gift far beyond anyone else in Ruthlen, except for myself," Tamat said. "That is as it should be. She will continue to develop her Gift as the years pass, until one day she will surpass what I now am."

"Have you no objection to that?" Reid asked. "Couldn't someone with such a Gift become dangerous?"

"I assure you, Reid, I am aware of Sidra's tendency to love power for its own sake, as I notice you are aware of it. But she has sworn to uphold the Chosen Way and its laws. I believe the heavy responsibility of being both High Priestess and Co-Ruler will cause her to develop a greater concern for others, along with the knowledge that power is not the only thing that matters. So it once was with me. So it will be with Sidra."

Reid was not so sure. He disliked Sidra because of the haughty and sometimes cruel way she treated Janina, and because something about her struck him as untrue.

"Janina, you are late again," Sidra scolded early one day. She had been waiting by the entrance to the temple complex and had stopped Janina before she could carry the filled water jar inside. "Every time it is your turn to bring the Water from the sacred grove, the rest of us must wait to begin our morning rituals. You are not only stupid and inconsiderate, you are incredibly lazy."

"This is my fault, Sidra." Osiyar, accompanied by Reid and the two scholar priests, had come out of his house in time to see Sidra waiting for Janina and to hear her verbal attack. "I delayed Janina earlier this morning when I stopped her to ask about Tamat's health. Tamat has eaten nothing for three days, and since yesterday she has seen no one except Janina. I feared she might be ill. I am surprised that Janina was able to walk to the grove and back so quickly. I assure you, she has not been lazy."

"Questions about Tamat's health ought to be addressed to me, Osiyar," Sidra said spitefully. "This foolish girl knows nothing. She constantly makes mistakes. You cannot depend on what she says."

"Perhaps her errors are caused by her fear of displeasing you," Osiyar suggested. "If you treated her more gently, she might make fewer mistakes."

"It is not your duty, but mine, to train the lesser priestesses, Osiyar!" Sidra's blue eyes held Osiyar's gaze for a long moment, until Reid, watching the scene, felt a tingling along his spine. He was certain Sidra and Osiyar were in telepathic contact, and he thought from the look on Osiyar's face that it must be a contest of two equally determined wills. After a while Sidra turned her head away. With one of her soft, rippling little laughs she gestured to Janina.

"Take the Water into the temple at once," she said. "The others are waiting for you. As for you scholar-priests, come with me." Without another glance for Osiyar, Sidra walked across the courtyard and entered the temple, followed by the two young men who were his students.

"Jealousy," Osiyar said, "is a terrible thing, a destructive force. I am glad I have never known it."

"Sidra reminds me of an older sister," Reid remarked, "who fears a younger child is her rival for her mother's affection."

"It is so," Osiyar agreed gravely. "Tamat is the only person Sidra loves, and so she sees Janina as a threat."

"Love does strange things to people." Reid was thinking about Janina. He had at first imagined that his strong feelings for her were the result of exhaustion, of the strangely beautiful and peaceful sacred grove, and of the aphrodisiacal scent of the red khata flowers. He had repeatedly tried to tell himself that he could not really care for an unknown girl, that he had known more than a few women before and never fallen in love with any of them. All his excuses and rationalizations were useless each time he came face to face with Janina. As the days passed, he felt more and more drawn to her. Just now, he had wanted to protect her from

Sidra's jealousy, wanted to see the hurt look in her mist-blue eyes dissolve into laughter. He had never heard Janina laugh. He wondered what the sound would be like.

"It is best not to love." Osiyar's voice startled Reid, making him wonder if the High Priest had entered his thoughts without permission. But it seemed Osiyar was talking about himself. "Because I love no one, I am not tortured by jealousy as Sidra is. When I am called upon to judge a dispute in the village or some quarrel between farmers, I am not cursed by affection for one side or the other. I can make an impartial decision. Because of that ability, I am respected by all in Ruthlen."

"Surely you loved your parents," Reid objected, recalling his own love-filled childhood.

"I do not remember them. They died when I was young, of an illness that suddenly swept through Ruthlen, killing many. On the day I was born I was dedicated to the temple, so when my parents died, Tamat took me in and gave me to the last High Priest to raise." Osiyar dismissed his youth with a quick movement of one hand, letting Reid understand it was not to be discussed again. "I hold Tamat in reverence, but no one else. Tamat has been a remarkable High Priestess."

"And Sidra?" Reid asked, thinking again of Janina and the loveless future she faced. "What kind of High Priestess will Sidra be?"

Osiyar's handsome face hardened. Reid

thought at first that the man was angry with him, but Osiyar's tone of voice did not change.

"Sidra is very different from Tamat," Osiyar said. "Sidra has . . . other attributes that will make her a powerful High Priestess. When her day comes to reign, I shall be her willing Co-Ruler, as I have been Tamat's. Sidra and I are well matched."

Reid said no more. While he liked Osiyar in spite of his apparent emotional coldness, Reid also felt sorry for him, believing his loyalty was torn between Tamat and Sidra in a way Reid could not fully comprehend.

Regardless of his claim to love no one, Osiyar treated the people of Ruthlen with unfailing kindness, employing his healing skills whenever needed, and, as far as Reid could tell, judging all disputes with scrupulous fairness. He treated Janina fairly, too, never scolding her as Sidra did, and for that fairness Reid liked him even better.

Each day Reid walked into the village with Osiyar and at least one of the two scholar-priests. There Osiyar dealt with any problems the villagers were having, while Reid and the scholars listened in order to learn from him. Always on these occasions, Reid could feel the women staring at him, assessing him. He was aware that the villagers had been informed of Tamat's plan for him. They seemed to accept it. The men, from whom he might have expected jealousy, were guarded and a bit brusque with him when he spoke to them, but they were not openly hostile.

"Your cousin and your friend are safe," Tamat said to Reid one day when they were alone.

"Are you certain of that?" he asked without thinking, then knew it was a foolish question.

"I would not tell you an untruth, Reid," the High Priestess said calmly, with no sign that she had taken offense. "While Commander Tarik slept, I implanted in his mind the information he needed to find the ones you call Herne and Alla. The following day, we modified the blanking shield enough to allow him access to them without revealing our location."

"If you touched Tarik's mind, you must know he would bring no harm to your people," Reid said. "Surely now you will let them come here, or let me go."

"For your sake, I regret that is impossible," Tamat told him. "You will remain with us, Reid."

"He won't stop searching for me."

"But he has," Tamat said. "Tarik and his wife, Narisa, both believe firmly that you are dead. I pity the sorrow they feel, but it was necessary to make them believe it is so in order to protect Ruthlen. They will search for you no more."

Reid stared at her, thinking of Alla and the grief she must be enduring for his sake, believing him dead. Poor Alla.

Just then, Janina came into the small private room where he and Tamat were. She bore a tray of fruit and the hot herbal brew they called *dhia*, for Tamat's midday meal. Reid promptly forgot his cousin in the pleasure of looking at Janina. He was so strongly attracted to her that he wondered how he could avoid going to her and taking her into his arms. He controlled himself only because he did not want to cause trouble for her. He told himself for the thousandth time that she was sworn as a virgin priestess, but it made no difference in how he felt.

While the personality of the High Priest allowed for little warmth, the tentative friendship between Reid and Osiyar grew stronger as Osiyar regularly defended Janina against Sidra's verbal attacks. Reid thought Osiyar saw Janina as a combination of pupil and distant niece or cousin. This idea was not at all unreasonable, since the population of Ruthlen was so small that after six centuries everyone was related in some way to everyone else.

Reid had several times answered Osiyar's questions about the way he had gained access to the sacred grove, and about his initial meeting with Janina. He never mentioned that they had almost made love, but one day Reid did speak of the presence he had sensed in the grove.

"An entity with feelings and intelligence," Reid said, trying to describe an incident for which words were inadequate.

"There is definitely something there," Osiyar agreed. "As a man, I am not permitted to enter the grove, but Tamat has told me of a presence we do not understand. Perhaps it is the spirit of the grove itself, or it might be the essence of this world."

"Has anyone ever considered investigating it?" Reid asked, intrigued. "There are simple, practical tests that might be conducted, even by the lesser priestesses."

"A sense of mystery is important to the beauty of life," Osiyar responded, shaking his head at Reid's suggestion. "It is not necessary to examine and record everything that exists, and in the case of the sacred grove the attempt would be well beyond the capability of even the most adept telepath. Like the far reaches of the stars, or the depths of the sea, the presence that exists in the sacred grove will remain an eternal mystery to us, adding beauty and unexplainable joy to our ordinary lives."

"Like a lovely woman?" Reid asked, catching sight of Sidra on her way to the temple with Janina. Osiyar followed the direction of his glance.

"That is a more mundane mystery," he said. "But, like the greater mystery, it is best left unpenetrated."

Reid stared at him, wondering if the usually serious High Priest had just made a joke. Osiyar looked back at him with a bland expression, and Reid dismissed the idea. But he remained puzzled by the words.

"Accept it," Osiyar said softly, his eyes returning to Sidra. "Simply enjoy what is beyond explanation. It is the way of Ruthlen. While you live here, make it your way, too."

With his own sight now upon Janina's slim figure, Reid's only answer was a shrug. There was certainly no explanation for what he felt about her. He thought perhaps Osiyar was right, and wiser than Reid could admit.

The days drew on toward the time of the double full moons, when Reid would be expected to mate with the village women who chose him. With each day that passed, Janina's heart grew heavier. She understood Tamat's deep sense of frustration about the gradual decline in the village population and her desperate hope that Reid would literally provide Ruthlen with new life. She accepted Tamat's reasoning, but still she could not bear the thought of Reid lending himself to some other woman. She had no right to think of him as her own, but she did.

When Reid talked with Tamat while she was in attendance, she tried not to look directly at him, though that was hard. She always wanted to look at him. Now that he was no longer so foreign to her she could see he was not ugly at all, only different from the people she had known all her life. With his face healed of its scrapes and bruises, and his beard gone thanks to one of Osiyar's razors, she could see how strong and masculine his features were.

She often caught him looking at her while she stood behind Tamat's chair in the small audience chamber off the central room. She believed

Tamat knew they looked at each other—how could Tamat not know?—but the High Priestess ignored the glances Reid and Janina cast when each thought the other's attention was elsewhere. And from the second time Sidra had caught them talking in the courtyard, after which she had subjected Janina to a long and very thorough tongue-lashing and hours of extra work, Janina had been careful never to speak to Reid when no one else was with her, nor to remain in private with him for even an instant—not until the day when Reid followed her into one of the smaller buildings behind the temple.

"What is this place?" he asked. "Osiyar told me all the smaller buildings not used for dwellings are storehouses for grain."

"They are." Janina gestured toward the casks neatly arrayed in rows along the wall, then to the vat in the center of the room. "You might say this is another way to store grain, for it keeps indefinitely. It's batreen."

"Never heard of it." Reid suddenly grinned at her. "But I have a fair idea of what it is just by the smell."

"The grain is fermented into a rather potent drink." Janina picked up a long wooden paddle and began to stir the contents of the vat. "It is used at the twin moons festivals. This batch is almost ready."

She looked down into the vat, unable to meet Reid's eyes lest he see in hers her bitter despair over what awaited him at the next festival. She knew of two women who had spoken freely of their desire to bed Reid in order to discover if he was any different from the village men.

"Do all the villagers become inebriated?" Reid asked. "Do you drink it, too?"

"I don't like the taste," Janina answered. "I only drink one cup, because it is required, but the villagers love it."

"All of them?" Reid asked. "Do they all drink far into the night? The priestesses and Osiyar, too?"

"All of them, except Tamat and me. Because of her age, Tamat stays only for the ritual and the first part of the feast. I always retire with her."

"But the others remain in the feasting area and drink heartily along with the villagers?" When Janina admitted this was so, Reid asked, "Don't they all have sick heads the next day?"

"For a while," Janina told him, "but the discomfort wears off quickly, and the drink has no dangerous aftereffect. In fact, it is quite nutritious. Why are you so interested in batreen?"

"I'm only trying to learn all I can about the life here, since it seems I'm fated to remain either in the temple or the village."

"Staying in Ruthlen won't be as bad as the alternative." He looked so unhappy that Janina could not help herself; she had to put down the wooden paddle and place both her hands on his arm. She thought he must be missing his friends, and while she had never had any friends to care about, anything that made Reid unhappy, made her unhappy. His hand came down on top of hers and she trembled at the contact of flesh with warm flesh.

"What is the alternative?" he asked. "What would they do to me if they decided not to let me live here any more?"

"You would be set adrift." Her voice was low. It was too horrible to speak about, so no one ever did. But in his ignorance, Reid had no qualms.

"Adrift? What do you mean—with no provisions?"

" 'Without sail, or oars, or rudder,' " she said, reciting from memory the most terrible punishment decreed by the Chosen Way. "It is against the law to take a life, because there are too few of us to waste life. But occasionally, if someone does something truly unforgiveable, that person is set adrift. There are dreadful creatures in the sea, Reid, huge monsters with tentacles that capture and crush their victims, then eat them. My parents died like that."

"They were set adrift?"

"No." She had never spoken to anyone about that terrible day. She had kept the horror locked inside her, but now she wanted to talk about it, to tell Reid what had happened. "They left in my father's littlest boat. It was just for a short time, to watch the sunset. Days of thick fog had just ended, and the breaking clouds were so beautiful, with the sky a deep blue. I can still see the scene when I close my eyes and think about it. The tide was full; the water came right up to the top of the sea wall. I stood on the wall waving to them.

"Usually, the sea monsters stay well away from shore, on the opposite side of the swift current, but perhaps because of the high tide, this monster had come in near to the wharf. It rose out of the water and took my parents. There was not time for them to cry out. They were simply *gone*. I saw it happen." She and her parents had never been close, but that had not made her loss any less terrible.

Reid said nothing. He just put his arms around her and held her tenderly. Janina had no tears to shed, but his concern for her was comforting all the same. Flouting the restrictions about priestesses avoiding any intimacy with men, not caring if Sidra might learn what she was doing and punish her, Janina let her arms slip around Reid's waist and rested her head on his shoulder. She felt his hand stroking her hair with a gentleness she would not have expected from a man so large and strong. After a while his hand left her hair. He tilted her chin upward, and at the same time lowered his head.

The kiss began in tenderness, in reassurance and comfort. It quickly changed into a wondrous heat that ignited Janina's very soul. She was stretched along the length of his body as though fastened to some instrument of exquisite torture. She wanted that contact, she craved it. She yearned desperately to be one with Reid, yet they dared not come together. It would mean certain death for both of them, a dreadful death on the sea. She could not do that to him, and she could not break her vows. Why then did she cling ever more closely to him and open her lips so willingly to take his tongue into the hot depths of her mouth?

Even as she asked herself the question she knew its answer. She had recognized Reid from the first instant she had seen his face during her Test. She had fought against her own feelings, had lied to herself and made excuses about Tamat needing her so she could spend as much time as possible in the same room with him and still not feel guilty. But now, in this deep, passionate embrace, she could no longer hide from self-knowledge. Reid was her one true love, the mate predestined for her. She wondered what cruel force had brought them together to suffer this violent conflict between duty and desire. It would have been better for both of them if they had never met, if neither had known the other existed. Still, she did know him, and loved him, and would never stop loving him. Wrong or not, she could not prevent herself from returning his kiss and wanting it to go on forever. It was all she would have of him, and even this much was forbidden.

It was Reid who drew back first.

"This can only hurt you if someone should discover us," he said, setting her aside and heading toward the door.

"And you." She faced him across the room, her eyes burning with unshed tears. "Three nights from now, you must lend yourself to some village woman and give her a child."

"I wish it could be you," he whispered harshly.

"Oh, Reid," she moaned, then bit off the reply that would have told him how much she wished the same thing. For his safety, she had to make him understand that he could never kiss her, or even be alone with her, again. "I am to take my final vows nineteen days from now, when both moons have darkened and become new again. Did you know that? Since first I came to the temple after my parents died, I have been waiting to be bound into my final place in the priesthood, though it will be a lesser place than Tamat wanted for me." She stopped, choking back a sob, knowing she had failed all the precepts she had been taught.

"Final vows?" Reid exclaimed. "I thought you were already a priestess. And what do you mean, bound? I don't like the sound of that. Janina, are you absolutely certain you want to become a priestess?"

"I am a scholar-priestess now, bound by primary vows, so I have no choice," she admitted, knowing she no longer desired what once she had wanted so badly. "It was decided for me on the day I was born."

"But do you want it?"

"I can't change what was decided by my parents," she said. "They are dead and can't change their plans for me, you see. I have been studying for ten years. Now my period of training is finished, and it is time for the last steps, my final profession of willingness, my tattoo, and the golden rope bracelets that can never be removed."

"Sidra and Tamat aren't tattooed," Reid objected, thinking about the tattoo on Osiyar's forehead. Janina's reply made it clear to him that she understood what he was thinking.

"Priests wear their tattoos on their foreheads," she informed him. "Priestesses wear theirs over their hearts."

"Can you refuse to take the final vow?" he asked, wincing at the thought of hot needles searing her tender flesh.

"No." It seemed to Janina that the space between them grew wider at the sound of that one small word. She saw Reid's expression close, so that she could no longer discern what he was feeling. His mouth became a hard slash.

"We should not be here together," he said, opening the door.

He left the brewery building with fury in his heart. He and Janina belonged together. He was certain of it. Yet she was being forced into a barren existence he firmly believed she no longer wanted, while he would be made to couple with some unknown woman in the name of genetic improvement. It was cruel and unfair, and he had to find a way to save them both.

"Reid, must you be so clumsy? You almost knocked me down." Sidra watched him from bright, suspicious eyes. She was so close that her sweet perfume filled his nostrils, reminding him of the crimson flowers in the sacred grove. "What were you doing in there? Only priestesses are permitted in the brewery."

"Janina was explaining how batreen is made. Don't blame her; I blundered into the place and then insisted she tell me." Reid had had enough of rules. These people were worse than the Jurisdiction when it came to trying to force everyone to conform. He'd be star-blasted if he'd follow their rules! He'd lie with no woman he hadn't chosen for himself, and he didn't care if Sidra knew everything he was thinking.

Sidra raised her elegant eyebrows at him. Reid, thinking she might know what was in his mind and expecting to be accused of corrupting a scholar-priestess, decided to attack first.

"I'm surprised you didn't know what I was doing in the brewery without asking me. I thought you were always aware of everything that happens in the temple complex."

"You know perfectly well by now that I cannot enter anyone's mind without permission," Sidra answered calmly, heading toward the temple and drawing him along with her. "That is our Chosen Way, Reid, and I will uphold it."

"Does no one ever break the law?" Reid wondered.

"I doubt there has ever been a law made that no one has broken." Sidra mounted the steps to the temple.

"Tell me, Sidra, is it possible to touch someone's thoughts without that person knowing it?"

"Not from telepath to telepath. To non-telepaths, yes, it is possible, because they don't understand how the Gift works. Why do you ask?"

"I knew it when Tamat examined me the first day I was here," Reid replied.

"She meant you to know." Sidra smiled, looking right into his eyes, and for just a moment Reid felt the hair on the back of his neck stand up, until Sidra spoke again. "I believe Osiyar is waiting for you in his house."

She pulled open the heavy wooden door and went into the temple. Reid stared after her, feeling rather than hearing her mocking laughter and knowing that beautiful, dangerous Sidra was fully aware of his frustrated passion for Janina. When the temple door had closed again and the silent laughter had stopped, Reid turned toward Osiyar's house, aware that he had learned two valuable facts that day. He knew about the effects of batreen, and he knew that despite her profession of respect for the Chosen Way, Sidra did not obey its laws.

CHAPTER 7

"*You will come with us to the shore this evening,* Reid," Tamat said. "Since you are to spend the rest of your life with us, you must begin to celebrate our festivals as we do. You will start by offering yourself, and the seed of new life that lies within you, to the full twin moons."

Janina saw Reid's mouth tighten. An angry flame sparked in his grey eyes. For an instant she thought he would turn on his heel and leave the central room of the temple—possibly even try to escape from Ruthlen itself.

"You need to master your proud spirit." Tamat had also seen his anger. "It is an honor to be required to sacrifice yourself for the community. Accept our will, Reid. Do as you are told."

"It is not my community." He was just short of open defiance, though still respectful of Tamat.

Janina held her breath, hoping he would do nothing to merit severe punishment. Surely Tamat would not want to punish him on this of all days, when his co-operation was so vital to her plans. "Nor is blind worship of two dead moons and an overlarge star a religion I can believe in," Reid added.

"The moons are not dead," Sidra declared. "They grow and change and then dwindle as the days pass. They rise and set at differing times, until the evening comes round when they rise and set together. On those sacred nights, they are either bright disks or else so dark they are only barely discernable. Are not such changes proof of life?"

Sidra regarded Reid with so much scorn that Janina feared the priestess would strike him. She trembled, waiting to see Sidra's hand rise. It was Tamat who soothed Sidra's temper and Reid's pride.

"You need not believe as we do, Reid," Tamat said. "Only respect our beliefs. That is all we require of you."

"I can do that," Reid said.

He still did not look happy, but when Tamat dismissed him he bowed politely and went away with no further protest.

"He will be difficult to control tonight," Sidra said, looking after him. "He is too independent to do what you want of him, Tamat."

"He is a young and healthy man who has lived a celibate life for many days now," Tamat responded. "Give him a few cups of batreen and a willing woman, and he will not resist for very long."

"You may be right," Sidra said. "Janina, why are you standing there listening to words that cannot concern you? Go to the kitchen at once. You were to help Philian with the bread baking, and you are late, as usual. Tamat dear, let me help you to your bed. You should rest before the great effort you will make at moonrise."

Janina found Philian hard at work. Preparations for the feast had begun at dawn, when several of the village women had arrived at the temple kitchen to lend their hands to the mixing and kneading and cooking that needed to be done.

"When it's time to take men tonight, I'll chose Reid," joked Senastria, one of the fisherwomen, who was well known for her love of men and her wild ways. "I like danger, and he looks dangerous to me."

"You have enough danger on the sea," retorted her friend Anniellia, slapping a pile of dough around on the table. "You worry about the sea monsters and leave Reid to me. I shall be the one to give the village its first dark-haired baby. He's so big, that Reid. Do you suppose that means—?" She glanced at the priestesses before whispering something to Senastria. The two of them went off into a fit of laughter.

"Stupid, crude fools," muttered Philian to Janina. "All they ever think about is lending themselves to men."

Janina punched harder at the lump of dough

she was kneading. She was angry with herself because she was as wicked as the two village women. She could think of nothing but Senastria in Reid's arms, kissing him while he put his hands on her. He would surely choose Senastria. She was much prettier than Anniellia.

For most of that day, Janina tried to shut her ears against the women's talk about lovers and their comparisons of the sexual skills of certain village men, mixed with speculation about Reid. She was greatly relieved when Sidra sent for her in late afternoon to help Tamat dress, so she had an excuse to leave the giggling women.

It seemed to Janina that Tamat was more fragile than ever. The aged hands shook often while Janina and Sidra robed her, and as soon as her headdress was arranged, Tamat sat down, looking as though she might not rise again.

"Dearest Tamat," Sidra said, "you are unwell. Shall I put on the headdress and go out to the people in your place? The walk to the beach will tire you badly."

"You are not High Priestess yet, Sidra," Tamat said with unaccustomed irritability. "Janina, help me to stand. Sidra, call in the lesser priestesses. It is time to go."

Despite her frailty, Tamat walked out of the temple with her usual dignified composure, nodding to Reid, Osiyar, and the two scholar-priests when they joined her. Moving to the entrance of the temple complex, she greeted the villagers who waited in the gathering twilight, then stepped onto the ceremonial road and began the procession to the beach with Osiyar by her side.

Reid fell into step next to Janina.

"What will happen at the beach?" he asked in a low voice. "Osiyar has told me nothing except to bathe and put on clean clothing, and then do whatever I am told to do."

Janina could see Sidra walking just behind Tamat and Osiyar. After her came the lesser priestesses and the scholar-priests. From that distance Sidra could not hear anything Janina and Reid might say, so they were safe from her scolding or criticism. The villagers who followed the group from the temple were also too far away to eavesdrop. For the next few moments it was safe to speak to Reid.

"I wish you well this night." She spoke quickly. "When Sidra tells you to kneel, do so at once. Beyond that I cannot advise you or explain what will be done. It is a power given only to those who are full priestesses or priests. Because I am not a telepath, I will never be capable of understanding it, nor will I be able to do what the others do. The ceremony is intended to honor the full moons, and tonight Tamat will also ask for new life to be given to Ruthlen."

She gave him a quick, slanting look. His face was flushed with anger, and she thought perhaps with embarrassment, too. Had she been in Reid's position, she would have been horribly embarrassed. She forced herself to stop thinking about the village women, or wishing she could be one of them. She had her own destiny to fulfill. As always, she would obey Tamat, even if obeying broke her heart.

Side by side, Janina and Reid walked in silence past the tumbled rocks of the headland that separated the beach from the rest of Ruthlen. They had almost reached their destination. Janina could think of nothing more to say to Reid that would not cause her, or him, great pain. There was nothing either of them could do to change what Tamat had commanded to happen this night. It was Reid who found words.

"Janina," he said, "I promise you I will not—"

She put up her hand to stop him, fearing that someone might overhear whatever he had been about to say, for now they had stepped off the end of the road and were walking across the sand. Tamat and Osiyar were standing together at the edge of the water, with Sidra just behind them. The other priestesses and the scholar-priests took their places behind Sidra.

"Come here, Reid," Sidra ordered. "Stand there, close to Tamat."

Janina remained alone, outside the half circle formed by white-clad backs. She did not belong in that circle, nor did she belong among the villagers. So it had always been. She stayed where she was, in case Tamat should need her.

In unison, Tamat and Osiyar began to raise their arms just as the full twin moons rose one after the other into the clear, purple-blue sky. The moons gave almost as much light as the sun, but in contrast to the sun's orange-gold glare, this was a pale, silvery light that pleased and rested the eyes. The ocean foamed pure white as it reached the shore, while farther out smaller waves sparkled silver in the trails cast by the moons.

Tamat and Osiyar, still acting in unison, lifted their arms over their heads and held them there. Emanating from their fingertips, sparkling particles of light began to pour in silver profusion, falling around the two figures at the water's edge until they were only indistinct shapes seen through flowing, glimmering beauty.

Janina heard the villagers' indrawn breath, then heard them falling to their knees in reverence, for though they were all telepaths, too, and had witnessed this ceremony many times, no one else had ever possessed the richness of power that Tamat held in her mind. With Osiyar's strength added to Tamat's, the spectacle the villagers now beheld was one of awe-inspiring wonder.

Then Sidra and the other priestesses all raised their arms, using their combined power to call down more of the moon-silver. The light they achieved was not so bright as that of Tamat and Osiyar, but still the space around them glittered and glowed.

By that light Janina read on Reid's astonished face all the mingled delight and amazement he was experiencing at his first sight of the full power of Ruthlen. Watching Reid, knowing he could not partake of the sacred ceremony any more than she could, Janina did not feel her usual sense of inadequacy and loneliness. His eyes met hers across the space separating them. He smiled at her through a sheen of glittering light. Janina smiled back. It seemed to her that the silver power of the telepaths dimmed and receded into the distant background. She saw only Reid and his longing for her, while in her open, innocent face and eyes she showed him her own hopeless yearning for him and knew he understood her emotions as she understood his. Then Sidra moved, chanting an ancient hymn, and Janina's visual contact with Reid was broken.

The light enveloping Sidra and the lesser priestesses faded. Sidra, still chanting, motioned to Reid to kneel. There followed a moment when he did not move, during which Janina wondered if he would defy the priestess. Then he went to his knees, but so awkwardly that Janina considered the possibility that Sidra had forced him down by the power of her mind and was holding him there on the sand.

Now Tamat turned from the sea, lowering her arms over Reid until the veil of silver light flowing about her fell across his bent shoulders like a mantle.

"Thou shalt bring new life to Ruthlen," Tamat intoned, "Strength and health and vital life."

Tamat's arms fell to her sides, the silver light around her dissipating. At the same time, the light surrounding Osiyar was gone, too, leaving a pale, tired-looking man. Tamat staggered in weariness. Osiyar and Sidra took her arms.

Tamat stiffened her back and pulled away from them.

"I am perfectly well," she said. "Come, Reid, walk beside me that the villagers may all see you. It is time for the feast."

It seemed to Janina that the return to the temple took a long time. She walked alone, isolated between the inhabitants of the temple in front of her and the village folk behind her. The warmth of the day had given way to coolness, since the season was turning toward the dark time of year. She shivered in her sheer, sleeveless white robe and was grateful to the two scholar-priests who ran ahead of the procession to light the giant bonfire that had been laid outside the entrance to the temple complex. Its warmth was welcome.

Soon the smells of hot vegetable and fish stews wafted across the festival area outside the temple wall, and piles of steaming, fresh bread were brought to the tables to the delight of the hungry villagers.

Amid the cheerful, noisy crowd, Reid and Janina stood together, not speaking. Reid's face still held an expression of wonder at what he had seen at the beach. When his look met hers, Janina felt as though they had pledged themselves to each other during the ceremony just completed. But how could that be when they were fated to be torn apart on this very night, when he must go to another woman's bed while she returned alone to her virginal duties in the temple? She was fully aware of the way the women were regarding Reid's tall figure and whispering among themselves about him.

"Reid, come with me," Sidra ordered. "You are to sit over there. Janina, you know where you are supposed to be; why aren't you in your place?"

As Sidra led Reid away, Janina noticed Senastria and Anniellia watching him closely. Dry-eyed and suddenly angry with fate, she went to stand behind Tamat, who waited patiently at the center of one of the long tables until the villagers had seated themselves and then quieted enough to hear her.

"The harvest will be a good one this year," Tamat said to them at the close of a short speech of welcome. "Therefore, feast and take your pleasure tonight, for the days ahead will require hard work from all of you, farmfolk and villagers alike, to fill our storehouses against the coming cold season. Let us celebrate the fertility of the land and the women of Ruthlen, and the continuation of our Chosen Way." She then sat down in an ancient carved armchair.

Pitchers and jugs of batreen were brought out to cheers and applause. Tamat was given the first cup. She drank it down without stopping, apparently gaining strength from the healthy brew. All of the priestesses, along with Osiyar and the scholars, then each drank a cup, after which the feasting began in earnest.

Sidra had seen to it that Reid was seated at another table from the one where the priestesses were, to give him the opportunity to talk with as many village women as possible. Knowing what he would shortly do with one of those women, Janina could not look at him again. If she did, he would surely see her pain and might be tempted to do something that would result in punishment for him. She directed her attention toward Tamat instead of Reid. But she could not help seeing on Tamat's other side that Sidra and Osiyar were whispering together.

"You do not eat, child." Tamat was looking at her untouched stew bowl.

"It's the batreen," Janina began.

"No, it's the man." Tamat patted her hand. "I understand how difficult it can sometimes be to hold to your vows. I'm old, girl, but my memory hasn't failed me yet. Stay with me tonight, in my room. We'll talk of other things so you need not think about what he will be doing."

Soon after this, Tamat rose to leave the feast. She took Janina and the two lesser priestesses with her. Sidra and Osiyar would remain to preside until the villagers had eaten and drunk their fill and had stumbled off to bed with whatever partners they desired.

With an aching heart, Reid watched Janina go. He wanted to hurry after her, to tell her he had no intention of coupling with any woman but her. Then he saw Sidra looking at him and knew he would have to be on guard lest she discover what he was planning. He tried to make his mind blank, to think about nothing but the food and the batreen and the dancing that had just begun. He let the village women take turns teaching him how to dance in the circular, four-partner steps that seemed to go on and on forever. After a while he saw Sidra and Osiyar talking to a pair of well-dressed elderly men, whom he assumed were important in the village. He decided Sidra would be too busy to watch him carefully.

He pretended to drink heavily, but over and over again he managed to dispose of his batreen onto the ground or into the bushes. He began to weave and shout the way the other dancers were doing.

"Come with me," urged a woman, catching his hand to pull him from the crowd of dancers. "I'm Anniellia, and I chose you for tonight."

As she dragged him away, Reid snatched up a large jug of batreen.

"You won't need that," the woman said with a knowing laugh. "I'm all you'll need or want until dawn."

"I like the taste," Reid declared, weaving drunkenly. "We'll just have another cup before we retire."

Anniellia took him to her home in the village. It was little more than a shack, set closer to the water than the other houses. She lit a lamp, then fastened the shutters tight over the single window.

"Have you cups for the batreen?" Reid asked.

"Only one," Anniellia replied, producing a dirty wooden specimen. "You shall use it. You are my guest."

"No, lady," Reid insisted gallantly. "You may use the cup. I'll drink from the jug." He filled her cup, then pretended to drink deeply, upending the jug.

"It's good," he said, wiping his mouth on his sleeve. He filled Anniellia's cup again. She drank only half of it before putting it down.

"Take off all of your clothes," she ordered. "You are mine for tonight, and I've never seen a man who looks like you. I want to watch your body while we're together."

To replace his soiled and damaged treksuit, Reid had been given the same loose grey tunic and trousers the village men wore. When Anniellia reached for the waist of his trousers, he stepped away from her.

"You first," he said, filling her cup to the brim. "I want to look at you, too."

Anniellia pulled off her grey dress and flung it into a corner.

"Well?" she asked, pirouetting in front of him. "Am I pretty enough to please you?"

"You are lovely," he murmured, hoping he sounded convincing. She was a slightly heavier, much coarser version of Janina. She had full, rich breasts and nicely curving hips. Her hair was a shade or two darker than Janina's and curly instead of straight. Her eyes were sky-blue. Reid felt not the slightest stirring of desire for her. She was not Janina.

Anniellia lay down on her narrow bed, spread her legs a little, and beckoned with a provocative smile.

"Come to me," she said. "I have been waiting for you all evening, and I'm ready. Just take me now, Reid. We can do it more slowly the next time."

"I'm flattered that you chose me." Handing her the cup of batreen, Reid sat on the edge of her bed. "I shall drink a toast to your beauty."

"Can't that wait until later?" she said peevishly, shifting her legs. "Reid, hurry."

"And you must drink a toast to me. I'll be hurt if you don't." Gently but firmly he urged the hand holding the cup toward her lips. "Drink all of it, Anniellia. That's the custom in my home village."

"I'm getting dizzy." Her voice was plaintive, the words slightly slurred.

"Have I done that, made you dizzy with desire?" He laid one hand on a bare breast and felt her squirm in pleasure. "Now, I want you to drink another toast, my sweet Anniellia. To your lovely right breast. That's it. Now another, to your incredibly beautiful left breast."

He made her drink toasts to her nose, to each of her ears, all of her fingers and half of her toes before she finally fell asleep. She'd have a foul head in the morning, but he had confirmed the information Janina had given him by asking the lesser priestess, Philian, and she had assured him that while enough batreen would send the drinker into a deep stupor, it never caused any permanent physical damage. It was a completely harmless, totally pleasurable drink. Reid might have enjoyed it himself if he had been free to drink it in safety.

He picked up Anniellia's dress from the floor and tucked it over her naked body. Then he splashed a little of the batreen around her so she would smell it in the morning, and finished the job by rumpling the bedclothes. Finally, taking the jug with him, he slipped out the door and headed back to the temple complex.

The feast was over, except for a few folk draped across the tables in sleep and a group of elderly women talking together, who broke off to stare at him as he went by them. Sidra and Osiyar had gone. Reid made his way toward Osiyar's dwelling, eager to find his own room and lock the door against the women of Ruthlen.

The moment he stepped inside the High Priest's house, Reid knew there was something different within the building, some unusual yet faintly familiar feminine scent. It reminded him of red flowers. He peeked into the rooms used by the two younger priestlings, but they were empty. While priestesses were severely restricted, it seemed the priests were free to spend festival evenings as they wished. Shrugging his shoulders, Reid started for his own room. A low moan stopped him. It came from Osiyar's chamber.

Thinking the priest might have imbibed too much batreen and become sick, Reid pushed open the unlatched door, intending to ask if he could help. There, within the chamber, he saw the source of the sweet fragrance and recalled on whom he had recently smelled it.

Sidra lay naked on her back upon Osiyar's bed, her softly waving golden hair spilling across the covers, her eyes closed. She was an incredibly beautiful woman in the full ripeness of maturity, who was obviously lost in the throes of passion. Beside her, but not touching her, lay Osiyar, also unclothed and in the same aroused state as Sidra. His eyes, too, were closed. Sidra moaned, and Osiyar answered her with a long, drawn-out groan. The room was filled with a tension so strong Reid could not avoid feeling it, with sexual need, with a woman's demanding urgency, and with that sweet, heavy khata-flower perfume which he now recognized as Sidra's.

Reid turned away in disgust, left Osiyar's bedchamber, and closed the door softly. He paused for a moment in the round central room of the building, feeling sickened by the perversion of a great power. Now he understood why he had disliked Sidra so much since first meeting her. Something in him had seen her basic falseness.

Sidra, High Priestess-Designate, was doubtless virgin in body, but in mind and soul she was as unchaste as the lowest prostitute on any prison planet. It took no telepathic ability to understand that the two in the room behind him had linked their minds to commit in spirit an act they were forbidden to perform physically. The dishonesty and hypocrisy of that act took his breath away. He thought he knew who had instigated it, who had the greater telepathic power. The only question unanswered by the scene he had witnessed was whether Osiyar had been seduced or was a weak and willing accomplice.

He wondered briefly if Tamat knew. Then he thought surely not. That knowledge would destroy her, would break her gallant old heart. For Janina's sake, who loved Tamat, and because, in spite of their differences about opening Ruthlen to outsiders, he had come to admire and respect the High Priestess, Reid decided not to tell Tamat what he had seen. He hoped she would go to her grave not knowing. He felt certain that Sidra's telepathic power was strong enough to keep her secret well hidden. But when Tamat was dead, how could he leave Janina under the rule of those two in the room behind him? And what would they plan for him, once Tamat was gone?

He did not remember leaving Osiyar's house; he simply found himself in the temple courtyard. Breathing deeply of the clean night air to get Sidra's perfume out of his lungs, he hurried toward the opening in the encircling wall. His overpowering need to get as far away from Sidra and Osiyar as he could propelled him into the feasting area just outside the entrance.

"There you are." A female hand reached toward him to pull him away from the temple complex and into the darkness.

"Who are you?" he demanded, trying to shake off the unwanted touch.

"Senastria the fisherwoman," said the seductive voice. "I want to lie with you, Reid. I want to bear your child. Anniellia said she would have your first son, but she was wrong. It will be me."

After what he had just witnessed, Reid wasn't certain he could have made love then, even with Janina. He felt sick and dirty. This woman did not interest him at all, but he did not want her to make an uproar about his unwillingness.

He followed her up the nearby hillside. There, on a grassy spot between two rock outcroppings, she pulled him down beside her. To his great relief, Reid realized that he was still carrying the batreen jug. He thought it likely from her behavior that Senastria had already imbibed a fair amount. She proved to be a more willing drinker than Anniellia had been. She gulped right from the jug, giggling, and giggled again when Reid pretended to drink, too. It was not long before she slept soundly on her rocky pillow.

Reid returned to the temple, where he spent the rest of the night sitting against one of its columns with the empty batreen jug between his legs.

"I understand that you lent yourself to two women last night," Tamat said. "I am pleased with you, Reid, and I will be even more pleased when they produce healthy children."

"No one can be certain they will have children," Reid said.

"They always do after the twin full moons festival," Tamat replied serenely.

Reid had not thought about pregnancy, he had

only been interested in avoiding women he didn't want. He saw Sidra smiling at him and tried to guard his thoughts. He could not look at Janina's set, unhappy face. He wanted to tell her he had lent himself to no women, because he wanted only her. Realizing that Sidra's lovely blue eyes were still on him, Reid tried to make his mind a blank.

"If there is something wrong with Reid, so that these women do not conceive," Sidra said with false sweetness, "he can always try again at dark moons time, when we will celebrate Janina's full admission to our ranks. That seems to me an appropriate night for Reid to prove his value to us by impregnating two, or possibly three women. We would like you to father as many children as possible, Reid."

Before you are destroyed. The message lay so clearly in his mind that Reid was amazed Tamat had not sensed it. But Tamat obeyed the laws and would not expect her designated successor to violate them. He stood mute, wondering how much of his thoughts Sidra had penetrated, wondering if she knew the contempt and disgust he felt for her.

"Reid will do what he is required to do," Tamat said, making Reid remember that in this room there were at least two conversations taking place at one time. Sidra cast a mocking look in his direction before excusing herself to discuss some temple matter with Osiyar.

Go to your lover, you false, vicious creature, Reid thought scornfully as Sidra walked past him in a sweet wave of khata-flower fragrance.

Be careful, Reid, she answered silently. *You don't understand the power you are tempting.* He heard her laughter in his mind just before he doubled over and fell to the floor in sudden, excruciating pain.

Tamat cried out in surprise, while Janina rushed forward to help him. In an instant, the pain was gone. Reid lay too limp from shock to move, with his head in Janina's lap while she mopped his damp forehead with a corner of her robe. When Reid was able to open his eyes, the first thing he saw was Sidra's dainty, silver-sandaled foot peeping beneath the hem of her soft blue robe. He thought for a moment that she would kick him or make the pain return with greater intensity. Instead, she spoke aloud.

"Reid, I believe you have consumed too much batreen and it has disagreed with you. Please be more careful at the next festival."

"I will be careful," Reid promised in the shaky whisper that was all he could muster. Sidra went away. Reid caught Janina's small hand and held it to his lips for a moment.

"Stand up, Reid, and face me." At Tamat's bidding, Reid took a couple of deep breaths and made himself get off the floor. Tamat looked hard at him. "I do not believe what just happened to you was the result of batreen. What is wrong?"

"Nothing, Tamat." He felt steadier now. The brief, unbelievable pain was only a memory—coupled with a fear that it would return. He recognized that fear as something Sidra had implanted in his mind in an attempt to gain control over him.

"You lie." It was said without anger. The aged High Priestess leaned her head against the back of her chair, watching him intently.

"I will not permit access to my thoughts," Reid said, bringing a look of surprise to her face. He could not let her know what Sidra and Osiyar had done together, or what Sidra had just done to him. Tamat was so old and frail that if she knew, it would destroy her, and there was no one else but Sidra to take her place. After this morning's demonstration, Reid felt certain he would not last long if Sidra were High Priestess, and she might well choose to harm Janina, too. Even if she did not, Tamat's death would cause great pain to Janina. No, he had to avoid doing anything that might shorten Tamat's life.

"I have right of free access, but I do not believe this matter is urgent enough for me to expend the energy necessary to cross the barriers you would erect against me. If you will not allow me to enter your thoughts, then tell me in words," Tamat commanded.

"I cannot," Reid told her. "Trust me, Tamat. Believe that I will resolve any problem in my own way."

"I know you are an honest man." Tamat let out a long breath. "Keep your thoughts to yourself then. Only remember, I am not without power."

If Sidra had said that to him, Reid would have

called it a threat. From Tamat's lips, the words were like a promise of help.

"Thank you, Tamat." She sent him away then, and he left without another look from Janina, who had resumed her demure stance by Tamat's side.

"Child," Tamat said when the door had closed behind Reid, "you must end this dangerous attachment. Reid's coming has disturbed everyone in the temple and the village, but you most of all. He is meant for the village women. You are meant for the temple."

"I have tried to dismiss him from my thoughts by every exercise I ever learned in concentration," Janina replied. "But since the day I prophesied his coming, he has lodged in my heart and I cannot tear him out of it."

"I wish I had never arranged that Test, nor made the potion you drank," Tamat muttered. "But unfortunately, I am unable to foresee the future and so I could not tell that the result of my actions would be pain and disharmony to your heart and mind."

"Don't blame yourself," Janina cried, going to her knees beside Tamat's chair. "What has happened between Reid and me isn't your fault—nor his, either. I don't want you to think it's his deliberate doing. It's just that we knew each other at once. I feel we were meant to meet. Reid is part of me."

"Sidra likes him no better than she likes you," Tamat said. "I fear for both of you when I am gone."

"Do you think Sidra made him ill just now?" Janina asked. "It happened so suddenly, and then, just as suddenly, he was well again."

"She would not dare."

Janina thought Sidra *would* dare, and furthermore, she thought Tamat suspected as much, though she would not admit it. There was something peculiar happening, an intense undercurrent to life in the temple in recent days. She had been so involved with her feelings toward Reid and her growing unhappiness at her own fate that she had walked through her days without consciously noticing the way Sidra and Osiyar talked in quiet voices or whispers and abruptly stopped when anyone came near. They had always done that, for as long as Janina could remember, but recently the murmurings and sidelong glances had increased. The two lesser priestesses had changed, too. Philian was now openly fearful of Sidra and clung to Tamat's side whenever she could. The other, Adana, spent most of her time with Sidra. Tamat did not seem to notice, but Janina was certain the High Priestess knew what was going on.

Among Janina's duties was that of walking into the village each day, to the market by the sea wall to select fish for the evening meal. The fishsellers had never shown any friendliness toward her, yet they dared not be too disrespectful because of her connection with the temple. On the day after the twin full moons festival, Senastria had the best fish, so Janina had to make her choices from the unexpectedly talkative woman.

"That's a rare man you keep at the temple," Senastria said, grinning widely. "He satisfied me better than any of these village dolts could ever do, and look at the catch I've made today after spending the night with him. He has brought me luck. I've heard that the next time he'll be lent to us is during the dark moons festival. I'll be first in line at the entrance, waiting for him."

Janina laid the fish in her basket and turned aside, unable to make any answer that would not embarrass her. She was not to be allowed to leave the marketplace easily, however. Anniellia stood blocking her way, legs spread, fists on her hips. Janina stopped, but Anniellia was not interested in her.

"You only had him for a short time, and after I had already finished with him," she told Senastria. "I had him for most of the night, and I can tell you, he nearly broke my bed with his passion. What a man! What endurance! I'll gladly bear all the children Tamat wants, so long as Reid puts them inside me."

"He was with me longer!" Senastria yelled.

"He was with me first!" Anniellia retorted.

"That's because you dragged him away from the feast," screamed Senastria. "He left you to come to me and he was so eager he couldn't wait to walk to my house. He took me right there on the hillside. My back is raw from the rocks we rolled upon, but he was worth a little pain."

"Liar!" shouted Anniellia.

"It's you who lie!" returned Senastria.

"You stupid fisherwoman! Everyone knows you are barren. I will have Reid's child," Anniellia announced triumphantly.

At that insult to her fertility, Senastria slapped Anniellia hard. Anniellia grabbed Senastria's hair and pulled it. The two women went down, rolling across the pavement of the waterfront market, shrieking insults at each other. A crowd quickly gathered to watch them.

Janina walked away, tears streaming down her face. No one took any notice of her.

Those women had had what she wanted from Reid, had been held in his arms and kissed, yet all they could think of to do about it was quarrel. And what of Reid? Had he enjoyed it? Had he found them lovely? She knew he had only done what Tamat had commanded him to do, and everyone always obeyed Tamat. She could not blame Reid for what had happened. Still, some part of her wished he had boldly refused, had claimed he would lend himself to no one at all since Janina was forbidden. But if he had done so, he would have been punished. He might even have been set adrift. She would not want that. If Reid was to live, he would have to lend himself to the village women over and over again, and she would have to learn to bear it. She did not think she could.

"Janina, what's wrong? Who has made you cry?"

The object of her unhappy thoughts stood before her in simple grey tunic and trousers. She looked at his beloved face and it was all she could do to keep from running away and throwing herself into the sea. Instead, she thrust out the basket of fish, using it as a barrier between them.

"Nothing is wrong," she told him. "I'm not crying, I've only been laughing till my eyes watered. Two women at the market are fighting over who had the better part of you last night. It was very funny. Half the village is there watching them."

"I'm sorry." He put out his hand to her. She sidestepped it and left him, hurrying toward the kitchen building. But with her new awareness of peculiar forces operating within the temple complex, she made note of Sidra standing in the shade of the temple colonnade, watching them.

CHAPTER 8

Tamat was ill. She lay in her private chamber, propped up on pillows, unable to rise from her bed. Janina stayed with her day and night, sleeping but little, and that on the floor beside Tamat's bed. She even stayed with Tamat each evening when Sidra came to make her usually private report on the daily events of the temple.

"You must know, dear Tamat," Sidra said on the second night, eyeing Janina with distaste, "that I only wish you well again. You need not fear to be alone with me."

"I have no concern for myself at your hands," Tamat said in a weak voice. "I know you love me."

"Then let me lend you what strength I have," Sidra offered. "Come, take my hands and look into my eyes and I will help you to recover."

"You would only exhaust yourself, Sidra, and you need all your strength to manage the affairs of the temple. The drain on your energy is great since you have taken my place as well as your own in maintaining the blanking shield."

"Osiyar has been a great help to me," Sidra said.

"Still, I will not consume your Gift for my personal benefit. Left to myself, I will recover in a day or two," Tamat promised.

"She fears," Tamat remarked to Janina after Sidra had left them, "that I will die before I have transferred the ancestral memories to her. If that were to happen, she would have nothing but her own Gift to sustain her as High Priestess. She will need, and she will certainly want, much greater power than that."

"When will you link your mind with hers?" Janina asked, hoping it would not be too soon. Tamat would need time to regain her strength before attempting the Sacred Mind-Linking.

"I think," Tamat said after some consideration, "it should be during the dark moons festival. We will all have fasted and prepared ourselves for your binding as priestess. Once that is accomplished, I will give Sidra what she wants without subjecting her to a second period of fasting. She has waited patiently, considering her character, and it is well past the time when I should have entrusted the power to her. I will not live much longer, Janina. This illness is but a warning of the future. I do not need the Gift of prophecy, my dear; I can see for myself what lies ahead."

Janina was too aware of Tamat's weakness to protest what she had said. She wondered if Tamat would live until the dark moons festival. And then she thought with a shiver that once Sidra had the ancestral memories, her oft-asserted love for Tamat would be severely tested, for Sidra would have no more need of Tamat. Only love would make her keep the High Priestess alive then.

Further, Janina knew that although once she was bound as a priestess, she would be physically safe from Sidra, there was much Sidra could do to torment her mind. When Tamat finally drifted into slumber, Janina crouched at the foot of her bed, laid her head on her hands, and wept silently in despair and fear.

Reid came to visit Tamat the next day. Seeing how weak she was, he stayed only a short time. He left believing she would not live much longer. From what he had learned of Sidra, he was convinced that he and Janina would not outlive Tamat by many days.

He had tried to stay away from Sidra as much as possible because of his disgust at the way she had broken the spirit of her sacred vows during the full moons festival. Osiyar he could not avoid, for they lived in the same house and the man was his instructor. Partly because he had grown to like Osiyar, Reid believed the illicit relationship between the High Priest and Sidra was mostly Sidra's doing. He thought Osiyar lacked that air of falseness which to Reid's perception was so great a part of Sidra's personality. To lend credence to Reid's conviction about the difference in character between them, Osiyar now went about his duties with an attitude of controlled tenseness which Reid interpreted as guilt.

That evening, Philian approached him as he stood alone in the courtyard watching one half-full moon set while the second moon, also half-full, still rode high in the purple sky.

"Tamat wishes to speak with you," Philian said.

"Is Janina with her?" Reid felt the quickening of his heart that occurred every time he knew he was to see Janina, but Philian shook her head.

"Tamat has sent Janina to her own chamber to rest, and she is sleeping soundly," Philian said. "I am to tell you also that Sidra and Adana are completely engaged in maintaining the blanking shield, while Osiyar is busy instructing the scholar-priests in ways of controlling the Gift. You and Tamat will not be disturbed."

Wondering why Tamat wanted a second interview with him in one day, and a completely private one at that, Reid followed Philian into the temple.

"Wait outside my door," Tamat instructed the lesser priestess. "Let no one enter, not even Sidra if she should come here."

"Yes, Tamat." Philian closed the door behind her.

"Sit on the side of my bed, Reid." When he had obeyed, Tamat went on. "There are eight days left until the time of the dark moons, when Sidra will draw the disk and crescent tattoo on Janina's left breast, and I will personally bind upon her wrists the golden ropes that will change her from a mere scholar to a lesser priestess. I will tie the unbreakable knots of gold, as my great-aunt once tied them for me."

Tamat paused, closing her eyes and waiting, as though she expected some comment. Reid could not make a sound. The thought of the unspeakably vile Sidra being turned loose to stab Janina's tender breast with a needle stopped his voice most effectively. After a moment of silence, Tamat continued, keeping her eyes closed.

"That night, we will celebrate the dark moons festival. Janina, as our newest priestess, will be the guest of honor, and you, Reid, will once more lend yourself to the village women."

Still Reid said nothing. He began to wonder if Tamat knew he had not really lain with either Anniellia or Senastria at the full moons festival, and if she was planning to scold him about it and perhaps threaten some punishment if he did not do what she wanted at the coming festival. He was not expecting her next words, nor the charge she laid upon him.

"The day after that festival," Tamat said, "as the newborn crescent moons begin their ascent into the evening sky, Sidra and I will perform the most difficult task for any telepaths. During the Sacred Mind-Linking, I will transfer to her all of my memory. Everything I received from the previous High Priestess's memory, back to the time before Ruthlen was founded, and all that I have learned during my own lifetime, will become Sidra's memories also, to use as she wishes. The act of transference will kill me."

"No," Reid said, taking her hands, thinking this had to be the time to reveal the truth about Sidra. "Tamat—"

"Do not tell me I will live for many years yet," Tamat instructed, opening her eyes at last and looking into Reid's face. "I know how much strength I have left, my friend. It will be just enough for the Mind-Linking. Oh, my body may breathe, or even eat and appear to be awake for a few days afterward, but my mind will be broken beyond repair. I have left the task until too late you see, because I always secretly hoped Janina would be capable of following me. But it will be Sidra. There is no one else."

Reid dismissed any thought of revealing Sidra's perfidy to this valiant old woman who already had a deep sorrow to bear. He squeezed her hands, wishing he knew how to lend her his strength. Tamat smiled at him, and for an instant he wondered if she knew his thoughts.

"I lay a command on you, Reid," she said. "I have tried to assure Janina's continued well-being by allowing her to become a lesser priestess even though she lacks the Gift. Once her wrists are bound with the golden ropes, she should be safe from harm by anyone in Ruthlen. Before the Sacred Mind-Linking, Sidra must make a vow to care for and protect all the priestesses. But of late I have begun to doubt Sidra's good will. Her desire for complete power, her lack of compassion for those weaker than herself—" Tamat stopped, swallowing hard. Reid thought he did not need to tell her about Sidra. In the blue eyes that never left his face he saw a despair too deep for words, and he was convinced that Tamat knew all about Sidra.

"There is no one else," Tamat whispered again, so softly that he had to bend nearer to hear her. Then, after a moment's pause, she spoke once more. "Reid, I command you to use all means necessary to protect Janina after she is bound as a priestess. I might have asked Osiyar, but he is weak in certain ways. You are the one I trust. You are strong and clever." The wrinkled eyelids closed again in exhaustion.

"I promise," Reid said, "that from the moment you bind the golden ropes on Janina's wrists, I will protect her from any harm whatsoever, even at the cost of my own life. Am I to witness the ceremony, Tamat?"

"It is for priestesses only," came Tamat's thread of a voice. "Until the binding, and the Mind-Linking, you both remain under my rule, Reid."

He said nothing to that, and after a moment more she relinquished her grip on his hands.

"Leave me now," she said in a stronger voice.

"Send Philian to me. Don't speak of this conversation to anyone."

"I understand." Reid returned to the temple courtyard, to stand in the silver dimness of moonset, considering all that Tamat had said. She must know how he felt about Janina. By extracting that promise from him, she had secured his good behavior toward the girl. But she had worded her command so oddly. He was to protect Janina, not from the instant he made his promise, but from the moment she actually became a priestess.

Reid believed Tamat when she said that the strain of the Mind-Linking with Sidra would kill her. After the time he had spent in Ruthlen, he also believed that Tamat would never willingly break any of the laws the telepaths had laid down for themselves.

But those who were not telepaths were not obliged to obey the telepaths' Chosen Way. And it was universally understood that prisoners were not required to obey the laws of their keepers. Tamat knew all of that as well as Reid did. Reid began to think the High Priestess, too scrupulous to enter his mind after he had repeatedly forbidden it, had been giving him a dangerous message in the only way she could—without actually speaking the words. It was up to him to interpret and act on that message.

Time passed rapidly until it was the day before the dark moons festival. Tamat insisted that she was completely well again and would be able to preside at the ritual which would bind Janina into her final vows, and at the feast afterward.

Reid had been called to the central room of the temple, where he found Sidra and Osiyar.

"Eat well today," Osiyar instructed. "Retire to bed early tonight."

"Drink no batreen at the feast tomorrow," Sidra ordered, "for when night comes you will be required to lend yourself to as many women as you possibly can, and we do not want you incapacitated by drink. Tamat is deeply disappointed that neither Anniellia nor Senastria has conceived. You must do better this time. You owe us that."

Reid said nothing, and carefully thought nothing, trying to keep Sidra from reading his thoughts. But once his interview with her was over and he was sure she would be completely occupied with Osiyar, he admitted his anger to himself.

He'd be star-blasted into atoms before he'd go through another night like the last festival! He had spent the past sixteen days as the unwilling subject of innumerable stories about the rivalry between Senastria and Anniellia, and their plans for him during the night of the dark moons.

On his daily walks into the village with Osiyar and the scholar-priests, he had borne the cold stares of the men and the knowing smiles of the women. He did not trust any of them. They had gone too quickly from the urge to stone him because he was unknown and different from anyone they had seen before, to a suspicious eagerness to allow him to father a large part of their next generation. He found it hard to believe they were as subservient to Tamat's wishes in that matter as they appeared to be. He felt more and more certain that the length of his life would be decided by the length of Tamat's life, which gave him two to four days more at best.

He was determined to get away from Ruthlen, and he had decided he would take Janina with him. She had become so precious to him that he wanted no other woman, and he would rather die than leave her behind to deal with the power-hungry Sidra. The more he thought about how to do it, the more convinced he became that it was what Tamat wanted, too. He believed that was the message she had tried to convey to him when she was so sick.

He thought almost constantly about ways in which he and Janina might reach freedom. He had heard enough about the horrors of the sea to know there could be no escape that way. The difficulties of procuring and provisioning a boat were further reasons to avoid the sea route, along with the obvious objection Janina had once voiced, that on the open water there was no place for a boat to hide after they were missed and the alarm was raised.

But there were hiding places on land. One of those places would never be searched by villagers looking for him. Even Osiyar could not go there. Only priestesses were allowed in the sacred grove.

Reid took himself to the kitchen building,

knowing he would find there the young priestess Philian, who was close to Tamat and who seemed to be a sensible person. When he told her he was hungry, she cheerfully gave him half a loaf of fresh bread and a cup of the hot, brewed herbs called *dhia*. While he ate, Reid fell into easy conversation with her, hoping to learn from her the timing of the next day's events, and pretending complete ignorance of them.

"I know nothing of the ritual planned for Janina tomorrow," he said between bites of crusty bread. "What will be done with her? Some kind of purification first, I should think."

"At dawn tomorrow, wearing a plain white robe, Janina will go alone to the sacred grove to fetch the Water for her purification bath," Philian informed him. "When she returns, she will be greeted by all the other priestesses and conducted into the central room of the temple. There she will be stripped and bathed with the Water she has brought. Tamat and Sidra will then examine her to be certain she is pure enough to be a priestess."

"Does the examination involve mind-linking?" Reid asked, wondering how Sidra could hide her falseness during such a linkage. "Is the tattooing done afterward?"

"You know too much about our rituals already, Reid," Philian said gently. "I cannot tell you more."

"I understand. Forgive me if my questions were rude. It is only that I'm interested, since Tamat says I'll be here for the rest of my life."

But he had learned what he wanted to know. Janina would go alone to the grove the next morning. Reid planned to be there waiting for her. Somehow he would convince her that they had to leave Ruthlen before she was irrevocably bound as a priestess.

They could climb down the cliff into the ravine, the way he had come. They would stay in the ravine, follow it to its southern end, find land that was more open, and then try to make their way back to Tarik's headquarters. It would take many days of walking, and he knew they might not survive to find Tarik and the others. Still, it would be better than being forced to service all the women in the village while Janina was nearby and knew what he was doing, yet was kept from him by vows he felt certain she no longer wanted to take.

"Don't waken me tomorrow morning," Reid said that night to the two scholar-priests in Osiyar's house. "All that ritual with the priestesses is nothing to me, and I need to rest for the coming night, when I probably won't sleep at all. I have been ordered by Tamat to lend myself to as many women as I can." He spoke with appropriate seriousness, and the young men gravely agreed that he must follow Tamat's bidding in all things.

Shortly before dawn, while it was still dark enough to provide some cover, yet light enough for him to find his way, Reid slipped out of the temple complex. He believed no one was awake, though he stopped several times to hide in the shadows when he thought he heard footsteps behind him, and once or twice he had the eerie feeling that someone was watching him.

He skirted the village on the landward side, keeping well away from the houses, until he came to the road leading toward the sacred grove. It did not take long to reach the steps which would take him to the opening in the mountain. He paused to look around, to make certain once more that no one was following him.

By now it was much lighter, and Reid could see a few farmers in their fields gathering the last of the harvest. Rather than chance being seen using the steps, he went up the hillside by scrambling among the bushes and briars that grew wild there. Glancing behind his shoulder one last time to be sure no one had noticed or followed him, he moved onto the wide stone terrace on his hands and knees, then ran for the cover of the tunnel entrance. It was as black as deep outer space, and he tripped repeatedly on the carved stone steps before he came out into the deeply shadowed early morning light of the little grove.

Janina came unwillingly to the grove, with her heart in torment. In just a little while she would stand in the temple naked and cleansed, awaiting examination. Tamat and Sidra would join their minds to hers and both would learn how impure she was, how undeserving of the tattoo and the golden bonds of a priestess. They would know how unfit she was for a life of purity and service, and how reluctantly she took her vows. She had failed Tamat yet again, for while her body remained unchanged by her desire for Reid, her mind and heart belonged to him alone.

Would Tamat understand how determined she was to be a worthy priestess, to fight her feelings for Reid, to do battle with them and win? She knew Sidra would not.

The grove was lighter than it should have been. Janina knew she had dawdled too long on her way, and the sun had risen too high. Unless she hurried, she would be late for her own purification. She washed her hands and rinsed the water jar in the separate spring where the tunnel opened into the grove, then went quickly to the pool to fill the jar.

Every time she came here she remembered the first time she had met Reid. This morning, a day when she ought not to think of him at all, he filled the sacred grove with his strong yet gentle spirit. Telling herself to shut him out of her mind, she lowered the clean jar into the pool and began to fill it.

"Janina."

At the sound of Reid's voice, she almost dropped the jar into the deep pool.

"Go away!" she cried, lifting the filled jar to stand it carefully on the moss before she stood to face him with heart-broken defiance. "You should not be here. You know that. Tamat told you never to come here again. You will be severely punished if anyone discovers where you have been."

"It won't make any difference," he said, catching her hands and then her shoulders, pulling her to him with rough tenderness. "I'm not going back to the village, and neither are you."

Janina was so surprised by his unexpected appearance in the grove and by his sudden action that she made no protest, nor did she struggle when he lowered his mouth to hers. He was all she wanted, all she could think of, and it did not matter if he had lent himself to every woman in the village. She cared only that he was here now, holding her, setting her afire with a passion that did not abate when he lifted his head to look into her eyes with an intensity that almost frightened her. And she knew, all her lifelong training told her, just how wicked her feelings for him were.

"You know you don't want what they will make you do today," he said urgently, his words echoing her own early-morning thoughts. "You aren't meant to be a priestess. You aren't even a telepath. You can be of little use to them."

"I have no choice. It was decided long ago. Please, I can't bear this," she cried, tears rising in her eyes. "Reid, leave me alone. Go away. Don't cause me any more pain than I'm already feeling. The things I've done with you before this day were a violation of my primary vows. I'm unfit, impure. When her thoughts touch mine, Sidra will challenge my bonding. Why can't you understand what you are doing to me?" she shouted at him in anguish.

"You do have a choice. I'm giving you one." In her emotionally tormented state she heard his words as a temptation beckoning her away from the path of duty. "Come with me, Janina." When she would have continued her protests, he took her mouth again, silencing her desperate words with his lips.

"Reid, Reid." She moaned his name between hungry kisses. Beside herself with fear and longing and unpardonable guilt, she clutched helplessly at his shoulders and threw her head back to let his mouth sear her throat with yet more kisses.

"Tamat won't live much longer. Anyone can see she's growing weaker every day," Reid murmured, his voice muffled against her soft skin. "Sidra and Osiyar have been doing obscene, disgusting things together. The temple is no place for you now, if it ever was. Come with me, Janina. We'll go back to headquarters by the same way I came. We'll find my friends. We can be free. *Free*. Don't you realize what that means?"

"I cannot," she cried. "I can never desert Tamat, and I can't abandon the Chosen Way. I know nothing else, no other way to live. Reid, please stop kissing me and tell me you understand."

"Listen to me," he said, lifting her off her feet and then sinking to the ground with her locked in his arms. "I promised Tamat I would protect you with my life." He broke off his explanation to kiss her again.

Janina knew she should tell him that the best way to protect her would be for him to stay away from her. It was sacrilege for him to embrace her on this special day, when she should be thinking only of the vows she would soon profess. But the place where he had laid her down was next to a khata bush covered with flowers. The sweet fragrance released by those crimson blossoms made her dizzy. She put her arms around his neck and pressed her cheek to his so he would not see how close she was to breaking into helpless tears.

"Janina, come with me," he murmured into her ear. "If we stay in Ruthlen, Sidra will destroy us both as soon as she is High Priestess. I know we can escape through the ravine, but I won't do it without you."

She had her mouth open to tell him she could not, must not even dream of escape, but before she could say the words his lips were on hers again. His tongue filled her, and she felt his hands on her breasts as he pressed her back against the soft, golden-green moss.

She thought with sudden wry humor that if he wanted to escape he was wasting precious time, but the scarlet khata flowers spread their perfumed magic through the air and all rational thought fled from her mind. Reid's hands burned on her breasts.

"Reid." She could say nothing but his name, over and over again. Suddenly she was beyond argument or resistance. Reid was all she wanted or could think about. He was the world. He was her heart.

Quickly, he removed her robe and sandals, then his own clothing. She moaned and called his name again when she felt the hard length of him against her, but she made no further effort to fight him. How could she resist something she wanted so badly? His large hands caressed her trembling body with surprisingly gentle strokes, moving from shoulders to breasts to hips to thighs and then upward across her abdomen to capture her breasts again. His mouth and tongue followed the trail warmed by his hands. Janina awakened into passionate awareness at his touch, knowing without conscious thought that Reid was her destiny.

She was pure feeling now, wild, passionate sensation and need, with no room for concern about consequences. So skilled was Reid, so attuned to each other were they, that when he began to push against her she quivered into deep, rapturous pleasure. She accepted his body with intense joy. There was no pain, there were no regrets. She and Reid were one being, as they had always been meant to be, as they would be throughout all eternity. And eternity was this moment, this instant of glorious, total union.

"Separate them!"

Before the angry words had fully penetrated a consciousness directed solely toward Reid, he was torn from her arms. Janina cried out in loss, reaching for him, to pull him back to her.

Someone caught her hands, jerking her to her feet to stare uncomprehendingly into Philian's shocked face. She saw Reid standing next to Adana, and she knew by his blank expression that Sidra was using her mind to hold him immobilized.

"What are we to tell Tamat?" Sidra demanded of Janina. "When Osiyar found Reid gone, I knew he would be with you, you disgusting creature. You and he were planning to escape, weren't you? But first you had to desecrate the grove and the sacred pool with your filthy lust. See what you have done! You have so angered the presence who lives here that the very Water boils in outrage."

Janina saw to her horror that the pool was bubbling and steaming, while miniature waves splashed onto the moss at its edge. At first she thought Sidra was somehow controlling the Water, until she realized that Sidra, too, was frightened by what was happening.

"Empty the jar into the pool," Sidra said to Adana.

"No," Janina cried. "I just took it out for my—"

"For your purification ritual?" mocked Sidra. "You can never be purified now, Janina. You are no longer even a scholar-priestess. Pour out the Water, Adana."

At Sidra's command, the young woman picked up the jar and dumped its contents back into the pool. The Water continued to bubble.

"We must return to the temple at once," Sidra

said with obvious unease. "Tamat and Osiyar should know about this."

Philian picked up Janina's white robe and would have handed it to her.

"Put that down," Sidra commanded. "She may not wear it now."

"But Sidra," Philian protested, "she can't walk naked through the village. Everyone will stare at her."

"Let them stare," Sidra said. "Reid will go naked, too."

"No," Janina begged. "Sidra, have pity. Let Reid at least put on his trousers."

"Why?" asked Sidra. "Don't you want the village women to gaze upon what should have been theirs to use, which you have unlawfully taken for yourself? There is blood on your thighs, Janina. There will be no doubt what you two have done."

"Release Reid," Janina pleaded. "He will go away. He'll go back to the forest the way he came and cause no trouble for the village or the temple. I'll take the punishment on myself. Let him go, Sidra. Please."

"Let him go?" Sidra's mocking laughter stabbed through Janina's shame to make her tremble in sudden terror for herself and for Reid. "He would never leave you, Janina. Indeed, he cannot. You and he are bound together forever. I know that, if you do not. You will therefore die together."

"Then if you will not let him go," Janina begged in desperation, "release him from your control. Let him walk back to the temple under his own will, like a man."

"He is too dangerous for that," Sidra insisted. Then, with a last worried glance at the still-boiling pool, she headed for the tunnel, calling over her shoulder in a falsely sweet voice, "Come along, Reid, follow me. And don't trip on the steps."

CHAPTER 9

Never in her life had Janina known such humiliation as she felt during that walk from the sacred grove to the village and thence to the temple. When the villagers had seen Sidra earlier heading for the grove flanked by Adana and Philian, they must have known something was amiss. Now they lined the streets to watch the fallen scholar-priestess and her lover being marched back to the temple in unclothed shame.

Because it was a festival day, there were more people than usual who were free to stare. The fisherfolk had not put out to sea, and many of the farmers had come into town with their families for the festivities. All were in their brightest holiday clothing. Every house in the village had been decorated with sheaves of grain and late-season flowers. Through this cheerful, sunlit scene Janina walked in despair.

Certain that Sidra would stop the procession in the middle of the village in order to publicly subject her to scathing verbal abuse if she demonstrated the least hesitation or failure of dignity, Janina tried to keep her chin up and her eyes straight ahead. For the same reason she held her arms stiffly down at her sides, instead of using her hands to cover her nakedness as she so desperately wanted to do. She knew this parade through Ruthlen was Sidra's cruel revenge against her for all the years during which Tamat had protected her when Sidra would have seen her banished from the temple, and she wanted to give Sidra no opportunity to enlarge upon that revenge.

Behind her set face and stiff yet steady forward motion, Janina's every instinct cried out in rebellion against Sidra's callous disregard for common modesty. Reid had held and touched her unclothed body. It should not now be revealed to all these uncaring people. She tried to remember how it had felt to be loved by Reid, to become one with him, but all she could feel was horror at the way they had been found, with Reid still deep inside her and no doubt at all as to what they were doing, no possibility of excuse or explanation. And now she would have to face Tamat.

"Were you jealous of me?" From the roadside Senastria's familiar voice broke into Janina's thoughts. Senastria yelled again. "You heard me boast how wonderful he was, so you had to try him for yourself, was that it? You fool, now you've spoiled it for all of us." She threw a rock, which grazed Janina's right cheek.

More stones followed. Several hit Reid. Being still under Sidra's control, he gave no sign that he felt or heard anything, but walked through the village like someone already dead. Yet Janina knew he was fully aware of everything that was happening to them.

The onlookers began to follow Sidra and her little group, enlarging the procession with crowding, taunting people who loudly declared their outrage and their determination to see justice done to the false would-be priestess who was no telepath as every priestess should be, and equal justice meted out to her monstrous alien lover.

Eventually they came to the decorated tables being prepared in anticipation of the feast that was scheduled to take place after Janina's binding, the feast at which she was to have been guest of honor. Those who had been working on the tables gave up what they were doing to follow the crowd to the wall surrounding the temple complex. As the group led by Sidra approached the entrance, Janina realized with a stab at her heart that she could never again walk through the opening in that wall.

The noisy, shoving procession stopped between the feasting area and the temple wall. Sidra sent Adana to the temple with a message. After a while Tamat appeared, supported by Adana and flanked by Osiyar and his two scholar-priests. Janina could see by Tamat's drained expression and Osiyar's scowling face that Adana had informed all of them of what had happened.

When she first saw Janina naked between Sidra and Philian, Tamat reeled backward. Osiyar caught her, holding her upright until she recovered from the shock. Janina wanted to run to her, to throw her arms around Tamat and comfort her, and be comforted in turn. But there was no comfort any more, not for Tamat or herself, and worse than the punishment she was certain awaited her was the pain of what she had done to Tamat.

"I found them locked together beside the pool, beneath the khata flowers, which they were shamelessly using to enhance their sensations during lovemaking," Sidra proclaimed loudly, so all who had followed them from the village would know the full extent of Janina's crime. "Even now the Water in the pool boils in protest at the desecration."

This announcement brought a murmur of fear from the onlookers.

"As the pool boils, so the mountains smoke." Osiyar added his verbal blow to Sidra's account. He lifted an arm, pointing to where two of the mountains behind the village were belching much more steam than usual. Again the villagers whispered and muttered their fearful concern.

Janina felt the familiar prickling of Tamat's mind touching hers. She did not resist. She wanted Tamat to understand how she felt about Reid. And she filled her thoughts with all the love and respect she felt for Tamat, the gratitude for Tamat's care of her. All of this she combined with a regretful farewell. She knew she would have no other opportunity. When Tamat's touch withdrew, Janina felt like weeping. She had sensed no understanding from Tamat. She did not know if that was because of her own lack of telepathic ability, or if Tamat was so angry at having her plans for Janina thwarted that she could not forgive what Reid and Janina had done. Very likely there was no forgiveness possible. Janina pressed her trembling lips together and waited.

"Sidra," Tamat said, "release Reid."

"He is dangerous," Sidra objected. "He might try to hurt you."

"Reid will not harm me," Tamat replied. "Release him."

Janina saw fear on Sidra's beautiful face, an emotion quickly smoothed away, but it puzzled Janina, even in her own fear and shame. Why should Sidra be afraid of Reid?

Janina saw her lover slump a little as Sidra relinquished her control over him. He straightened at once, then stood flexing his hands as though they hurt.

"You have broken our laws, Reid," Tamat told him. "You knew the grove was forbidden, yet you went there. The first time you set your feet in that sacred place was a mistake. At that time, you were a stranger and knew not our laws. You were forgiven because of your ignorance. But the second time you entered there, you went with knowledge of what you were doing. You deliberately broke our law. And for what? To meet a woman untouchable by men. You have therefore erred doubly. And she, who is sworn to death rather than break her vow of perpetual virginity, knows what the punishment is."

"It was entirely my fault," Reid interrupted. "I seduced her. Don't punish her for my error, Tamat."

"Punishment is not mine to give or withhold, Reid," said Tamat. "Janina, proclaim your own punishment, and his."

Janina's mouth was dry, her tongue immovable. She tried to swallow but could not.

"Say it, Janina." Osiyar spoke with the sad dignity befitting the occasion.

"Say it!" Sidra's voice was full of triumph.

"Adrift," Janina whispered.

"Louder," Sidra demanded. "Let all of Ruthlen hear your own admission of guilt."

"I shall be set adrift." Janina had found her voice again. She said the awful words of the Ultimate Verdict in hot defiance of Sidra, who had never loved her, who felt no sorrow at this terrible ending, who would not pity Tamat's grief at what had been done this morning. "Forbidden to return to Ruthlen under any circumstances, without food or water or clothing, without sail or oars or rudder, I shall be cast adrift to face the elements and the monsters of the deep, until I die."

There was a soft murmur of respect from the villagers for one who could so bravely accept that most dreadful of all fates, who could speak the proscribed words without weeping or pleading for mercy. The murmuring stopped abruptly when Janina fell to her bare knees before Tamat.

"I beg your pardon for my crime," Janina cried, "and I ask one last favor, Tamat, from you who have always been so kind to me."

"Have you no pride or shame?" asked Sidra in great indignation. "There is no forgiveness for what you have done."

"Set Reid free." Janina would not be stopped by Sidra's protests. There was only one thing that mattered to her now. She boldly spoke what was in her heart, addressing Tamat and Tamat alone. In the High Priestess lay her only hope for the man she loved. "He is still unfamiliar with our ways and should not be killed for not adhering to them. I lured him on because I wanted him. The fault in this is mine. I accept my fate, but let Reid go."

"I cannot do that, child." Tamat looked straight ahead, not at Janina. "You will die together."

"Tamat," Reid said suddenly, "enter my thoughts."

"What nonsense is this?" Sidra cried angrily. "This day is dreadful enough for Tamat. She does not need the added strain of enduring your barbarian terrors over a just punishment. Tamat, pay him no heed."

"I grant you permission," Reid said to Tamat.

"I give you free access to my mind. Learn from me before it is too late."

"No." Sidra spoke angrily, fearfully. "Not before all the villagers. Tamat, this man is mad with fear."

"I am not mad," Reid declared loudly enough for everyone in the crowd to hear. "There is much you can learn from me, Tamat. For example, I did not couple with either Senastria or Anniellia. Instead, I gave each of them too much batreen to drink, until sleep overcame their desire. That is why they did not conceive, and all their talk about my wonderful lovemaking was imagination, because I will lie down with no one but Janina. There is more information in my mind, Tamat. Take it while you can."

"Tamat!" Sidra's voice rang clear in the astonished silence of villagers and temple folk alike. "Tamat, I beg you, do not exhaust yourself over this barbarian outcast. He can tell you nothing of value or interest."

But Sidra spoke to a woman concentrating on someone other than herself. Tamat's eyes held Reid's. Sidra gave one tiny whimper of fear before she recovered herself. Janina saw Osiyar look anxiously at Sidra, then at Tamat and Reid. A moment later, Tamat relaxed and Reid turned his head to look at Janina. From somewhere inside her shocked, terrified being she found the strength to smile at him. It was the only way she could thank him for his public admission about the village women and about his feelings toward her.

"I thank you, Reid," Tamat said softly. "You have been helpful. I know now what must be done. I regret I cannot alleviate your sentence."

"I understand," Reid replied calmly.

Without another word, Tamat began to walk toward the village. The crowd parted for her, then moved even farther away, as if unwilling to press too close to the condemned pair who would follow the High Priestess to the place where their sentence would be carried out.

In accordance with temple rules, Janina had fasted for three days before her planned initiation. Now she felt light-headed, as though she might faint. Determined that at least in these final few moments of her life she would do nothing to shame Tamat any more than she had already done, she made herself keep walking while she tried to ignore the ringing in her ears and the black veil threatening to cloud her sight. The pain in her feet, which were cut and bruised after her long walk on the hard stone road, helped her to focus her thoughts on taking one step after another. When she took a deep gulp of air and her sight cleared for an instant, she saw Reid glaring about as if he wanted to attack everyone surrounding them. She hoped he would restrain himself and go to his death bravely. It would be an unbearable humiliation if he had to be tied with rope before meeting his fate. She had accepted their just punishment; she wanted him to accept it, too.

To her relief, Reid did not try to fight what was happening. Led by Tamat, Sidra, and Osiyar, escorted by all the other priests and priestesses and the villagers, he and Janina retraced their steps along the road until they came to the wharf.

"The tide is exceptionally low today," Sidra remarked. "Tamat, perhaps it would be best if you wait here instead of trying to walk all the way to the end of the wharf to reach the water."

Tamat, ignoring her assistant's advice, did not stop until she had traversed the length of the wharf. There, where the sea usually rocked the largest of the fishing boats of Ruthlen, shallow puddles had formed amid the depressions in the sticky mud.

"I have never seen the tide like this," said Osiyar, looking down at stranded shellfish and rapidly drying seaweed.

"Never mind," Sidra told him. "It won't stop the punishment. See, the men are bringing planks." Behind Tamat's rigidly held, frail back, Sidra flashed a glance of gloating triumph in Janina's direction, a look that clearly conveyed all the ill-willed pleasure she must have felt at this total ruin of the young woman she had for so long considered her chief enemy in the contest for Tamat's regard.

Turning from Sidra's exultant beauty, Janina watched Tamat instead, seeing the grey weariness in that dear face and knowing she had caused it, knowing Tamat would not live long with the grief of this terrible day weighing upon her heart. The aged blue eyes met hers for one last moment, then looked away.

"Let the sentence be carried out," Tamat said, her voice unwavering. "Let all who witness this punishment know that the laws governing Ruthlen and its temple may not be broken without swift retribution."

Planks were hastily laid to extend from the wharf to the edge of the water. Speaking in solemn, measured tones that revealed no emotion at all, Osiyar commanded Janina and Reid to descend a ladder at the end of the wharf. Then, with Senastria and a fisherman leading them, they were taken along the planks to one of the few fishing boats still afloat. The tiny boat in which they were to be set adrift was brought and tied to the stern of the fishing boat. The condemned pair were ordered into it and told to sit down. Senastria and her friend got into the larger boat, raised the anchor, and headed for deeper water.

Janina sat huddled on one of the wooden seats in the tiny craft, looking backward toward shore. She could still see Tamat standing at the end of the wharf. She knew the High Priestess would stay there until Senastria and her friend had returned after making certain that Reid and Janina were well adrift.

"How far out will you tow us?" Reid called to the man who sat holding the tiller at the stern of Senastria's boat.

"Just a little farther, until we are well into the swift current," the man replied, eyeing Reid with surprise. "Why aren't you pleading for your life? Or for a quick, painless death?"

"Would you grant me either?" Reid asked.

"And put myself in peril of the same punishment as yours?" the man responded, laughing. "No, never."

"Then I will never plead," Reid replied, eliciting another look of surprise from the man, this one mixed with more than a little respect.

"You ought to be pleading in terror." Senastria turned from trimming the sails to stare at Reid for a moment. "You lied to me, Reid. You let me think you had put a child in me, you let me believe I would be honored for bearing new blood and bone to this community. You made a joke of me. I hope a sea monster eats you slowly, part by part."

At the mention of a sea monster, Janina moaned in terror, then clamped her mouth tightly shut, grimly repressing the fear now threatening to crack the thin veneer of composure she had so far maintained. She did not want Senastria to carry tales of her cowardice back to Tamat—or to Sidra and the other villagers.

"This is far enough," Senastria said, unfastening the line holding the smaller boat to hers and tossing the free end of the line to Reid. She looked out to sea with a concerned expression. "The mist is rolling in fast, and I think the tide is still ebbing. It's unnatural for it to be so low. Who knows what's waiting out there in the deep water? I want to get back to shore before the wind dies completely and we have to row." She and the man brought the fishing boat around and headed for land.

The smaller craft in which Reid and Janina sat was indeed well into the current. It spun around twice before, with sudden surprising speed, it began to move parallel to the coastline. Within moments, the mist had enveloped them. Senastria and her friend, along with the village and all the rocky coastline, disappeared from sight.

"Tamat, there is no need for you to wait until Senastria's boat returns," Osiyar said. "Come back to the temple now."

"The fog will help," Tamat said, as though speaking to herself. "No one will see them."

"Come with me, Tamat dear," Sidra urged. "I will have Adana brew hot *dhia* for you, to drive away the chill."

"Nothing will ever remove the chill cast by this day," Tamat answered.

"You must not grieve for Janina," Osiyar told her. " 'Those who wickedly betray our trust rightly deserve whatever punishment is decreed for them.' So says the Law of Ruthlen."

"Osiyar, have you never loved?" asked Tamat.

"Never," the priest replied proudly.

"Love," said Tamat, "is a force even I cannot command or control. I felt it once, long ago, but turned from it because I was a priestess born. Others are not so fortunate as I have been. I pity you, Osiyar."

Osiyar did not answer. Tamat watched

Senastria drop the anchor of her boat. When the fisherwoman and her friend reached the wharf, treading on the planks laid down earlier, Tamat thanked them for their help before she sent all the villagers home.

"I want you and Osiyar to return to the temple," Tamat then said to Sidra. "Leave the young ones with me. I have a final lesson to teach them."

"Final?" Sidra looked at Osiyar, and Tamat did not need telepathy to know what her assistant was thinking. Sidra imagined Tamat's heart had been broken by the events of that day, and she believed Tamat would soon die, leaving Sidra to rule. Sidra feared Tamat's death would come too soon, before the Sacred Mind-Linking had been performed, yet she dared not betray her concern that she might be deprived of that anticipated additional power.

With her usual lovely grace, Sidra bowed to Tamat before obeying the High Priestess's command. Turning, she walked along the wharf, back toward the shore, her pale blue robe floating out around her. Tamat watched until she saw Sidra and Osiyar on the road out of the village. Then she faced the four young people who stood awaiting her orders.

"Philian," Tamat said, "you are to be the leader of this party. Take Adana and these two young scholar-priests and go into the ravine. Avoid the sacred grove. Instead, climb down by the secret stairs I told you of the last time you went to gather medicinal plants. Do you remember the way?"

"Yes, Tamat, but I don't want to leave you alone."

"How could I be alone with Sidra and Osiyar to guard me? Now, when you have reached the ravine, this is what I want you to do." Tamat gave them directions that would send them to the far southern area of the ravine. "Stay there until I send for you. It may be a very long time. Go at once, without returning to the temple, and guard your thoughts well against any intrusion. Your lives depend on that."

"Yes, Tamat." They were accustomed to obeying her. They did not question her orders. One by one they knelt to her, there upon the stone wharf, with the mist closing in. She looked down at them fondly.

"I release you from all your vows except the vow of complete obedience to me," Tamat said. When Philian would have objected, Tamat added, "The reason for this will soon become apparent to you. Now, go."

When she was alone, Tamat turned to face the sea. In the shallow water just beyond the oozing mud of the exposed harbor bottom, a small fishing boat lay at anchor. Investigating it with her mind, Tamat found it well-stocked with food and other supplies. She lifted one hand, pointing toward the boat. Using all her concentration, she commanded the anchor chain to rewind itself. Slowly, silently, the heavy anchor lifted until the boat was free and had begun to move into the windless fog. Tamat sent it straight out, toward the swift current, and waited until the current caught it.

Then, releasing the boat to move on its own, she gathered her strength once more and let her thoughts leave her body to fly swift as a great seabird along the current, searching in the thick fog, listening, watching, until she found what she sought.

Reid would probably notice the tiny craft in which he and Janina rode had stopped moving. He knew how to sail and would be alert to such things. Janina, shaking with terror and cold, would not know.

A wisp of fog brushed Janina's cheek, soft as a kiss. Tamat saw Janina lift one hand to touch the spot, then relapse into her former huddled posture. Reid leaned forward, watching her.

It's up to you, now, Reid, Tamat thought. *I've done all I can, but I must save my remaining strength for one last task. Treat her gently, my friend.*

Reid looked up, searching the fog as though he felt her presence. Then Tamat's mind returned to her body, and she was back on the wharf, dizzy with fatigue, her head aching.

"Now," she muttered aloud, "it is time to hasten the inevitable before Sidra can cause any more pain."

All was ready. Philian and the others were safe. By casting her senses outward, Tamat could feel them making their way through the ravine on the far side of the mountains.

The planet itself would help her. The tide was lower than it had ever been before. The mountains belched clouds of steam. The pool in the sacred grove was hot and bubbling. With her senses still open, Tamat reached toward the spirit that had inhabited the sacred grove since long before the first telepaths had come to Ruthlen. She waited patiently for the contact. When it came, she knew with mingled sorrow and relief that she had been right. Sidra had broken the harmony that had lain between Ruthlen and the grove for six centuries; she had perverted the meaning of her most solemn vows, had used the Gift to invade the minds of others without permission, had violated her oath of chastity in her mind if not in her body—and her evil desire for complete power had reached outward from the temple to contaminate all of Ruthlen.

There was only one cure, for Sidra and for Ruthlen. And for Tamat, who had failed to keep her sacred charge, Ruthlen, safe from defilement. What Tamat planned to do was no more than fair retribution. Sidra, with her mind not yet expanded by the Sacred Mind-Linking, would remain incapable of understanding the consequences of her deeds, or the need for a terrible Cleansing.

The contact with the Other was broken now, leaving Tamat still standing at the sea end of the wharf. She put her back to the water, to face the simmering, molten mountains. For just an instant she felt young again, and strong, as she had been eighty years before when she had first become a priestess. Then she raised her arms over her head one last time and called down all her power.

CHAPTER 10

A stone-faced Janina had remained in one position since she first sat down in the boat. She was drenched in cold moisture from the fog. Periodically she shook with long tremors brought on by cold and fear. She stared straight ahead, knowing that at any moment a terrible death would come to her out of the thick greyness. The sea monster that had once taken her parents would return for her.

She deserved what would happen to her, but that did not make it any less horrible. Reid did not deserve his cruel end, for everything that had happened was her fault. She had prophesied his coming, and by that prophecy had brought him to Ruthlen. She had not warned him immediately that she was unattainable, but instead had allowed him to kiss and caress her, thereby awakening in him the desire that had led to his downfall. She, and she alone, was responsible.

And how badly she had hurt Tamat, who loved her, who must be suffering silent anguish right now because of foolish, wicked Janina.

A wisp of mist brushed against her cheek. Her deep depression lifted a little, and Janina had the strangest feeling that Tamat was there with her, touching her with love and telling her not to lose courage.

Save Reid, whispered a voice in her mind. *Help Reid, Janina.*

The prickly sensation lasted only a moment. When Janina raised one hand to touch her cheek, the feeling faded, and her hand fell listlessly back into her lap. She knew she had imagined that whisper because she wished so strongly that Tamat could forgive her. But what she had done was unforgivable, and there was no hope for her—or for Reid.

The little boat felt as if it wasn't moving at all, though it was difficult to tell in the heavy fog. Janina noticed Reid looking around curiously. Then she heard what he must have heard, the sound of a large body slipping through the water, and she knew the sea monster had come to claim them. Deep apprehension stabbed through her.

A dark, indistinct shape loomed through the mist. Seated as she was in the stern of the boat and close to the water's surface, the thing approaching them looked immense.

She did not cry out. No one would hear or

help, and with a faint glimmering of nearly destroyed pride, she knew she did not want Reid's last thoughts to be of her cowardice. She would accept her just punishment with as much bravery as she could manage. She caught her lower lip in her teeth, biting down hard to help her remember to keep silent. Squaring her shoulders, she braced herself to meet horror and unendurable pain.

Reid was standing up, something Janina knew should never be done in a small boat. She almost told him to sit down before she heard him laugh aloud. She thought for a moment that perhaps Reid planned to tip over the boat, to dump them into the sea to drown before the monster could eat them. Her heart swelled with a strong resurgence of tenderness for him, for his brave, laughing attempt to make their end more merciful.

Reid did not tip the boat over. Instead, he reached out to touch the approaching monster. He grasped some dangling part of the creature's body and held on, moving so quickly that their boat almost did tip. Janina sat numbly, rocked by the sudden motion, while Reid's laughing voice sounded around her.

"Tamat!" Reid shouted into the fog. "Thank you, Tamat! Thank you!"

Janina did not understand why he was so elated, or what he was doing—not until he picked her up with one arm and rather roughly tossed her onto a wooden deck. Then she saw that what had nearly run them down was no sea monster but one of the fishing boats from Ruthlen.

Reid finished tying their smaller boat so it would trail after the larger one, then came back to Janina, who was still crumpled upon the deck where he had left her.

"It's no use," Janina cried. "The fisherfolk will throw us into the water for the monsters to eat. They have to, Reid. They dare not save us for fear of their own lives when they return home. Don't you understand that?"

"There are no fisherfolk," he replied, lifting her to a sitting position and holding her in his arms. "There is no one else aboard. Tamat would not have sent us a manned boat."

"Tamat?" Janina pulled away to stare at his damp, shining face. "Tamat would never—" She bowed her head in grief at the thought of Tamat and of what she had done to that kind, beloved old woman.

"She did send the boat to us. I know it." Reid held her so she had to look at him. "When I told Tamat to enter my mind, I filled my thoughts with anything that might be useful to her. I told her what Sidra and Osiyar had been doing, and I told her I remembered sailing when I was a boy. I let her know that if she could provide a boat, I could sail it."

"Do you know what Sidra is doing? She and Osiyar whisper together all the time. I worry about Tamat." Janina had seized upon the one statement that made sense to her. Reid shook her a little, stopping the flow of her words.

"Sidra and Osiyar are irrelevant just now. I'll tell you all about it some time later. The important thing is that Tamat sent us this boat."

"She did not," Janina stated firmly. "We have broken the law and must be punished. We must die, Reid. The sea monsters must eat us."

"Didn't you feel the little boat stop? We were dead in the water, becalmed, yet the current flowed all around us. For a while, I almost believed one of your sea monsters had caught hold of us, until I saw this boat. Janina, all of the fisherfolk stayed home today, because of the festival. All the boats were moored at the wharf or anchored off-shore, and all but a few of them were on their sides in the mud because the tide was so low. Yet this boat followed us, and found us. Tamat did this. She is powerful enough, isn't she?"

"Reid," Janina insisted, "we have been so wrong. We have broken the law. We deserve to be punished." She stopped trying to convince him of that simple fact when she was overcome by another spasm of shivering.

"Come below." Reid pulled her toward the cabin. "There should be at least a blanket to warm you a little. Come on, Janina."

Reid's hasty search of lockers and the hold revealed not only blankets but several changes of clothing in waterproof bags, along with a full store of preserved food in the galley. Reid wrapped Janina in a heavy blanket, toweled her dripping hair, then brewed herbs and made her drink two large cups of strong *dhia*. Finally, he pushed her down on one of the bunks and covered her with a second blanket.

"Sleep," he ordered.

"I can't sleep. The sea monsters—" She stopped, afraid she would begin to cry. He bent low to kiss her, his mouth warm and tender on hers. He was still naked, as he had been since they had removed their garments in passion in the sacred grove. When he straightened, she caught at his hand. Though she was close to tears, and ashamed to have him see how cowardly she was, she did not want him to leave her.

"Janina." He sat down beside her. When he tried to put his arms around her she cringed in renewed shame and guilt.

"Very well," he said sternly. "I will tell you now what I had planned to tell you much later—or perhaps never tell you. I believe Tamat wanted me to escape from Ruthlen. I also believe she wanted me to take you with me. She knew you would never be safe with Sidra in power. I think Tamat understood what we did today in the grove, and despite what she had to say in public, she did not condemn us, for she certainly sent us this boat." He told her all that had been said during his last interview with Tamat, and why he thought she had given him an unspoken directive.

"If she had implanted the idea in my mind, which would have been the easiest way to make me do what she wanted, Sidra might have discovered what Tamat had done and could turn the information against her. But this way, even if

Sidra were to invade my thoughts, it would seem to her that I had thought of it myself, which was true. Thus, Sidra could not hold Tamat to blame. Do you understand this, Janina?"

"Yes." She was not so agitated now. Reid's words had calmed her enough to allow her to think more clearly. "What you say makes good sense. Tamat would think that way."

"Don't ever forget that Tamat wants us to live." Reid pushed gently on her shoulders, forcing her backward onto the bunk. "You need to sleep. I'll wake you if anything important happens."

She almost told him that if the really important event—the arrival of a sea monster—happened, he would have no time to waken her, but she knew that if she started to think about the sea monsters again, she would never sleep, and he was right—she needed to rest, so she could help him.

She lay back, mulling over his account of his meeting with Tamat. She knew Tamat had a reason for everything she did. If Tamat had saved Janina and Reid, it was because she wanted them alive for some specific purpose.

She touched her cheek, recalling the fleeting sensation of a kiss, and the whisper in her mind: *Save Reid. Help Reid.* And she *knew*, as certainly as she could have known if she had truly been a telepath, that Tamat's purpose in saving them had been to send Reid back to his own people. Tamat had found a way to grant Janina's plea to save him, and to answer Reid's frequently repeated request to let him leave Ruthlen. Therefore, Janina was dutybound to do everything in her power to help him. It was what Tamat wanted.

Sighing, almost asleep now, she turned over onto her side. Through half-closed eyes she saw Reid rubbing himself dry. His body was so beautiful, so large and strong-muscled, so utterly masculine. She felt a thrill of pleasure just watching him draw the rough towel across his naked skin. She thought with a drowsy smile that what they had done earlier that day wasn't such a terrible crime after all. She wanted to put out her hand to touch him, but she was too weary even for that small gesture.

Her last conscious thought was that she did not know what she could do to help Reid, because she was such a coward, and as Sidra had so often told her, she was not very intelligent. But she would try. She would do her best—for Tamat, and for Reid.

Just before Sidra and Osiyar reached the temple, the ground began to shake. Sidra stumbled, weaving her way awkwardly through the entrance in the surrounding wall. She quickly recovered her balance before turning to the High Priest with an eager expression.

"This rumbling won't last long. Come to my room," she urged. "We will be safe there, on my large bed. Adana and Philian surely won't return for some time yet, not if they walk back from the wharf with Tamat. Lately, Tamat walks so slowly

I often grow impatient with her. Come and lie down with me, Osiyar. Lend yourself to me once more. This day has been so exciting. I want you to end it by giving me pleasure. And I will please you, too, as well you know." Her blue eyes shone; her lovely face glowed. She caught at Osiyar's hand to pull him along with her. Osiyar stood unmoving, holding her loosely by one wrist.

"Tell me, Sidra, why were you so afraid when Reid suggested that Tamat enter his thoughts?"

"I wasn't afraid." Rocked nearly off her feet by another earth tremor, Sidra shot a surprised glance in the direction of the smoking mountains. "What a lot of steam. They shouldn't be doing that. What do you suppose is wrong?"

"Answer me." Osiyar's hand tightened around Sidra's wrist until she winced. He spoke with his usual cold precision. "If you do not answer, I will ask Tamat when she returns, and she will tell me."

"Perhaps not. She may not want to speak to anyone. She will need to preserve all her strength for the Sacred Mind-Linking. I think Tamat may not live very long after that is completed, so she will be too weak to tell you anything then, either."

Osiyar dropped her wrist abruptly. When he spoke again, it was with deceptive quiet.

"You forget, Sidra, that I am High Priest and Co-Ruler with Tamat. By our ancient laws, I can command your obedience and set limits to your power. I think I have been too lenient with you, too indulgent because of your beauty and your . . . skills." He drew himself up until he towered over the shorter Sidra. "Tell me why you were afraid of Reid."

"I touched his mind once or twice," Sidra said reluctantly.

"Without permission?" Osiyar was deeply shocked at such a breach of an immutable law.

"Reid was an alien, an unknown factor," Sidra said. "I wanted to be certain he was not concealing some greater telepathic skill than ours, that might be harmful to us."

"Only Tamat is permitted free access," Osiyar said. "You know that full well, and you know Tamat is satisfied that Reid is harmless to us."

"*Was*," Sidra reminded him. "Reid is dead now, along with that stupid Janina, and I am glad of it. He had seen us together, Osiyar, in your room. The barbaric fool was filled with disgust at what we so enjoyed."

"As am I, now." Osiyar stared coldly at her, not heeding the renewed trembling of the ground beneath their feet. "Did you plot his downfall, along with Janina's? Did you think to break Tamat's heart and thus destroy her so you could become High Priestess at once?"

"I shall be High Priestess by tomorrow night," Sidra shouted over the sudden roar of the mountains. "You and I shall be Co-Rulers."

"Of what?" asked Osiyar, struggling to keep his balance. "Of this? Look around you, Sidra. The mountains have awakened to rain fire and death upon the village, as our ancestors claimed they did in times long past. When the mountain spews its insides across Ruthlen and into the sea, will you help the villagers then as a High Priestess ought to do? Or the farmers? Will you tend their wounds and bless the dying? Or will you retire to your khata flower-scented bed to dream of lust and sweet degradation?"

"If not with you, Osiyar, then I will find someone else." Sidra glared at him, her long golden hair whipped by a sudden gusty wind, her blue robe billowing. Then she smiled her lovely, false smile. "Come, I will forgive your cruel words. The temple is the strongest building. Let us go there. It will be the safest place until this storm passes."

"It is no mere storm, and it will not pass," Osiyar said. "Do you not realize that if Reid knew what we have done, Tamat also knows? This is her Cleansing."

"If it is, then Tamat is dead by now, killed by her own Gift, and I am High Priestess already." Sidra gave a wild, high-pitched laugh of triumph, but at Osiyar's sudden threatening movement, she stepped back, away from him. "Why, Osiyar—I thought you loved no one."

"I may not be able to love, but I am capable of respect. I know goodness when I meet it day after day. I know evil when I see it naked before me."

Osiyar stopped talking. He retreated inside himself, concentrated, and found Tamat. He experienced a burst of joy at the contact, and thanked the twin moons and the sun that she was not dead, though he could tell she was weakened by her last great effort.

I am here, Tamat. Accept my help. He opened his mind to her, let her fully know his foolishness and vanity, his loveless dalliance with Sidra, and his deep remorse over the laws he had broken.

You may enter my mind, Osiyar, Tamat told him, *but know this task I have set for myself will kill me and may well kill you, too, if you choose to aid me.*

How else can I redeem myself? asked Osiyar. *My life means nothing unless I give it to you now.*

Come then, High Priest, and do my bidding. Join with me.

Tamat opened her mind to him completely, letting Osiyar know her great wisdom, the centuries of stored memories, her anguish at what must now be done, and her understanding of his own guilty pain. With the ground rolling and trembling beneath his feet and Sidra screaming at him, Osiyar, High Priest of Ruthlen, stood in the temple complex, withdrawn and silent, his mind totally linked to that of Tamat on the shaking wharf.

The mountains split open to spill molten lava toward the sea as the Co-Rulers, in complete accord at the last, joined together to destroy their corrupted domain.

CHAPTER 11

"*Tarik, come outside and see what has happened to the lake. There is no wind, but the* water has suddenly churned up into high waves, and they are reaching far up the beach, almost to the trees."

"Tarik, look at this." At the same moment that Alla entered the headquarters building and began to talk, Narisa spoke also, pointing to the screen above the computer-communicator to show her husband the finding that had so startled her. "Is it an earthquake? A volcanic explosion? What do you think?"

"It looks like both," Tarik said. "That's strange—it's near the area where we picked up Herne and Alla. But there are no volcanoes there, only forest and cliffs. I don't understand this new information. It makes no sense. Alla, you say the lake is covered with waves?"

"Yes. Do you think there might be some connection to what Narisa is seeing on the screen? Could an earthquake so far away make the lake water here so rough?" Alla, while hurrying across the central room to see for herself what had disturbed her friends, glanced down at the table containing the computer-generated holographic model of the continent. She stopped, staring at it, not believing her eyes at first. It took her a moment to find her voice, and when she did it was not like her own voice at all—it crackled with excitement, and the words tumbled over each other in her haste to speak them.

"In the name of all the stars! Tarik! Tarik, look—see here! The cliffs are gone—*look*!"

Before she had finished speaking, Tarik was at her side, regarding the model with the same fascinated astonishment that Alla felt. The computer model was generated from information gathered by the spaceship *Kalina*, which had been placed in permanent polar orbit above Dulan's Planet. They had traveled to the planet aboard the *Kalina*, and now Tarik kept one or two of his people there at all times to maintain the ship and monitor the information sent to his headquarters.

"My readings indicate that part of the eastern coastline is slowly changing shape," Narisa said, joining the other two at the model table. She looked from the model to her husband. "Gaidar is on duty on the *Kalina* until noon today. Shall I check with him, in case it's an instrument malfunction?"

"Please do. It's the first thing we should investigate, but somehow I don't think it's the instruments." Tarik did not take his eyes from the model. Where once it had shown cliffs, six steep mountains now rose, while on the far side of the mountains a narrow crescent of lower land edged the sea. After another glance at the model, Narisa returned to her post. She spoke into the computer-communicator while Tarik and Alla waited.

"Gaidar says he was just about to contact you, because something strange is happening down there," Narisa reported. "In addition to the topographical changes we can see on the model, there has been a series of violent explosions."

"We can tell that from here," Alla said impatiently. "Hasn't he got any more information? If Reid is still alive in that area—" She did not finish the sentence, but stood watching as the top and side of one of the mountains on the model split open.

"Gaidar says," came Narisa's calm voice, "that it is as though some kind of shielding mechanism is slowly being shut off, allowing the true contours of the land to be gradually recorded on our instruments. He says it looks as though the cliffs and part of the forest were false readings."

"A shield?" Alla repeated. "And Reid is caught in that?"

"Or," Tarik said slowly, his eyes still fastened

on the model, "it's like a magical spell that dissolves as the wizard who wove the spell dies."

"Spells? Wizards? Are you mad?" Alla tried to laugh, but could not. This was too serious for laughter. "A shield has to be generated by someone—someone with considerable intelligence and technological skill—which makes me wonder if Cetans are on Dulan's Planet without our knowledge, and if Reid is not dead, as I've been telling you all along, but is their prisoner."

"Not Cetans," Tarik said. "Telepaths."

"*What*?" Alla cried, and saw that Narisa had turned from the computer-communicator to stare at Tarik.

"Do you remember when we found you and Herne?" Tarik asked. "I awakened that day absolutely certain we would find you exactly where you were. Narisa, don't you remember how we laughed about it afterward? We thought then that the Chon had something to do with our sudden ability to locate them."

"Of course," Narisa replied. "It could be telepaths. But, Tarik, it would take incredible mental powers to create such a shield and keep it in place over a long period of time. You see, I know you well enough by now to believe I know what you are thinking." She smiled at her husband, and he smiled back at her in complete understanding.

"If I'm right, that shield has been in place for six hundred years," Tarik said softly.

"I know you love fantastic stories, Tarik," said Alla, "but that sounds impossible to me. It would be much more practical to suspect the Cetans of having a secret monitoring base on this planet, just as we have."

"We're all only speculating." Frowning deeply, Tarik watched the still-changing model. "Whether it is Cetans, or telepaths, or some peculiar natural phenomenon, we need to know for certain. I think another expedition to that area is in order."

"Surely," Narisa exclaimed, "you aren't going directly into that mess now—with volcanic debris in the air, hot ashes and lava, repeated earthquakes? Not to mention dangerous gases? If the computer is right about what is happening, that's what you will find."

"We'll monitor it carefully for a day or two," Tarik decided. "If the earth tremors our computer is reporting settle down, and if this model stops changing shape, we can fly over the area in a shuttlecraft for a visual inspection. Care to come along, Alla?"

"You couldn't keep me away," she responded promptly, wishing they could leave at once, but understanding Tarik's caution. She would be as patient as she possibly could, and keep her growing excitement under control. Smiling broadly, she added, "Herne is not likely to refuse if you ask him."

"I had planned to do just that," Tarik replied, grinning back at her, making her believe that he, too, thought Reid might still be alive. "Just in case we discover we need a doctor."

The great wave rolled beneath the boat sometime during the night. Thrown off balance, Reid fell down from the cockpit where he had been standing watch and tumbled through the hatchway. He landed on top of Janina, who had been thrown out of her bunk by the sudden lifting and settling of the sea.

Certain the sea monsters had come for them, Janina screamed in terror. She clutched blindly at Reid's rough tunic and buried her face in his chest. Freshly awakened from an exhausted sleep as she was, she had not had time to remind herself to pretend to be brave. Fear swept over her, making her shake uncontrollably.

Reid pulled her to her feet, steadying her until she could stand by herself. Then he raced for the cockpit, grabbing the ladder and hoisting himself up it with remarkable speed. Fully awake now and determined to face their mutual death at his side, Janina followed him.

The boat had righted itself and lay rocking gently on a calm sea. There was no sign of any monster. The fog had dissipated. All around them the world was empty and black—except for the sky behind them, which flamed with a lurid red glare.

"Is it a huge fire?" Janina asked.

"I believe one of the volcanoes is erupting," Reid answered. Seeing her blank look in the ruddy light, he added, "One of the mountains behind the village. Do you remember how the pool in the grove was filled with boiling water? And how low the tide was when we put out to sea? I would say there has been an eruption, and probably an earthquake, too. What rolled us about just now was most likely a great wave racing toward shore. Which means—"

"Tamat!" Janina stretched out her arms toward the red glare. "Reid, take us back. I have to find Tamat, I have to help her. Sidra will think only of herself. Take me to Tamat."

"We have been forbidden to go back." Reid held her fast, as though he were afraid she would throw herself into the sea and try to swim to the village. "We would be killed the instant we set foot on shore. We don't know what has happened in Ruthlen. Tamat may be dead already. We have no choice but to go on."

"No. Tamat needs me. I have to find her. I can't fail her again!" She began to fight him. Screaming and weeping, she pummeled his chest, biting and scratching and shrieking, while Reid tried to hold her. The blanket she had been wrapped in fell away, leaving her naked. She felt Reid's hands on her, touching her, inflaming her overwrought senses. And suddenly, irrationally considering their desperate situation, she wanted him to make love to her, wanted him in her arms.

"Stop yelling and listen to me!" Reid ordered, shaking her hard. "If I'm right—if that was a great wave we felt—then the water will recede quickly and there will be another, and possibly a third wave, until the force of it is expended. We are too near the shore for safety. We have to sail into deep water before we are caught by the waves and thrown onto land. If that happens, the boat will be wrecked and we will be killed."

"Not deep water. The sea monsters live there!" Hysterical now, she flung herself at him, wrapping her bare arms and legs around him. She cried his name over and over, as though he were the only thing she could depend on in a world gone mad. "Reid, Reid, hold me. Please hold me. I'm so frightened."

The boat began to rock violently. Reid shoved her away from him, slamming her onto the seat by the tiller and holding her there.

"If you don't stop screaming, I'll hit you," he shouted, his voice like a slap across her face. "Get yourself under control. Go below, find a packet of clothes, and put them on. Then come back here and help me raise the sails. And be quick about it." He watched her as though he feared a renewed attack of hysteria.

The sound of a cataclysmic explosion roared through the night, nearly deafening them. Flames poured into the sky from a mountain far astern. An incandescent cloud above the mountain began to expand, lighting the night with its glow. The once-calm sea began to roll and heave; the wind began to blow.

"You are right, Reid." Janina slumped on the seat, drained of all emotion in the face of that spectacle, at last accepting what had happened and willing to stop fighting what could not be changed.

Ruthlen must be destroyed by now, she thought, and though its people had teased and tormented her during much of her youth and no one of them except Tamat had ever loved her, still Janina felt pity over so great a loss of life at one blow. She even pitied Sidra for the swift obliteration of everything that cruel and imperious woman had wanted to rule. Osiyar's end caused Janina greater regret, for he had never deliberately been unkind to her, and he had always respected and cared for Tamat. It was Tamat's death that made her heart ache most of all, yet even as she grieved she knew it was a loss that could not have been postponed much longer in any case.

"Tamat is certainly dead after that explosion," she told Reid in a remarkably steady voice, "and I said good-bye to her this morning, knowing then that I would never see her again. I'm sorry I have been behaving so badly. I won't weep any more, or cause you any trouble. I'll try to help instead. I know a little about handling a boat, although I haven't been on the water since my parents died. I'll get dressed."

She felt amazingly calm. From somewhere within her battered spirit there now arose a new determination to remain alive. She reminded herself that Tamat had sent them the boat so they could live. She would do whatever Reid asked of her and, coward though she was, she would try her best to hide her fear of the sea monsters.

She started below. She was halfway through the hatch when the shock wave hit them. The pressure of it lifted their boat out of the water before smacking it down hard against the surface of a wildly churning sea.

Reid had been standing by the tiller. Janina saw him fly overboard just before she fell downward into the cabin. She hit her head, then sat on the deck for a while, too dazed to move, while the mad rocking of the boat made her dizziness even worse. When she could see in single images again, she crawled up the ladder and stuck her head through the hatchway. Reid was nowhere to be seen.

"Reid! Reid!"

A groan answered her, a half-strangled sound coming from below the stern. Grasping the tiller for balance she bent over, straining to see through the red-tinged darkness. Reid was in the sea, hanging on to the rudder.

Nearly blind with fear, certain that a sea monster would appear at any moment to snatch him away from her, Janina grabbed at his clothing and began to pull. It took a long time to get him into the boat. She lost her hold on him several times while they bobbed about on the dangerously rough sea. Each time Reid reached for the railing, he was washed away from it, until a wave caught him, lifting him higher. He took advantage of it, clutching the railing, his chest now at a level with it, and at last Janina, by bending far over the stern, got a good-sized piece of his trousers between her hands. Reid hung there uncertainly for a long moment when the stern began to sink again, until Janina pulled once more, using all her strength. The stern lifted. Janina pulled again, Reid helping as much as he could while still holding on to the railing to keep himself from falling back into the water.

As she finally hauled him over the stern, the bow of the boat plunged downward into the trough between two waves. Reid and Janina rolled over and over together, nearly falling through the hatchway before Reid put out a hand to stop them. They lay there for a while, catching their breath. Janina's bare back and buttocks were pressed hard onto the deck by Reid's weight. Reid was dripping seawater all over her. She felt his sudden hardness, sensed rather than saw that his mouth was about to touch hers. She lifted her face to his.

The boat rolled again, throwing them across the cockpit once more. Reid let her go and reached for the tiller.

"Do you know how to raise the sails?" he asked, shaking his head hard as if to clear his brain of the last vestiges of his fall into the sea.

"I—I think so," she replied in obvious uncertainty. "It has been so long since I helped my father on his boat."

"Here, take the tiller." He seized her arm and put her hand on the smooth wood. "Just hold it steady. I'll get the sails. It's not too different from the rigging I'm used to."

Janina sat watching his red-outlined figure in the darkness while he worked with the practiced movements of an expert sailor. The wind was rising, making the sea even rougher. She struggled to hold the tiller steady.

"Go below and put on some clothes," Reid ordered, dropping into the cockpit once more.

"You first. You're dripping wet," Janina said.

He did not argue. A moment later she saw a dim glow from the cabin and knew he had found the switch for the solar bulbs. By the time he returned in fresh, but too-small tunic and trousers and a heavy jacket, she was shivering and glad to follow his command to finally put on some clothing. She took the opportunity to make two cups of hot *dhia* and find some slightly damp bread. These she brought to Reid at the tiller. She stood beside him, swallowing her share while he ate his. She was not hungry, but she knew that if she were going to be of help to him at all she would have to stay healthy and capable of work.

They scarcely knew when night changed into day. The sky was dark with clouds of volcanic ash that blotted out the sun and fell upon the boat and the sea until the waves were coated with the pale grey floating particles. Reid ordered her to brush as much of it as she could off the boat.

"It's so light, it's hard to move it," she complained, sneezing through a cloud of fine grey-white dust.

"If it piles up, it will be heavy," he replied, "and heavier still when it gets wet." Then he sent her below to find cloths to wrap around their faces so they would not inhale the dust with each breath.

Janina was greatly relieved when Reid, deciding the danger of more great waves had passed, began to sail closer to shore. The wind continued strong at their back, and the current added its northward motion to help carry them along parallel to a rocky, barren coast that offered no harbor inviting enough to make them want to stop. Another night and day, followed by a third night of steady sailing took them well beyond the immediate debris thrown out by the volcano to a dawn of hazy blue sky and pale sunshine.

Among the ship's stores, Janina located several pair of the slit eye protectors the fisherfolk used against the dazzling sunlight. When she took a pair to Reid, she found him watching the shore, which had changed in character. No longer did precipitous rocks fall off abruptly into the sea leaving no place to drop anchor. Now a strip of green scrub-land edged the water, with a range of low, worn-down hills in the background. Reid adjusted his eye protectors before once more turning his gaze shoreward.

"There's a river," he said, pointing. "I think it's time to stop and rest."

He moved the tiller and sheeted the sail, sending the boat toward land. A short time later they were sailing between green banks overgrown with bushes and a few stunted-looking trees. Reid continued up-river along its meandering course until they were well away from the sea, and the river had narrowed considerably. Only then did he order Janina to lower the sail. He dropped the anchor in a little cove with a gravelly beach backed by a single clump of trees.

"This looks safe enough," he said. "The trees will shade the boat from the late-day sun."

After the rough seas they had endured, it was strange to be at rest. In this sheltered place, the boat hardly moved at all.

"Now," Reid said, "before anything else, we sleep."

They had had only short snatches of rest for three nights, taking turns and always on guard against the weather or another great wave, or—in Janina's case—against the sea monsters she still expected to appear and destroy them. She needed no prodding to make her lie down upon her bunk while Reid took the narrow berth opposite her. He rolled over once, wrapping the blanket around himself, then lay silent. In the unaccustomed stillness, however, it some time before Janina could fall asleep.

It was almost evening before she was awakened by a movement on deck, followed by a loud splash. Lifting her head in alarm, she saw that Reid was gone from his berth. Fearing that something terrible had happened to him, Janina leapt from her bunk and climbed up into the cockpit to look for him.

When she emerged from the cabin, she found

a scene of peaceful beauty spread before her. The sun lay low in the sky, bathing the distant hills with orange-gold light. The trees edging the shore shook out their leaves in a sun-sparkled, windy dance. Yellow-and-white flowers starred the rough grass and ran across the gravel beach on slender vines.

"Join me," called a voice from below.

Janina looked down to see Reid floating on the smooth surface of the cove.

"What are you doing?" she cried, too frightened to move.

"Jump in," he invited. "Or climb down if you'd rather. Use the ladder at the stern. I found it in one of the lockers. Too bad we didn't know about it when I fell overboard."

"Why are you in the water?" she asked.

"After three days of hard work, I needed a bath." He laughed up at her, mocking her fear. "So do you. Come in, Janina. Don't look so frightened. The water is much too shallow here for your huge sea monsters. That's one reason I sailed so far upriver before stopping, just in case they do exist."

"I'm afraid of the water. I don't know how to float on it the way you are doing." It was worse than that. She could see that Reid had taken off all his clothes before he went into the river. She would have to do the same. She wasn't sure she could bear it if he tried to touch her or wanted to kiss her. Thinking about what had happened in the sacred grove and immediately afterward, she felt a terrible shame. Remembering how she had wanted him to make love to her their first night on the boat, she was embarrassed at the very thought of Reid holding her.

"It isn't deep," he said encouragingly, apparently not seeing her confusion. "Look, I'm standing, and there is no current in this spot. You won't drown. I won't let you."

I'll drown in your eyes or your kiss, she thought, *and whatever you say now, you will let me.*

"If you don't come in," he said, "I'll climb aboard and throw you in."

She thought he probably meant it. He probably found her unwashed body repulsive in the close quarters of the boat. She turned her back to him and began to strip off her tunic and trousers, noticing as she did so the bruises on her arms and legs and hips, evidence of how many times she had been thrown against something hard during their days at sea. Perhaps Reid would consider those black-and-blue and yellow marks unattractive and would not want to touch her.

She went down the ladder awkwardly, hating the thought of immersing herself in the river. At the temple, daily baths were taken in a carved stone tub with the sides comfortingly near. But the temple was gone, and this limitless space was all she had, this empty world peopled only by Reid and herself.

The bruises did not deter him. As she had feared, he touched her. When she reached the bottom of the ladder, he put his arm across her back to float her away from the boat. At first she was terrified, stiff with tension, crying out when he tried to make her lie back and float on her own. She threw her arms around his neck in fear, nearly sinking them both. Reid bobbed to the surface, putting out one hand to hold on to the ladder. He kept Janina safe within the circle of his other arm, drawing her closer to him. Beneath the water their legs tangled in a lazy rhythm. She rested her head on his shoulder while she wiped the hair out of her eyes and caught her breath again. Reid pulled her closer still, his eyes on her mouth.

"No." She turned her head aside. How could she fight what she felt for Reid? How could she obey the laws that had compelled her all her life when the only thing she wanted was to be held in his arms like this, to feel the long strength of him against her trembling body? She thought that if she did not drown in the river, she would surely drown in her own confusion.

"Janina," he whispered, "don't be afraid. You really will float, my dear. Let me show you how." He gently pushed her onto her back.

She went under a few times, trying to fight him, before she found to her astonishment that he was right. She would float on top of the water so long as she did not struggle. It was a delightful, careless, relaxing feeling. Tired of struggling, she gave in to that feeling, letting her fear of what Reid might want to do and her embarrassment about their nakedness drift away on the river.

Her long silver hair swirled around her, the tops of her breasts stood up like small hills above the gentle plain of her chest and abdomen. She laid her head back in the warm, clear water and let Reid guide her where he wanted.

He was behind and beneath her. She could feel his strong legs kicking steadily. His arm curved around her left side, his hand splayed across her abdomen as he pulled her slowly along. Above them the sky arched in misty purple-blue, decorated by deep green leaves when they neared the shore. Janina relaxed a little more, closing her eyes. She felt Reid sink to some lower level beneath her, before he rose out of the water with her in his arms, to walk a few steps onto the gravel.

He laid her down on a soft bed of creeping vines and yellow-and-white flowers that released a sweet, powdery fragrance when her slender body crushed them. A cloud of blue butterflies that had been hovering above the flowers dispersed into delicate winged fragments of color, then flew away.

"Beloved," Reid whispered, and Janina's bones melted while her blood ran hot within her. She had wondered more than once if their lovemaking in the sacred grove had been the result of true desire or of the influence of the khata flowers, whose fragrance was said to encourage passion. Now she knew. In this cove there were no khata bushes, yet she wanted Reid with a yearning of both body and spirit that overcame the last of her qualms. There was no shame here, no embarrassment. There was only love—and a sweet, insistent desire.

She opened her arms and Reid lowered himself into them, taking her mouth with firm assurance. He began a tender and very thorough exploration of her body, loving her with a slow relish that had been denied them in their first encounter. Nor did this loving end as abruptly as that earlier coupling. Here there was no one to interrupt them so cruelly, and as if to erase the memory of anything that had gone before, this time Reid taught her how to love him in return, telling her with quiet words and showing her with gestures what he wanted her to do, until she was certain he must have reached the same state of rapturous delight that she was enduring. She was trembling from head to toe; she could feel his body quivering, too, each time she put her hands on him.

Finally, when she thought neither of them could bear any more of this increasingly fervent desire, when she thought it was impossible for desire to rise to any greater height, she learned she was wrong. He took her slowly, deliberately, with a rich and gentle tenderness that moved her nearly to tears, until he was buried deep within her and she was his completely. Then she knew pleasure beyond anything she had ever imagined could exist.

It was at that moment of shimmering intensity—when they were one body, one consciousness, one spirit—that for her the laws of Ruthlen dissolved into nothingness, for how could a law made by mere mortals mean anything at all when a man and woman were predestined to meet and love as she and Reid loved?

CHAPTER 12

The sun was sinking behind the low hills. Purple shadows lay across the land. High thin clouds of volcanic ash, colored by the setting sun, streaked across the sky in a glorious tangle of deep red and gold or purple and green. The boat rocked gently in the cove. The river rippled past, making quiet whispering sounds.

Janina turned her head to look at Reid. She could not believe now that she had ever thought him ugly. He had a harsh, strong face, but there was beauty and goodness in it. Such a face could never be ugly, only unfamiliar until one knew him. As she knew him now. As she loved him now.

Reid stretched and rolled over on top of her, to plant a long, deep kiss firmly on her mouth.

"It's going to be dark soon," she whispered

when she could speak. "Shouldn't we go back to the boat?"

"Are you so eager to get into the water again?" he teased, nibbling at her earlobe.

"I'd feel safer there, in a smaller place," she said, trying to catch her breath.

"Smaller means more intimate." He rose, pulling her up too. "I do like that idea."

She went into the water with much less fear this time, partly because Reid was holding her hand. She walked until she could no longer stand and then she floated, letting Reid put one hand on her breast to move her along while he swam. But he would not keep his hand still. He rubbed and teased at her flesh until her nipple stood up hard and rosy, at which point he lovingly attacked her other breast.

By the time they reached the rope ladder slung over the stern, Janina could hardly think. Reid let go of her, laughing softly, then pulled her around to face him. Janina moved closer, putting her hands beneath the water to caress the needy hardness of him. Reid held on to the ladder with one hand, pressing her hips against his with the other hand, letting her feel his eagerness. Janina put her arms around his neck when he kissed her. Then, unwilling to wait any longer, she spread her legs and wrapped them around his waist, pushing herself onto him until he filled her.

Reid's gasp of surprise at her sudden action, followed by his groan of pleasure was all the encouragement she needed. When he stroked into her, she shivered into instant, intense fulfillment. She hung about his neck, her head resting on his shoulder, while he took his pleasure. She saw his hand clutching the rope ladder tighten, heard his sigh, and felt life pouring into her from him. Locked together, they floated in the water, unable to move apart or speak, Janina marveling that two acts of love could appear to be so different and yet each have the same ability to touch her very soul. It was good to know that love with Reid included laughter as well as gentleness and intense passion.

"It's growing cold," Reid said at last. He helped her up the ladder, then pulled himself out of the water.

They stood facing each other, the setting sun painting their bodies with orange-gold light that glistened where droplets of river water formed. The heavy length of her hair hung over Janina's shoulder, trailing down between her breasts in a moist stream of water-darkened gold.

Reid thought he had never seen anyone so beautiful, or so graceful. There was a depth of passion in her too, along with an unexpected playfulness. That sudden advance of hers just as he had been about to boost her up the ladder had been delightful. He wondered what had made her think of it. He found himself grinning at her, wanting to tell her to dress herself immediately or he'd have her again, standing right there in the cockpit—and any other way he could think of.

He'd better not say that. She was still a bit shy

of him and might not appreciate the humor. That would change. He had a feeling that they were going to be alone together for quite a while. He just hoped he could vanquish some of her foolish fears—about immersing herself in water, for instance, and about obeying the laws of a land and people now totally destroyed, if that explosion they had witnessed was any indication, and most of all, about the existence of terrible sea monsters. He thought the best way to change her ideas was to expose her to the truth of their situation.

He waited until they had dressed and used the solar heating unit to prepare a fish and dried-vegetable stew, which they ate with the last of a loaf of stale bread. Reid moved an empty crate from the storage area in the hold into the cockpit to use as a dining table so they could enjoy the soft twilight and the evening breeze, which in this haven was more pleasant than the wind they had been exposed to while at sea.

"There are some bags of flour in the drybox below," Reid began, watching her closely to gauge her reactions to what he was planning to tell her. "Do you know how to use it?"

"I can cook and bake, Reid," she said quietly, her mist-blue eyes soft upon his face. "Every girl of Ruthlen learns how to do both. I also know what wild plants can be safely gathered for food. If you catch any fish or wild animals, I can prepare them, and cook them, too."

"Good," he said, pleased that she had surprised him again. "Can you read a map?"

"What is a map?" She looked blank. Reid thought she might have known maps under another name, so he hastened to explain, then pulled out a battered sea chart he had found in one of the lockers. He spread it on the crate, smoothing down the creases while she looked at it with great interest.

"The fisherfolk must have used this," he said. "It's primitive, but you can see these are the six mountains behind Ruthlen. This is the village, with the wharf jutting out into the bay. I think these lines and markings must represent water depths."

"The bay is shallow," Janina said, understanding the chart at once. "This line must be the strong current, sweeping along offshore. And here is the beach where first I saw your face and foretold your coming—where Tamat later dedicated you to Ruthlen."

She was silent for a moment, staring down at the scraped-skin chart. Reid, pleased by her ready comprehension, decided not to allow her time to think about what might have happened in Ruthlen. He flipped the skin over and produced the marker he had found with it.

"I'm going to draw another map," he said, "based on what I remember from the models Tarik generated on the computer back at headquarters. This one will begin where the other map ends. See, here is the rocky coast we have sailed past since we left Ruthlen. Here is where we are now, in the river. And this is the coastline beyond this spot."

He sketched rapidly, remembering in detail, for he had been vitally interested in the planet and had paid close attention to everything Tarik said about it.

"We are heading toward the northern polar region. That is how Commander Tarik has designated this part of the planet." He drew an arc across the top of his impromptu map. "It will grow much colder as we approach this area, and it will be dangerous sailing. But once we round this cape"—he pointed to a sharp angle of land where he had drawn rocks extending far out into the sea—"on the other side we should be protected from the worst of the polar gales, and the land should be more hospitable when we need to drop anchor to rest. If we can sail farther along the coast, to this point here, then we can beach the boat and walk the rest of the way. The journey will take all the strength and courage we have, Janina, but I believe we can reach headquarters before it becomes too bitterly cold to travel in these latitudes."

"Must we go by sea?" She did not look up at him. She kept her eyes on the chart, but he heard the fear in her voice. "Couldn't we walk the entire distance by land? Wouldn't it be the shorter route?"

"No, because here"—he made swift marks on the chart—"like the backbone of the continent, is a range of tall, steep mountains. They would be nearly impassable to us during warmer weather, and with the cold season coming there will be early snowfalls at those altitudes. We can't travel as quickly on foot as we can by sea. With the current to help speed us along, and the wind at our backs, we could be at headquarters before the worst of the cold weather arrives. If we are lucky, the Chon will find us before then. For some reason they don't live on this side of the mountains, but once we round the cape at the north of the world, the possibility of meeting them will increase with every day. Once they have spotted us, the chances are good that they will let Tarik or Narisa know where we are."

"I wish I were a telepath." Janina spoke sadly. "If I were, I could communicate with the Chon sooner than you will."

"Never mind." Reid refrained from pointing out that if she were a telepath, she would not be sitting there with him, she would be a dead High Priestess-Designate, buried beneath molten lava. "Telepathy won't help us on the journey we face. Courage and resourcefulness will."

Janina bowed her head at those words, believing courage was the very quality she lacked. She promised herself she would try her best to keep him from learning what a coward she was.

They slept together in one narrow bunk that night. The lack of space did not stop Reid from making love to her with skill and inventiveness. But in the chill morning mist it was a newly efficient Janina who took charge.

"We will need food for our journey," she said. "This is a small boat, but there ought to be enough storage space in the hold. I think we should begin by scrubbing out that part of the boat. It probably reeks of fish and will make everything we put into it smell and taste of fish. Then I will teach you which plants to dig or pick, and you will teach me to be a better sailor so I can be of more help to you."

She had a few other suggestions, to most of which Reid agreed at once. He was well pleased by the way she had accepted their circumstances. Her fragile appearance was deceiving. She was proving to be tougher and far more resilient than he had expected, considering her restricted and sheltered background.

They worked quickly, not wanting to waste any more good weather than necessary. The little boat was soon spotless. They packed the newly clean hold with roots and berries which Janina guaranteed would last for more than the twenty days Reid estimated their journey would take. She cut wild herbs and hung them from the mast to dry so they would be able to brew hot *dhia* to help keep them warm in the polar chill. They would not have time to dry the fish Reid caught each day, but they found salt in the hold along with a few containers intended for the storage of fish in brine, and these they packed full. They saw no animals large enough to justify expending the time necessary to hunt and snare them. Janina insisted they could live quite well on what they were storing.

The fisherfolk had apparently gone barefoot while aboard, and so did Reid and Janina. Knowing warmer gear would be needed soon,

Reid used lengths of heavy cloth he found packed in a locker, which were originally intended as material for sail patches, to make clumsy shoes for both of them. Among the clothes they had found on the boat were several pairs of heavy stockings, which would provide added warmth for their feet.

Janina had found a pair of oars stored beneath one of the bunks, so they were able to use the smaller boat, in which they had been set adrift, to ferry supplies from shore to the larger boat.

To range farther and find more food, they sailed the boat up and down the river until Janina handled it with easy familiarity. Reid tried to teach her to swim, and Janina did her best to learn, knowing it might be necessary to know how. She never spoke of the terror she felt about returning to the open sea. She thought they would probably be killed on the northward voyage, if not by sea monsters, then surely by cold and ice. She had heard tales of the bitter polar regions when stories about the ancestors were recounted, though no one in Ruthlen had ever dared to travel so far.

The nights were becoming noticeably colder. A golden haze lay upon the land each afternoon. Ripe fruit or small nuts hung from every bush.

"Tomorrow we will rest and eat all we can of food that won't travel well," Reid decreed on one especially lovely evening. "The following day, if the weather holds, we will leave here."

"I suppose that is best," Janina agreed. "We

can't wait much longer, can we? It will be too cold." She promised herself once again that she would not let Reid know how frightened she was. She wanted to suggest they stay where they were until the cold weather had come and gone, but she knew he would never agree to that. He was too eager to see his friends again and to learn the fate of his cousin, Alla.

Since they would be forced to remain on the boat for many days to come, they took blankets and slept ashore that night. Reid made a fire and cooked fish. Janina contributed bread made from their precious store of flour, and flavorful roots roasted among the coals. They finished with a selection of delicate yellow-and-purple striped berries.

Twin half moons rose one after the other, shedding a hazy silver mantle over the landscape, their light diffused by the volcanic ash still drifting high in the atmosphere. Reid drew Janina into his arms.

"There won't be much time for this after tomorrow," he said, kissing her brow. "We will both have to work constantly, and take turns sleeping."

"I know." They sat on a blanket with their heads together, holding each other close. After a while Reid lifted her tunic, sliding his hands along her ribcage, and then up her arms, flinging the garment onto the gravel after he had removed it. He knelt beside her and buried his face in her breasts. Janina caught his head, holding him hard against her. It was always like this. He touched her and began to caress her and instantly she was lost. She could think of nothing but Reid.

He pushed her back onto the blanket, then pulled off his own clothing. Janina lay watching him in the firelight, admiring the way his smooth muscles moved beneath his bronzed skin, feeling the heat of desire lapping up inside her, threatening to overwhelm her. She smiled up at his darkly handsome face when he bent over her.

"But you are still half dressed," he murmured, laying his hands on the waist of her trousers. He slid the trousers down a little and lowered himself to kiss her tender flesh. Janina began to tremble. He pushed the trousers lower still. She lifted her hips to help him. His hands cupped her buttocks before slipping around to caress her belly and move down into the tangle of silver hair between her thighs. Her trousers were gone, her legs fell apart, and Reid's hands were driving her mad. And his mouth. She had never known, never guessed, anything like that was possible. She grabbed at him, holding him in both hands, reveling in the way he responded so eagerly to her touch. She cried out in disappointment when he pulled away from her. But his own hands stayed where they were and she knew she could not endure much more of his loving torture.

Then, just as her body began to explode, he

entered her, not in his usual gentle way, but with the hard, driving force of his own passionate need. She met him with a matching desire, pushing upward against him, clutching him to her, fingers digging into his back. An instant later her wild cry of fulfillment echoed through the night, followed by Reid's deeper expression of ultimate pleasure.

The next morning they spent playing naked in the water. Janina endured the final swimming lesson with laughing good humor, enjoying the caress of Reid's hands when he helped her to move her arms correctly. His lightest touch could ignite her senses. To cover her sudden desire for him, she laughed and teased him, then squealed in mock fear when he dove under her, caught her across his shoulder, and staggered out of the water to toss her laughing onto the beach and take her with no further preliminaries. His body was cool and wet, his manhood hard and demanding. She closed her eyes and gave herself up to him with unquestioning love.

They slept the afternoon away, then ate their evening meal on the beach. They made love one last time before dowsing the fire and rowing back to the boat. Janina had expected to be unable to sleep, but she drifted off at once. She did not waken until Reid called through the hatch to say the sun was up and all was ready for their departure.

She pulled on her clothes, then went above to help him. But she took a moment when Reid was busy with the sails to look shoreward and whisper a regretful farewell to the peaceful cove and the land surrounding it, the place where she and Reid had first truly acknowledged their love, the place she would always think of as the Golden Land.

CHAPTER 13

"I *have never seen such devastation before." Alla* watched the viewscreen in horrified fascination as the shuttlecraft flew over the area between the volcanoes and the sea. "The lava flow has covered almost all the land."

"The lava was channeled far out to sea by that ridge of rocks." Tarik indicated a dark grey area on the viewscreen. "It must have been a high promontory once, and if there was a bay beside it, which appears likely, it is gone now."

"No one could live through something like that," Herne said sadly from his seat next to Tarik. "We won't find Reid alive down there—or anyone else, either."

"Tarik, are those buildings?" Ignoring Herne's pessimistic remarks, Alla pointed to the viewscreen in sudden eagerness. "There, just beyond the volcanic flow."

Tarik maneuvered the shuttlecraft so they could see better.

"By all the stars!" he exclaimed. "That never showed up on the computer model. It looks like a ruined version of our headquarters. Herne, how do your instruments read?"

"The volcano appears to be quiescent," Herne reported, adjusting a dial. "There are occasional seismic rumblings, but they are not strong enough for us to feel them, or to cause any damage to the shuttlecraft. If they increase, we can lift off. I'd say it's safe to land, if you want a closer look."

"Please," Alla begged. "If there is a chance we could discover what has happened to Reid—"

"Say no more," Tarik told her. "I want to find Reid, too—but more than that, this area is a mystery that must be solved before any of us can feel safe in our own settlement. We need to know why and how our computer model was falsified, though I believe we can see below us the reason why it recently changed shape."

Tarik brought the shuttlecraft down well away from the still-smoking lava, landing on a small patch of smooth rock that looked as though it had been swept clean by a giant broom or whirlwind. Alla was the first one out. She stood blinking in dazzling sunlight that reflected off ruined white stone buildings. The light seemed unnaturally bright because of a lingering thin haze of volcanic ash that splintered the sun's rays and hurt the eyes.

"The damage is worse seen from the ground." Herne joined her, squinting against the sun. He was followed by Tarik, who strode past them, heading toward the remnants of the white building.

"Look at this," Tarik called to them. "I was right about this place. Here is a knee-high wall, like the one around our headquarters, and when it was standing that building in the center must have been a larger version of ours."

"There were several smaller buildings," Alla observed.

"This was possibly an important center for whatever society built it," Herne guessed, "but I doubt if anyone is alive here now." Then, seeing Alla's determined look, he added, "Still, I may as well survey it, just to be sure." He pulled a small heat sensor out of his waist pocket and headed for the ruins. Knowing that the sensor would detect the body heat given off by any living organism, Alla followed him, holding her breath in hope.

The six smaller buildings had been destroyed to their foundations. Most of the large building was in rubble, only a curved portion of the outer wall and two columns remaining upright, but those columns were identical to the ones around the headquarters building.

"We could have learned so much from these people," Tarik mourned.

"You don't know there was anyone living here before the eruption," Herne pointed out. "It is reasonable to assume these buildings date from at least the same period as our headquarters, and they may have been vacant even longer."

"How long do textiles last in the sun and open air, Herne? Not six hundred years, surely. This is recent." Alla had pounced upon a piece of sheer, pale blue fabric that was partly caught beneath a fallen column. She tugged at it, then stopped. "Tarik, come here."

Hearing the stricken note in her voice, he went to her at once and fell to his knees to push at the stone.

"Herne, come help me," Tarik called. "Let's move this piece to see what's beneath it."

Herne hurried to his side, handing the heat sensor to Alla. The two men pushed hard until the stone rolled over. They all stared at what lay beneath it, until Alla turned her head aside, refusing for pity's sake to look any longer.

"She must have been beautiful when she was alive," Tarik said softly.

"She's not long dead," Herne said. "In this extremely dry heat, I'd say four or five days at most."

"Then there were people living here!" Alla cried. "Reid could have reached these buildings. He could still be alive!"

"'Could' doesn't mean 'did,'" Herne responded sharply. "Tarik, I suggest we roll the stone back to cover her again. We'd never get the huge piece off that's pinning her legs, and there may be scavenger birds or animals. I'd hate to leave her exposed like this."

Tarik agreed, and the two men fell to work. Alla moved out of their way, still holding the heat sensor. It began to click. Because she had been clutching it in both hands and holding it close to her body while the woman was uncovered, Alla thought she might have overheated the sensing mechanism inside the device. To cool it she laid it down in the shade of a large section of a column that was leaning crookedly across another column. The heat sensor began to hum.

"Either I've broken it," Alla said to no one in particular, "or there is something alive in that pile." She picked up the sensor.

"You've probably broken it." Herne had come up behind her. With an annoyed expression, he took the instrument out of her hands. "I wish people with no mechanical aptitude would leave my equipment alone."

"You gave it to me to hold!" Alla flared. "Tarik, there is something under that column."

"Thanks to you, this is broken," Herne declared, holding up the sensor. "You just had a false positive reading."

"Get the spare and doublecheck the reading," Tarik suggested.

They waited until Herne returned from the shuttlecraft. Alla was in a state of uneasy excitement. Could it possibly be Reid buried beneath the columns? Had he found his way out of the forest and walked across the mountains to this place? All her intelligence told her it was impossible, but her heart was filled with hope.

Laying the second heat sensor down in the shady spot where the first had been, Herne switched it on. Immediately it began to emit a loud hum.

"Find the exact location," Tarik instructed. "We don't want to move heavy stone unnecessarily."

"I think we should call for another shuttle. We need more help," Herne said.

"There isn't time!" Alla cried. "You said that woman had been dead for four or five days. What if someone has been trapped under those stones for all that time? Before the others can get here, he could die."

"*He*?" Herne frowned at her.

"She's right." Tarik was inspecting the jumble of broken columns and other debris. "Let's try to haul this big stone out first. I think then we ought to be able to see if anything really is inside this pile."

It took all three of them, but they managed to do it without disturbing the precariously balanced columns.

"Alla, you are the thinnest one here," Tarik said. "Can you squeeze into that space?"

"I think so." She got down on her hands and knees, and crawled beneath the columns until she was flat on her belly with her left arm jammed down at her side and her right hand at chin level. She did not care that it was dangerous. This might be Reid—or it might be someone who could tell her where he was. It was worth the risk. Tarik slid his hand in to pass her a flexible tubelight. When she switched it on, she drew in her breath in amazement, forgetting to be disappointed because it was not Reid.

She had never seen so perfect a male face. It appeared to be chiseled out of the same smooth white stone as the columns. She might have thought it was a statue except for the blue dot and twin crescent tattoo on the forehead and the fact that the man breathed in short, noisy gasps. Balancing the tubelight between her left shoulder and her chin, she inched her right arm forward until her fingers touched his cheek. Pale eyelids rose. Sea-blue eyes stared at her, then closed again. Alla was stricken by the pain and hopelessness in those eyes.

"We will help you," she told the unknown man. She was fully aware that the chances were good he could not understand her, but still she wanted to reassure him and the sound of her voice might do that. "We will get you out of here. I promise it won't take long. Just stay alive. Please, please, stay alive."

The ground shuddered a little. Small pieces of shattered stone rained on Alla's head. She felt the columns above her shifting. Heavy white dust sifted downward, coating her out-thrust right arm and hand, along with the still face before her, making the man look even more like a statue.

"Alla?" That was Tarik, sounding urgent. "Alla, are you all right?"

She began to back out of the cramped space.

It was hard to do. After a few moments of struggle, she was glad to feel two pairs of hands on her lower legs, pulling her free of the stones. Then she sat in shatteringly bright sunlight, breathing deeply, but still refusing to admit to herself that she had been afraid.

"There is a man in there," she finally was able to say. "I think he has been badly hurt, but he is alive. I told him we would get him out."

"What?" Herne glared at her, looking angry, while Tarik helped her to stand.

"It's not Reid," she said, nearly weeping with disappointment. "Not Reid."

While Tarik and Herne hurriedly discussed how best to employ the equipment they had aboard the shuttlecraft to free the injured man, Alla stood staring at the pile of broken stone columns where he lay. She was fighting hard to control both sorrow and elation. To be part of saving a life that surely would have ended soon without help was cause for rejoicing—but where was Reid? Was he here, buried under rubble like the man at her feet? Was he somewhere else, and was he safe or hurt? Was he dead, as Herne believed? She could not think so. She could not *feel* that Reid was dead.

When Tarik ordered her to take one of the heat sensors and use it to survey the entire walled area, she examined every atom of the temple complex along with any likely places within walking distance. There was no other sign of life.

Extracting the man from the unstable rubble

surrounding him was a tedious job, made more dangerous for him and difficult for his rescuers by the occasional earth tremors that shook the area. They got him out toward evening, strapped him to a stretcher, and laid him in the cargo hold of the shuttlecraft, where Herne at once began using his diagnostic rods and various treatment instruments.

Alla sat beside Tarik on the flight back to headquarters.

"Perhaps, when he can talk again, he'll be able to tell us about Reid," she said.

"Don't expect too much," Tarik warned. "According to Herne, he's seriously dehydrated and badly enough injured that he might not live. It will be a long time before he can speak, if he ever does."

"He will know something about Reid," Alla whispered, half to herself. "He will. I know it."

Reid and Janina sailed due north on a sea as deeply blue and calm as the sky above them. They stayed within sight of land, riding the current that swept toward the polar region. Once they had left the low green area around the mouth of the river where they had stopped for several days, the coastline quickly became a dull, lifeless grey-brown.

The sky, however, more than made up for the colorless land. Each evening, they were treated to a vibrantly brilliant sunset as the volcanic ash still in the upper atmosphere turned purple, green, and red in startingly beautiful combinations. Sunrises were almost as colorful, and Janina much preferred them. Coward that she was, she feared the long nights, during which sea monsters might creep up on them to devour them before they even saw the terrible creatures. Sunrise, on the other hand, meant that they had survived another night and had hours of daylight ahead of them when they would be able to see any lurking monsters and at least try to sail away from them. She did not tell Reid of her fears, but she knew he was aware of them. She also knew that he did not believe the sea monsters really existed.

On the sixth day after leaving the river, they reached an area of dark red-and-gold striated rock cliffs, which had been eroded by sea and wind into wildly improbable shapes. The topmost layer of rock hung far out over the sea, like a canopy. Well beyond the cliffs, individual rocks rose out of the water in striped, treacherous beauty. Foam broke the surface of the sea in many places where Janina could see no rocks, but she knew they were there, hidden and dangerous.

"We are going to stop overnight," Reid decided. "I don't want to navigate this part of the coast in the dark if I don't have to, and if I remember the computer model correctly, there won't be any other places to drop anchor so we can rest until after we have rounded the cape."

He then proceeded to maneuver the boat so close to the overhanging rocks that Janina began to be afraid they would be dashed onto them.

Before long, Reid found what he was searching for, a sheltered inlet with a narrow opening to the sea. Inside it, the water was quiet and crystal clear, allowing him to easily navigate around the many rocks that jutted out of the little harbor.

"Time for a bath," Reid declared once they were safely anchored. He flashed her a grin, reminding her of the baths they had enjoyed together at their first anchorage. But this was a very different place from that sunny cove.

"It's too cold," Janina protested, "and those rocks look dangerous."

But Reid was already pulling off his clothes. He stood poised on the stern for a heartbeat of time, a tall, strong, magnificently proportioned man. Then he was gone, cutting into the water with hardly a splash.

Janina hung over the side, looking for him. She wished she could be as brave and carefree as Reid was, instead of constantly worrying about sea monsters. Reid surfaced farther away from the boat than she would have believed possible. He waved to her, beckoning her to join him.

Vowing not to show her fear of the water, not to let him know what a quivering coward she was, she removed tunic and trousers, then quickly went down the ladder. The water was unbelievably cold. Left to herself, she would have dipped no more than one foot in it, but Reid was calling her and she wanted him to think she was as indifferent to danger as he was. She decided that the best way to go in was all at once. It would be less painful that way.

She released her grip on the ladder, letting herself fall into the icy wetness. Just as she plunged beneath the surface she remembered to hold her breath, but the cold made her gasp, so she choked on the salty water. She thought she had fallen to the center of the world before she began to rise again, too slowly for her empty lungs. She bobbed to the top, gulping for air, shivering violently from the cold. Then, recalling Reid's lessons, she lay on her back and began to float. She was certain she would freeze to death within a moment or two.

"Swim," Reid ordered from just beside her. "Turn over and move your arms and legs. It will warm you."

It did help a little. Still, she was glad to climb out of the water onto a striped rock that angled upward at one side of the inlet. Here, where they were sheltered from the wind, a late-season sun had warmed the rock. Janina sat down on it, pushing wet hair out of her face. She saw the boat riding at anchor more than half the distance across the inlet.

"Did I swim that far?" she asked in amazement.

"You are better at it than you think." Reid perched beside her, resting one hand on her thigh. "I regret there is no soft beach we could use for a bed tonight. This rock is hard, and the bunks are so narrow."

She met his dark eyes and melted into them. Then she felt the rough rock against her back as Reid's weight bore down on her, his mouth searching for hers. She cried out in pain. He pulled away from her at once.

"This bed is too rough for you to lie on," he said. "Shall we swim back to the boat?"

"Can you wait?" she asked, surprised at his suggestion.

"Not very happily," he teased her, "but wait I will. I don't want to hurt you."

"I thought"—she blushed a little and her tongue stumbled as she recalled their romantic interludes in the cove—" I thought when the man wanted, it had to be done at once."

"Sometimes it is sweeter for waiting," he answered, mischief lighting his face. "I'll show you."

He rose and went back into the water. It looked to Janina as though he simply walked off the rock into the sea, but when she tried it, she slipped on a wet spot and fell hard, knocking the air out of her. She skidded across the wet edge of the rock and fell into the water. Reid caught her hair and pulled her to the surface, then towed her away from the rock.

"Can you swim or are you injured?" he asked, his face filled with concern for her.

"I can swim," she sputtered, unwilling to let him know how the salt water stung the scrapes on her legs or the scratches on her back. Knowing that he cared what happened to her made her feel braver. Somehow she made it to the ladder at the stern of the boat. There Reid stopped her.

"I want you," he said, and kissed her hard.

Janina responded eagerly. He was so warm, and they had not made love since leaving the river. There had been no time, for they had taken turns sleeping and sailing the boat. She did not trust the unknown water of the inlet. It was deeper than the river cove had been, and any kind of terrible sea creatures might lurk there. But if this was where Reid wanted her, in the same way in which she had once wantonly assaulted him, then she would not resist. She could feel his hardness against her when he held her. Her arms were around his neck. He caressed her body quickly with eager, knowing hands, and suddenly the water did not feel cold any more. But she thought it likely they would both drown if he did not hold on to the ladder when he finally took her. Then she heard his deep chuckle.

"Later," he said, lifting her toward the ladder. "We are going to wait, remember?"

She stood in the cockpit watching him climb aboard. He wanted her. One glance at him told her that. She sighed with a mixture of relief and anticipation. The bunks in the cabin below were too narrow for two people, but at least they were not the water.

Reid put out one hand to touch her face and smooth back her dripping hair. Janina forgot that she was half-frozen by the icy water, forgot her fear of the sea, forgot everything but Reid.

Then he did an odd thing. He held her by the shoulders, keeping her at a distance so their bodies could not touch while he leaned forward to kiss her. His mouth was sure and warm, his tongue a tormenting delight inside her. Janina put out her arms to pull him closer, but Reid kept her away from him. She ended the kiss with her hands clutching at his upper arms, her nails digging into hard muscle. When he let her go, his fingertips teased at her breasts before he moved away from her.

Janina drew in her breath with a quick, hungry gasp. She half expected him to urge her down to the cabin so he could make passionate love to her at once. With her blood pounding in response to his touch, she would not have resisted him. Instead of making for the cabin, he reached to the deck and pulled on his recently discarded trousers.

"For safety," he said, grinning. "Until we have eaten, at least."

Eat? What was wrong with him? Didn't he know how much it hurt to want him and be denied? She did not know how to react to this peculiar treatment, and she was still too inexperienced in the ways of men to make any protest.

"It would be wise," Reid told her while fastening his trousers securely, "for you to cover yourself, too. Since we are planning to wait." Still grinning, he ducked through the hatch and disappeared.

Janina wrung out her hair, twisting it hard to let the excess moisture drip over the side of the boat. She picked up her clothes, but decided she did not want to put them on again. She had worn the same tunic and trousers for days. She wanted a change. In one of the storage lockers, she found a pale yellow, lightweight blanket. This she wrapped around herself, twisting and tying it to hold it tight. It covered her from armpits to ankles, leaving her shoulders and arms bare. The fabric was thin but warm, so the evening air did not chill her.

Reid was at the solar unit in the galley, busily preparing their meal. They were to have several kinds of the roots Janina had dug and stored, which he had sliced and was stewing with herbs. There was a kettle of hot *dhia* brewing for them to drink. He looked around when she joined him, raising his eyebrows in appreciation of her costume.

"That's very seductive," he said, planting a kiss on her right shoulder. "Shall we eat on deck? I don't think it will be too cool, do you?"

"Reid, I don't understand what you are doing," she began.

"You will, later," he promised, kissing her other shoulder. "Just have patience. Will you bring the bread and the cups?"

She followed him back on deck, where he set the hot bowl of stew on a bench. The sky was flaming orange and gold. The tall rocks that formed the inlet were glowing with golden light on one side, while on the opposite side of the inlet they were shadowy silhouettes against the radiant sunset. Calm water lapped quietly at the hull of the boat.

Reid went below again, to reappear with bowls and spoons and the kettle of hot *dhia*. As he seated himself beside her, he leaned over to lightly brush her lips with his. Then he filled a bowl with stew and handed it to her.

"Eat," he said. "Enjoy a meal without rocking around at sea." There was laughter in his eyes when he looked at her.

"You are teasing me," she accused.

"Are you enjoying it?"

"I'm not sure." The stew was hot and tasty, the roots still crunchy, as they should be. Refusing to look at Reid any more, Janina bit into a piece of root, savoring it.

I can tease, too, she thought. When Reid reached across her for the bread, which she had laid on the bench next to her, she leaned forward so that her breasts brushed against his arm. He turned his head to look directly at her. She smiled innocently, lowering her eyes. Reid settled back on his side of the bench, munching on a chunk of bread. She thought she heard him laugh under his breath.

"May I have more stew?" He held out his bowl. Janina took it from him and leaned forward to pick up the ladle from the larger bowl. When she did so, her wrapped garment fell slightly apart, revealing one of her knees and half of a thigh. While both her hands were occupied in ladling out the stew, Reid placed one of his hands on her exposed knee, then moved it upward so that it slid under the edge of the fabric to the top of her leg. He left his hand there for a moment, fingers spread, one finger edging provocatively into the hair between her thighs.

Janina nearly dropped the stew. Reid withdrew his hand to take his bowl from her shaking fingers.

"Thank you," he said politely, and began to eat.

It took a few minutes for Janina to regain her composure and think of a suitably titillating response to what Reid had just done. Smiling to herself, she rose from the bench and went to the kettle of *dhia*, which Reid had set on the deck.

"Perhaps you would like something hot to drink," she suggested, kneeling by the kettle. As she moved downward she made certain her knees pulled on the fabric just enough to lower the upper edge of her garment until her breasts were half uncovered. When she leaned over the kettle she knew he could see the curving space between her breasts. Her amused excitement at this stimulating game they were playing, coupled with the rubbing of the fabric against her nipples, made them stand up noticeably.

She did not look at Reid while she poured out the *dhia* and handed him his cup. She thought that if she met his eyes she would burst out laughing—or she would throw her arms around him and plead with him to take her at once. Either action would spoil his pleasure. She would wait, and let him set the pace. Meanwhile, she would continue to tease him, and to let him tease her into heightened awareness of his masculinity and of what they would surely do together before much longer. This game was exciting, and it was fun.

Reid reached for the cup of *dhia* she held out to him, but before he took it he flicked a finger across one of her hard, tight nipples. She almost erupted into wild laughter. She almost tore off the blanket so she could fling her naked body into his arms. She did neither. It took great effort, but she restrained herself.

"Come sit beside me again," Reid invited with apparent calmness.

She rejoined him on the bench at the stern, but she coyly kept her distance, making certain not to touch him. Reid laughed and put one arm around her, pulling her back to lie against him. Giving up coyness, Janina leaned her head on his shoulder. His arm now lay along the railing behind her.

The sun had set. The sky grew dark, then lighter again when the moons rose, spreading twin silver trails across the water.

"They are more than half full," Janina observed, trying to think about something other than the strength of Reid's shoulder beneath her head. "That will make sailing at night a little easier."

"Hmmm." Reid was nibbling at her earlobe, his breath warm against her skin. Then she felt his mouth along the side of her throat. His arm slid off the railing to lift her nearer leg, separating the fabric again as her knee bent. She felt his hand stroking from knee to thigh. His other hand moved across her shoulders, pausing to dip into the hollow space between her breasts.

"Reid," she whispered in surrender as he gently bit at her shoulder.

"I think it is time to clean the dishes," he said softly. He sat her up, straightened the blanket over her legs, and began to collect their bowls. "Will you pull up a bucket of water to wash them, or shall I?"

In the surge of frustrated desire she now felt, she was sorely tempted to push both Reid and the dishes into the sea. Instead, with a toss of her head she flung her hair over one shoulder and went to draw a bucket of cold water. When she bent over the bucket to wash their cups, Reid's arms came around her from either side. He had a spoon in each hand, and he plunged both into the water, moving closer to her, letting her feel his hardness against her back. His fingers laced through hers inside the bucket. His tongue drew a fiery line from the bared nape of her neck to the edge of her now-imperiled wrap. She was afraid the blanket would come loose, leaving her naked for him to tease and play with. When he reached for the stew bowls, she slipped under his arm and moved to the far side of the deck where she could adjust her costume in safety.

"Here." Reid handed her the clean, damp dishes, piling one into the other. "Take these below."

Presented with her back, he ran one hand across her buttocks, while with the other he lifted her hair to kiss behind each ear. Janina began to tremble so violently that she almost fell through the hatchway. Behind her, she heard the splash of the bucket being emptied. She hastened to put the dishes in their storage rack.

Reid lit a small solar bulb in the cabin, then closed the hatch against the suddenly cold night air. The bulb shed a soft golden light over the little sleeping area. There was so little room to move that he accidentally brushed against her several times while he removed his trousers. Or perhaps it was not by accident.

Now his fingers were busy at the top of her wrap, unfastening it. When her hands came up to hold it against her bosom, he let go of it and sat down on one of the bunks.

"Put it on the other bed," he said.

Janina turned around. For some reason she did not want him to watch her while she removed the covering. She pulled the blanket off and folded it carefully, then laid it down, smoothing it with both hands. She was still unable to face him. She continued to stand with her back toward him.

He caught her by the hips, pulling her backward to sit on his lap, adjusting her position until his distended manhood probed upward between her thighs.

"Now," he said in her ear, "we will do it very slowly."

She could not move. Her head lolled on his shoulder while he played with her breasts until she cried out, begging him to stop. His hands ranged across her abdomen, leaving her trembling with aching desire. He separated her thighs and moved his hands between them with agonizing slowness. Looking downward, Janina saw his manhood, huge and hard. Galvanized by the sight, she caught it between her hands, held the hot, throbbing length and began to stroke it.

"No," he whispered hoarsely. "There's no hurry. Let me go, Janina. Let me love you this time. Afterward you may do whatever you want."

A short time later he told her to stand up. When she did, on shaky legs, he turned her around to face him and sat her down again so she was straddling him. And at last she had what she wanted. He was inside her; he had never filled her so completely. Her head thrown back, she gripped his shoulders, moving to an instinctive, sensuous rhythm.

Reid lay back on the narrow bunk with Janina on top of him, letting her move however she wanted for a while. Then, just when she thought her heart would stop from the intensity of her feelings, he moved again, separating them a little, letting the building tension cool without withdrawing from her completely. He clasped her in his arms and turned over so that Janina was beneath him. She felt his weight on her and the full force of him driving into her, over and over, the tension building again now, until it carried her out of herself into a glorious, shattering climax that took both of them at the same instant and left them drained and quivering long afterward.

They slept until the next day was well begun, and neither minded the narrowness of their bed. Nor did they rush to leave their safe harbor.

"You were right," Janina murmured, her face against Reid's shoulder, feeling his hands on her, knowing what he could do to her. "It can be exciting to wait, and to make love slowly. But not always. Sometimes there is an urgent need."

"Urgent," he whispered, pulling her hard against him, entering her as though he understood exactly what she wanted and needed at that moment. "I love you, Janina."

"Oh, Reid." But before she could tell him how much she cared, how much he meant to her, he began to move in her so that she was unable to speak, and it seemed to her that words were unnecessary. Their bodies explained everything.

Before they sailed onto the open sea once more, the sun was as high as it would rise so near to the polar region at that time of year. The wind was stronger, pushing them along with the current, but also chilling them. Janina brewed kettle after kettle of hot *dhia* for them to drink, and they piled on every layer of clothing they could find in the lockers. Still their faces grew red and chapped, and whenever their hands got wet, their fingers were soon numb.

"Just another day and night after this until we round the cape." Reid answered Janina's unspoken question as the sun sank below the cliffs.

"Then the weather should become warmer and the days will grow a little longer as we travel toward the equator."

Janina stood next to him, nursing a cup of hot *dhia*, trying to warm her hands on it. She scanned the sea around them as she had done so many times during their voyage, searching every bit of the ocean as though by keeping a constant watch she could ward off what she most feared.

She froze. There, just above the water off their stern, lay *something*.

She struggled with rising panic, with her desire to avoid revealing her cowardice to Reid against the need to warn him of danger—and with her hope that she had been mistaken. She looked away, then looked back again. *It* was still there.

"Reid." He glanced at her, appearing surprised at her tone. "The sea monster has come for us."

He looked astern, in the area she indicated, then shook his head.

"I don't see anything," he said. "It is so late in the day that the light may play tricks. It could have been a long shadow cast by an unusually large wave. The sea is rising."

"I know what I saw," she insisted.

"Whatever it was," he replied, "we can't do anything about it except try to sail away from it. The only weapon we have is a fish spear."

Janina did not sleep at all that night. She stayed beside Reid in the stern except for an occasional quick trip to the galley to refill their cups with *dhia*. She would not leave him—not until the sea monster killed them both. Until then, she would remain by his side, and, so that he would not know how terrified she was, she would keep silent about the creature she knew was lurking in the sea, waiting for them.

CHAPTER 14

When Tarik's group of ten settlers first arrived on Dulan's Planet, Herne had appropriated one room of the building they called their headquarters, decreeing that it would serve as hospital and sickroom for anyone who needed to be isolated while ill or injured. After the shuttlecraft returned from the site of the volcanic eruption, he ordered the still-unconscious man they had rescued carried into the bare white room. Alla offered her services as his assistant in any treatments that might be required, as did her friend, Suria.

"I fail to see how anyone who is both spaceship navigator and midwife can help me," Herne said to Suria. "And as for a botanist-zoologist—you would only get in my way, Alla."

"I have done a lot of dissection work," Alla protested.

"On humans or on peculiar animals?" retorted Herne, looking irritated. "What we should have among the colonists is another physician."

"If you had one, you would only find reasons to quarrel," Suria observed tartly. "What you need for this man is two people who can serve as nurses so you can sleep occasionally. A decent night's sleep might improve your temper."

Herne did not answer her. He was too busy cutting off the man's clothing. When he had finished, he took up the laser knife to cut through the golden bracelet the man wore on each wrist. He tossed the jewelry aside with the rest of his patient's tattered belongings, leaving it to Alla to rescue the bracelets and lay them in a safe place. Now Herne used the diagnostic rod to check his patient's condition one more time before he began the necessary repairs to the battered man.

Suria moved silently to the instrument table. Without being asked, she began to hand Herne what he needed, while Alla monitored the life-recording machine. Repair of the man's severe internal injuries was completed first, following which, at Herne's order, Suria started an infusion of universally acceptable artificial blood. Next Herne quickly cleaned a deep laceration on the man's left arm, removing a pressure dressing he had applied during the return trip and resealing a torn artery before melding the skin back over the wound with practiced precision. Then he went to work on the man's leg wound, cleaning it and setting the broken bones before melding the skin there, too. Finally, he immobilized the leg while he used sonic instruments to fuse the shattered bones back together.

As Herne worked, Alla watched the life-recording machine carefully, wanting the strange man to live with an urgency far beyond normal concern for a fellow being. She could see from the readouts that the man was so deeply unconscious he needed no anesthesia during the repairs Herne was making. In fact, with his near-fatal injuries, anesthesia would have been dangerous to him, but had it been required, Alla would have administered it. There had been only a few minor medical emergencies since they had come to Dulan's Planet. Each time Herne had grumbled sourly about his lack of staff and the lack of medical training of both Suria and Alla, and then he had allowed them to assist him. They were growing used to him by now. Flame-haired Suria made a face at Alla over Herne's bent head, and Alla smiled back.

"He'll live," Herne said, tossing the skin melder onto the instrument table and turning off the sonic instruments. "He will be unconscious for a while, probably until his fluid levels return to normal. He is badly dehydrated and in a state of shock. That broken leg will take a long time to heal completely. At least seven days, I'd say."

"I will sit with him," Alla volunteered.

"You will not," Suria told her. "You need to

eat, and to think about something beside Reid and this man for a while, or you will be Herne's next patient. I will stay with him until you are rested."

"Now that you have disposed of the man and the nursing schedule between you, I may as well get some rest myself," Herne said, and walked out of the room.

"You go, too," Suria ordered Alla fondly. "I promise I will call you if he wakens and is able to talk."

"He might know what happened to Reid," Alla said. "But if he doesn't—"

"If he doesn't, we will still find Reid. I know Tarik. If there is a chance Reid is still alive, he won't stop searching, not after the discoveries of the last few days."

But when Alla wakened after a long nap, the computer model showed that there had been another volcanic eruption, with more clouds of ash and steam billowing out of the mountains.

"We can't search that area again until the air clears," Tarik said, his dark face taut with strain. "The shuttlecraft engines would be destroyed if large amounts of ash were sucked into them. I am sorry, Alla."

"I understand." Her only hope now was that when the rescued man regained consciousness, he would be able to give them information that would help in the search for Reid.

She was alone with him the following evening when he began to stir, opening his eyes to see her bending over him. The sea-blue color of those eyes was dulled by pain, and Alla thought very likely by emotional shock, too, if he had been aware of what was happening to his home before the columns crashed down on him.

"The earth no longer trembles," he said in a hoarse, weak voice.

"You are in a safe place," Alla assured him. "We are well away from the volcanoes."

"Not at Ruthlen?" The voice became firmer as he spoke, as though he had tapped a reserve of strength far inside himself.

"If by Ruthlen you mean the place where we found you, no. We are half the continent away from there." She could sense him thinking about that and gradually understanding that he had been rescued by people from outside his home. A few moments later, he spoke again.

"My bracelets are gone," he said, rubbing at first one wrist and then the other.

"Our physician had to remove them," Alla explained. She picked them up from the shelf where she had laid them the day before and handed them to him. "I am sorry they were damaged, but I think they could be fixed without much difficulty."

"How appropriate that they should be cut off." He took the bracelets, turning them over in both hands. "A just punishment."

"One of our colonists is very good at metal repair," Alla offered. "I will ask him—"

"Don't bother. I am no longer worthy to wear them, and what they once represented is gone." He dropped them back into Alla's hands.

"Did you find others alive?" he asked.

"We found no one," Alla said, wondering for whom he was concerned. She added quietly, "We did find a body near you. A woman in a blue dress."

"Sidra." He gave a deep, painful sigh. Then came a response that made Alla wonder all the more about this man. "Sidra is gone. I am free."

"I need to ask you a few questions." Alla decided it was time to steer the conversation to the subject that most interested her.

"Your speech is different from mine," he said. "You speak as Reid did."

"You know Reid?" Alla bent forward, her hands clenched tightly together to keep her from grabbing at him in her excitement. "Please, he is my cousin, and we have been searching everywhere for him. If you know where he is, tell me so we can find him."

"So you are Alla." The blue eyes were sharper now, searching her face. Alla stared back at him, caught by his marvelous beauty—and by the possibility of finding Reid. She thought he was going to say something, but at just that moment Tarik appeared.

"Here is our commander," Alla said, and watched the man look Tarik over with remarkable thoroughness.

"You are Jurisdiction," the man said to Tarik.

"I am, but if you are a telepath, you have nothing to fear from us," Tarik responded.

"I do not fear," the man said. He looked from Tarik to Alla, then seemed to make a decision. "I am Osiyar, former High Priest and Co-Ruler of Ruthlen. What do you wish to know?"

"Where is Reid?" Alla asked before Tarik could speak.

"He is dead," Osiyar replied, and saw her face crumple. "You cared for him. I regret the need to cause you pain, but you requested the truth."

"Tell us everything," Tarik ordered, "from the time you first met Reid until the last moment you can remember."

Osiyar began to talk. Herne came into the room in the middle of the story to check on his patient, and then to remain, listening as intently as Alla and Tarik. In answer to Tarik's questions, Osiyar explained that the blanking shield around Ruthlen would have kept the scanning computer aboard the *Kalina* from recording evidence of the true conformation of the land beyond the forest, and of the people living there. He spoke briefly about Sidra and her intrigues. Finally, he told them how Reid had arrived in Ruthlen and what had happened to him and to Janina.

"Bedding a virgin priestess," Herne grumbled at this point. "The man ought to have better sense. No wonder your High Priestess punished him."

"So Reid isn't dead." Alla wasn't interested in Janina, only in her cousin. She knew she was grasping at a meager hope, but she could not help it. "Reid is familiar with boats. He might have managed to safely beach the one he and the girl were in. He could be trying to reach us over land."

"That's not very likely," Herne put in. "I was in the forest, too, Alla, and I know as well as you how impassable it is. Not to mention the wide desert and the prairie lands if they got out of the forest, or the mountains if they started walking from farther up the coast. No, I think it is more likely they never reached land. The two of them are drowned, or dead of thirst and starvation by now."

"There is something else you should know, Alla," Osiyar said when Herne paused for breath. "I told you Tamat and I joined our minds to hasten the volcanic eruption she knew was imminent. I remained linked with her to the end. In the last instants before her death, she thought of Janina with relief. The image in her mind was of Janina on a larger, well-supplied boat. I had no time to think more of it because the earth was shaking and the temple columns fell on me. But now I wonder if Tamat sent another boat after them."

"You mean, she sent someone to help them?" Alla asked eagerly.

"No," Tarik said with a certainty that impressed Alla. "He means Tamat sent them a boat with her mind."

"She could have done it," Osiyar agreed.

"Which reminds me, Tarik," Herne interrupted. "How are we to protect ourselves against this telepath? Who knows what he has already learned about us, or what use he will make of the information?"

"I am too weak to use the Gift," Osiyar said.

"Even if I were not, I still would not use it without permission. That is the law."

"We don't know that we can trust what you say," Herne objected.

"No more than I can trust you and Tarik when you tell me you will not turn me over to Jurisdiction authorities." Osiyar smiled, making Alla catch her breath at the perfect beauty of his face. "I believe, Herne, that we are forced to trust one another in this situation in which we find ourselves."

"Can you use your Gift, as you call it, to contact Reid or the girl?" Tarik asked.

"When I am stronger, perhaps," Osiyar said. "Janina's portion of the Gift is locked so deep within her mind that I do not think it can ever be reached except by use of a harmful herbal potion, so there is little chance that my presently weakened skills could touch her mind firmly enough for me to understand where she is or what has happened to her. She cannot send her thoughts outward, you see. Reid is another matter. Tamat believed he had some latent power which he himself did not suspect."

"That can't be true!" Alla declared, much shaken by this assertion. "If Reid had any telepathic ability, I would know it, and I tell you, he hasn't."

"You know nothing about such things," Osiyar retorted sharply. "Do not dispute Tamat's knowledge or her ability to search another person's mind to learn what lies within it. Her belief in Reid's unrecognized ability was one reason she decided to allow him to mate with the village women.

"As for contacting either Reid or Janina to try to discover where they are, you must all understand that such a use of the Gift would be exhausting for the most healthy telepath. If I were to try before I recover fully, I would surely fail, and if I die attempting what you want, I would be of no further use to you."

Alla watched him, intrigued by the coolness with which he spoke of his own demise and wondering if he did not care whether he lived or died. It was possible, considering that everyone he had known, as well as his home, was lost to him forever.

"Had you friends in the village as well as the temple?" she asked with sympathy. She considered his response no real answer to why he was so cool.

"There was no one I cared about. I love no one," he said, then looked at Tarik. "May I remain with you until I am well? I swear I will harm no one, whether by mind or by physical force."

"You are welcome to stay as long as you wish," Tarik told him, adding, "There is a Cetan among us, but he is a friend. I should also tell you that the remnants of the Chon live here at the lake."

Osiyar went perfectly still, staring so hard at Tarik that for a moment Alla wondered if he had already broken his promise not to use his Gift. Then she saw him relax.

"A Cetan. If you say he is friendly, I will

believe you. As for the Chon, Reid told Tamat that they still live," Osiyar said. "Before he came to Ruthlen, we had believed them all killed by the Cetans. Herne, how soon may I get up? I must meet them."

"Two or three days at the most," Herne said. "You will need a crutch for your broken leg until it has completely healed, but you should be able to move about fairly easily."

"If the Chon will accept me," Osiyar told Tarik, "we may be able to use them to search for your friend long before I am strong enough to try."

"Then get well," Alla said. "I know Reid is alive. I am absolutely certain of it. Osiyar, I beg you, recover quickly and use all your powers to help us find my cousin."

CHAPTER 15

For Janina the time of greatest terror was the period between the setting of the moons and the rising of the sun. During that dark time she expected the sea monster to attack at any moment. When the sun finally rose, she could hardly believe she and Reid had lived to see daylight come. As soon as it was light enough to see clearly, she scanned the water astern of the boat, and then all around it. She saw nothing but wind-driven waves. The monster had disappeared. That made her even more apprehensive. On the sea, the monsters ruled, and they would never let their prey elude them. Janina thought the creature was tormenting them, biding its time, letting them think they could outsail it.

There was no way they could escape by land, either. Any attempt to beach the boat would be prevented by the enormous grey-brown cliffs, weathered and barren, that soared straight out of the water to a height so far above them that Janina felt like a tiny speck against their chilling grandeur.

"They are at least two thousand space-feet high," Reid told her when she asked him about the cliffs. "Look at the ice in the crevices and along the shore. That is a sign that we are nearing the cape."

They entered an area of floating ice, and Reid sent her forward with the long fish spear, telling her to try to push the huge chunks aside. Each time she leaned over the bow, Janina expected the sea monster to snatch her from the boat. She gritted her teeth to stop them from chattering and without objection followed Reid's instructions. If they were going to die at any moment as she believed, then she would spend those last moments pretending to a bravery she did not feel, so Reid would never know of her cowardice.

She drew a long breath of relief when they sailed into open water again, with only an occasional tall iceberg to be seen far out in the deepest water. By now it was much colder, and the cliffs edging the coast were completely covered in ice and snow. It seemed to Janina that the icily beautiful world was entirely composed of the cold blue of sea and sky and the glittering white of the land.

They reached the cape late in the day. The high cliffs ended in a tumble of ice-rimmed rocks and crashing waves, swirling whirlpools and unexpected changes in current. Reid took a wide course around this dangerous, northernmost end of the continent, sailing so far out into the sea that Janina's teeth began to chatter again, this time with fear and cold combined. Then he swung the boat southward, tacking into the wind, fighting his way across the sweep of the current they had been riding, which continued its northward direction beyond the end of the cape.

The land looked no more hospitable on this side of the cape, and now, with the wind blowing against them, they were not making the rapid progress Janina would have liked. But they would soon be in a different part of the sea, and still the monsters had not claimed them. She allowed herself to begin to hope they might be spared. When Reid sent her below to rest, she had no trouble falling asleep.

When she awakened, it was morning again and they were uncomfortably far out at sea, tacking toward land. She could only make out the part of the shore that lay at sea level. The higher land was covered with heavy fog and clouds.

"It will rain soon," Reid said. "I have a feeling there is going to be a bad storm. I would like to find a protected inlet or a river. I don't want us to be blown back to the cape and dashed onto those rocks."

His face was pale and lined with fatigue, but Janina knew that she was not a skillful enough sailor to have taken the tiller to round the cape the day before while he rested, nor to sail the boat now under the present conditions. Still, she could see they had to stop somewhere soon so that Reid could sleep.

At least she could serve as lookout. She watched the shoreline, searching for a place where they might land. She saw nothing but the same grey-brown rock everywhere she looked. She turned back to tell Reid—and stopped with her breath caught in her throat. She could not move or speak, she could only stare transfixed in horror at the thing she had feared for most of her life. It had come for her at last. Her heart quaking within her, she saw the sea monster rise out of the water just off the stern of their boat.

It was huge. The half of it she could see was as wide as three men standing side by side and twice as tall as a man. It was even more hideous than she remembered, covered with dark gold scales, its green eyes bulging at either side of its snakelike head. Below its sloping shoulders and long slender neck, appendages similar to fins were extended to hold it steady in the water. At each side of its great, gaping mouth, twin tentacles writhed, searching the air for the food it would scrape into that moist orange maw. The tentacles were reaching toward Reid, who had not yet seen the danger behind his back.

Janina was unable to give voice to the scream that would have warned Reid of the presence of the creature or told him it was moving closer to him. She remembered in anguish how quickly her parents had died, before any warning could be given. She knew it would be the same for Reid if she did not act at once.

Her realization of the monster's presence and of what it was about to do took only an instant. An instant more and the terrified paralysis that had held her in its grip had disappeared. Never taking her eyes off the monster, she reached for the fish spear she had left in the cockpit the day before, picked it up and ran the few steps to Reid's side.

He must have thought she had lost her mind and was trying to stab him with the fish spear. He ducked, moving the tiller sharply and sending the boat wheeling in a half-circle. The sudden maneuver saved him. When the monster lunged, he was out of reach of the tentacles. But he was safe only for a moment or two, until the creature tried again.

Janina went sliding across the deck, the fish spear still in her hand. Reid caught her arm, pulling her to safety when she would have tumbled overboard.

"Damnation!" By now he had seen the monster, too. "Get down and hold on!"

He swung the tiller again. The boat heeled over. With a crack of wind the sails filled suddenly, pushing the starboard side of the boat even lower into the water. Janina screamed as the sea poured into the cockpit.

It was the monster that righted the boat. It crashed across the port railing, lunging at Reid a second time, and its weight stabilized them.

Miraculously, Janina still held the fish spear. Though terrified, she was determined to protect Reid. Not thinking at all about her own safety, she jabbed at the monster with the spear, stabbing it just below one eye. In a pool of foaming black blood, the monster slid back into the sea, where it lay wallowing on the surface beside the boat. Standing in the cockpit, ankle-deep in sea water, weeping and shuddering, Janina clutched the fish spear with white-knuckled fingers.

Reid was still at the tiller. The sails were empty now and flogging wildly as the small boat faced directly into the wind. With their forward motion slowing to a stop, they began to roll and pitch on the rough sea.

"We're in irons," Reid muttered. "We're going nowhere. Janina—"

Before he could finish the order he intended to give, she pointed in horrified silence. There, in the sea behind Reid, was a second sea monster.

One glance over his shoulder showed Reid the source of her renewed terror. She could see by his face that he was frightened, too. He leapt away from the tiller just as the monster raised itself out of the sea and, with a loud sound of splintering wood, thrust itself across the stern.

Two tentacles wrapped themselves about Reid's left ankle. Two more fastened around his right leg at the knee, and the huge creature began to draw him toward its mouth. At the same time it began to sink back into the sea, the weight of its body lowering the stern to a level dangerously close to the water. A wave splashed over the stern and into the cockpit. Reid caught at a line with desperate strength, pulling hard, swinging the sail to a new position as the monster relentlessly dragged him closer to the stern and that waiting, open mouth. His face contorted with pain, Reid held on to the line, fighting the inexorable pull of a creature many times his size.

Janina began jabbing at the tentacles with the fish spear. Her fear was gone. All she could think of was Reid. She had to make that hideous monster let him go. She stabbed again and again until, after what seemed to her an incredibly long time, the hold of the tentacles slackened. One tentacle suddenly released Reid to snake around Janina's bare left wrist. Flaming agony shot up her arm. She was now too close to the creature to use the spear effectively, but with a wail of rage and pain she grasped it near the sharp end and forced it upward into the gaping mouth.

The monster released Reid and an instant later let Janina go, too.

"Push it back!" Reid shouted, trying to stand up. "Push it into the sea."

She pulled the spear out first, ignoring the gushing black blood that turned the deck slippery. Then, forgetting any danger to herself, she put both hands on the cold, scaly head and pushed hard. The monster's tentacles grabbed at her again briefly, then loosened as it returned to the water.

Now Reid was at her side, looking over the stern, but not at the creature sinking below the waves. He was staring at the rudder.

"It's badly damaged," he said. Turning away, he began to limp about the deck in obvious pain, flexing first one leg, then the other, wincing as he did so. But in spite of the discomfort he was clearly feeling, he continued his assessment of what the sea monsters had done. "The dinghy is gone, too. The creature must have smashed it to bits. It was certainly big enough to destroy it easily."

"Reid, if they come back—" Janina began. He did not let her finish the thought.

"I don't believe they will," he told her, pointing. "See there. I think the first creature must have gone after the second one you wounded."

A short distance away, the sea was achurn with two writhing bodies. The sea monsters were fighting each other, and Janina could see it would be a duel to the death.

"We will have plenty of time to get away from here before the winner of that battle can finish its meal," Reid said, his arm across her shoulders, holding her close for a moment before he let her go so he could limp to the stern again for a second inspection of the rudder.

"How can we sail if the rudder is damaged?" Janina cried.

"We will just use what we have left," he replied. "Fortunately, the wind is rising. That will help to move us away from this area even if we do nothing, and we can try to steer with the sails."

There was no time to tend to their injuries. Reid rubbed his legs a few times, after which he seemed to forget they pained him. Choosing to ignore her own sore arm, Janina jumped to obey his commands. For all of that terrible day, she marveled at his sailing skill as he fought to keep them afloat and on some kind of steady course while the wind blasted at them, the sea rose in gigantic swells, and the rain pounded down. The monsters disappeared from sight and temporarily from Janina's mind. There were more urgent problems to confront. With the sky cloaked in thick, dark clouds, they could not tell in which direction they were being driven by the raging storm. They did not know whether they might be blown toward the northern pole and dashed upon the rocks at the cape they had just rounded, or tossed upon the inhospitable nearby shore—or, worst of all, forced so far out to sea that they might never find their way back.

The storm abated as night fell in a pall of total darkness. There was no light anywhere, no sign of moons or stars through the thick clouds still covering the sky. Reid refused to allow a light on the boat for fear it would attract more sea monsters.

They had little to eat, for, with the exception of the flour and a small quantity of other food stored in the drybox, everything on the boat was soaking wet. At least the viscous black blood spewed by the sea monsters had long ago been washed away by the waves that had swept across the deck from side to side during the worst of the storm. That was the only advantage Janina could find to the beating they had taken from the elements.

"Reid," she said after the sea had calmed a little more, "go below and sleep. You are half dead from weariness after the last three days. I'll stand watch." She did not add that it would do no good, that neither of them could have seen anything in the enveloping blackness. She could barely make out Reid's form. If the sea monsters attacked again, she and Reid would not know it until too late.

"I'll stay here with you," Reid said. Knowing how exhausted he must be, she gave him a none-too-gentle push toward the hatchway.

"I'm not afraid any more," she told him. "Go below."

She thought she saw him nod. Then she heard him stumbling down the ladder in the dark. After he had left her, she felt her way to the seat next to the tiller and dropped onto it, rubbing her left wrist. The place where the sea monster's tentacle had wrapped around it ached with a fierce, burning pain. She had been able to put it out of her mind while she and Reid fought to keep the boat from capsizing in the storm, but now that the immediate danger was over she could think of little except her discomfort.

Grimacing at the need to bring more water onto an already drenched boat, she dipped a bucket over the side to fill it. Then she plunged her left arm into the icy water. After a while the ache in her wrist lessened. She wasn't certain whether the salty water had actually helped or whether the injured part was just numbed by cold, but she didn't care which it was. She took her arm out of the bucket and rested it across her lap. She felt with her foot for the fish spear, pulling it closer in case she needed it again. Then she sat staring into the empty blackness.

She wasn't afraid any more. She hoped never to meet another sea monster, but her abject, unreasoning terror of the creatures was gone. She had dared to fight two of them, had injured both and caused the death of one. The sea monsters were not immortal, not impervious to all attacks. Even a single fish spear could serve as a weapon against them in determined hands. She had proven that. She might not be a telepath, but she was a valiant warrior. She had saved Reid.

She straightened her shoulders and sat a little taller, feeling as though a great weight had dropped from her heart. She felt free, capable of facing any challenge. She wished Tamat could know. Tamat would be proud of her.

Shortly after sunrise the clouds dissipated. Janina searched the horizon, eager to find land. There was nothing but calm, purple-blue sea, broken here and there by small white waves. The air was much warmer than it had been the day before, but she could tell by the position of the early morning sun that the boat was headed in the wrong direction, back toward the polar regions. She struggled with the damaged rudder and with the single sail Reid had left raised, but she lacked his ability to make the boat obey her wishes. Nothing she did had any noticeable effect on their course.

The noise of her efforts must have wakened Reid, for he stuck a tousled head through the hatch, then climbed into the cockpit. When he crossed the deck to her, Janina saw that he was limping.

"Sea water helped my wrist," she said, assuming he was suffering from the effects of the sea monster's tentacles. "You might want to soak your ankle and leg."

"I will have a chance to do that at once," he replied, leaning over the stern and reaching down to test the rudder. He pulled out a handful of wood fragments. "We have to repair this while the sea is calm. The rail is splintered, too, but that is an easier repair."

"You should eat first," she advised, wondering if the solar heating unit would still work. If it did, and if the flour was unspoiled, she could heat water for hot *dhia* and make some bread.

"Later. Come with me. You can't do anything here, so we may as well drift for a while." He paused in the galley to set the solar unit on recharge and pick up a few tools. Then he led the way to the hold. The supplies they had stored there were awash, but Reid seemed unconcerned about that. Wooden planking ran down the center of the hold, forming a short walkway that made it possible to get to the stored items. Reid knelt and began sawing across one of the planks. When he had finished, he reached below and hammered upward on it for a while until the portion of wood came loose. This he gave to Janina to hold while he searched among the coils of rope piled in one cargo bay.

"This will do nicely." He had selected a thin line, and this he carried back to the stern of the boat. While Janina watched, he used another tool to shape the plank into a crude imitation of the rudder.

"You will have to help me," he said, removing tunic and trousers. "Take off your clothing, Janina."

She did not hesitate. She stripped off her own damp clothing and spread the garments with Reid's on the forward deck to dry in the sun until they needed them again. Then she followed him down the ladder and into the water. She was concerned that the sea monsters might return, but she no longer felt the paralyzing horror she had once known at the mere thought of those huge creatures. If they came back, she and Reid would fight them off as best they could, but she would not waste time speculating about something that might not happen. For the present, she owed Reid all her attention so they could lash the wooden board he had prepared onto the damaged rudder. They worked together, treading water, Janina holding the board in place against the original rudder while Reid wound the rope around and around both, binding them together.

Before long they were out of the water again, standing in the stern, shivering in the bright sunlight and looking at each other. Around Janina's left wrist was a wide, angry red welt. Reid had similar marks on his right knee and left ankle. Each of them showed many bruises, both recent and old. Reid had the beginning of a rough, dark beard, and Janina's long hair was matted and tangled.

"We are certainly no beauties," Reid said, touching her bare shoulder lightly. "We need a quiet harbor with fresh water, where we can dry out and rest for a day or two before we go on."

"First we have to find land," she replied.

"At this time of year, the sun is low in the sky because it is moving southward," Reid said, squinting upward. "We will keep it on our starboard side. Eventually, we should come closer to land."

"Eventually." She put her arms around him and felt his instant response.

"Thank you for everything you did yesterday, and for your help today," he murmured, his face pressed to her damp, salty hair. "You saved my life, Janina.

"You are freezing," he said a moment later. "Come below. Let's see if we can find some dry clothes."

There was nothing that was not wet. Even the thin mattresses on the bunks were sodden.

"Can we move them on deck?" Janina asked. "Will they dry in the sun?"

"It's worth trying," Reid replied.

Together they dragged the mattresses out and spread them across the roof of the cabin, along with blankets, pillows, and a few pieces of clothing.

"This boat looks like a sailing laundry," Reid said, laughing.

"The clothes I laid out before we fixed the rudder are almost dry," Janina said, lifting Reid's tunic. "We can put them on again."

"Not yet." Reid took his tunic from Janina and placed it on the deck on top of hers. "For just a little while, let me love you. There were moments yesterday when I thought we would never hold each other again."

He knelt on the deck, pulling Janina down to him. They lay upon their still-damp clothing, naked bodies stretched out in the sun. Reid's hand brushed her hair back from her face, then caressed her cheek, traced the pure line of her throat and shoulder, and came to rest upon one breast. Suddenly Janina wasn't cold any more. When his mouth and hands had teased her breasts to aching fullness, warmth exploded inside her. She touched him, too, wanting to warm him, feeling his hard muscles beneath her searching hands.

There was a difference in this loving. She was no longer an inexperienced girl, terrified by her inner fears and the perils of their journey. She had fought the worst of her fears and overcome them. She was now a woman who knew what she wanted from her mate. She felt no shyness at all about kissing him with growing fervor, or about reaching down to handle him boldly. She laughed in delight at his ecstatic groans, and climbed atop him with no invitation, using his body freely, joyfully allowing him to use hers in return. Still laughing, she let him roll her over until they were perilously close to falling into the sea.

"There was a time," he whispered, his deep voice husky with love, "when you never laughed. I thought then that I would never hear that sound."

"Oh, Reid." She looked up into his beloved face, almost a silhouette against the purple-blue sky, and saw him laughing down at her. Then his mouth covered hers and they gave themselves to each other completely, Janina reveling in his hard, assertive masculinity, Reid treasuring her deeply receptive femininity. It seemed he could not get enough of her, for he stayed with her, taking her to repeated heights of pleasure before allowing his own release. Even then, he held her tightly in his arms, rolling them away from the edge of the deck, back onto their crumpled damp clothing to rest there in relative safety.

Janina felt the sun on her back and Reid's warm chest beneath her cheek and knew utter contentment. This was where she wanted to be—with Reid, in his arms. No danger was too great to face, no journey too long, if the effort made would keep them together.

His hands stroked down her back. She pressed herself closer to him, enjoying the pressure against her thigh as he became aroused again.

"Once more before we stop," he whispered harshly. "It's the danger that does this, that makes me so hungry for you. I need you, Janina."

"I thought it was because I'm irresistible," she teased, sliding a hand down between them to catch at him.

"You are," he said in a choked voice. "I love you with all my heart."

"Then stay as you are and this time let me give you pleasure, to show you how much I love you."

She pushed away from him to kneel, straddling his thighs. She played with him, teasing, bending forward to nibble at his nipples, running her hands over his body, caressing his rigid manhood with a gentle touch that made him moan and gasp. He offered no resistance, but lay spread out upon the deck with his eyes closed while she did whatever she wanted. His growing excitement was evident, but still he let her set the pace. He did not touch her. He let her do it all.

The astonishing thing was that even without his usual caresses, her own arousal was rapidly becoming an unbearable ache. Suddenly, she had to have him inside her. At once. That instant. She moved forward, raised herself a little, and then lowered herself onto him. She felt as though *she* were taking *him*, as though she was inside him at the same time he was inside her. She leaned forward, balancing on her hands and moving the way Reid moved when he entered her.

He opened his eyes and smiled at her. She smiled back; she was so happy she could not keep from smiling. It was beautiful. Incredible. Amazing. Each was part of the other; they were together in body and heart and mind. She watched his moment come to him, saw his face shine with joy just before she was swept away by a climax so rich and fulfilling that she collapsed onto him in mindless ecstacy and lay there for a long, long time, sobbing in breathless happiness.

"My love," Reid murmured over and over again, "my love, my love . . ."

They tacked back and forth, progressing only slowly until Reid accidentally steered the boat into a cold current that apparently flowed from the polar region toward the equator. After that, they shivered constantly, and even the wind seemed colder, but with the help of the sweeping current, they traveled more rapidly. Halfway through the second day, they sighted land again. It did not look very welcoming.

"This northern part of the continent is nothing but mountains and cliffs," Reid muttered.

Janina said nothing. In growing disappointment and frustration, she stared at jagged peaks of grey rock ramming upward in row upon row as far as they could see. There was no green at all, and when they drew nearer, no beach or inlet where they could anchor.

"We keep going," Reid said, answering her unspoken question.

They rode the current all night. At Reid's insistence, Janina slept a little, until she was awakened near dawn by a howling wind and the sound of breakers crashing upon rocks. Above all the noise, she heard Reid shouting for her. Tumbling out of her bunk, she pulled herself up the ladder.

Reid stood at the tiller, holding it with both hands, trying to control the spinning, wheeling boat.

"The current is pulling us toward the rocks, and I can't get out of it," he shouted. "There must be some kind of whirlpool or giant eddy ahead. It's too dark to see anything but the breaking waves."

Janina could just discern the white foam beyond the bow. The wind, and an implacable current, were driving them forward. Reid struggled with the tiller. Janina leapt to the sail, following his shouted orders, as they tried to tack away from the rocks. The boat heeled over, the deck tilting dangerously.

Janina lost her footing. She grabbed at anything she passed, trying frantically to slow her fall into the water. For long, agonizing moments she clung to a line. Then a huge wave smothered her, filling her eyes and nose and mouth with salty water. The force of the wave tore her hands from the line. She made a last desperate effort to catch it again before she sank into the foaming, raging sea.

Reid saw Janina fall overboard. Knowing he ought to stay with the boat, ought to wait so he could throw her a line when she came to the surface, understanding what was the sensible thing to do—even so, he dove in after his love.

He was immediately sucked downward, until he was so far beneath the surface he thought his lungs would burst. And still he was dragged deeper. He felt something brush his hand. He thought it was some seaplant until his fingers tangled in it and he knew it was hair.

Janina! He pulled on the strands he held and felt her limp body brush against him. With his free hand, he caught her around the waist, but he would not let go of her hair. Not yet, not until they were both above water. He dared not chance losing her.

His feet touched the solid rock bottom. He kicked hard, and then, with incredible speed, he and Janina shot upward, breaking through the surface of the water in the midst of a swirling, foaming maelstrom.

They were doomed, and Reid knew it. He had no idea in which direction the shore lay, nor was he capable of reaching it. He could hardly keep Janina and himself afloat. He could not see the boat. For all he knew it was at the bottom of the sea.

Janina's head lolled against his shoulder. She

might be dead already. They would both surely be dead within minutes. He was filled with rage at their fate, with fury at the unfairness of it after they had survived so much.

"Tamat!" he screamed, his words half choked by roaring water, "Tamat! Hear me! Help us! Help!"

CHAPTER 16

"Help! Help me! Help!" When the lights came on with eye-shattering brilliance, Osiyar was sitting up in bed, shaking and shivering. "Help! Drowning! Help!" he shouted at the people crowding into his room.

"It's a delirious nightmare from the fever he's had for the last few days," Herne said. "I'll prepare an injection to sedate him."

"Osiyar." Alla sat on the bed, taking both his hands in hers. "Wake up. You were dreaming."

"I am awake." Behind Alla's concerned face, Osiyar saw Tarik with his wife Narisa, and Suria with her lover Gaidar the Cetan warrior. Beyond them were two other members of Tarik's colony. All of them were in nightclothes. Herne had disappeared. Osiyar looked into Alla's grey eyes and shook his head.

"It was not a nightmare," he said. "It was a vision. I saw Reid."

"Where was he?" Her hands held his tightly while he concentrated, trying to bring back what he had seen.

"In the sea," he said slowly. "He was drowning. He and Janina."

"Please." Alla looked as though she would weep. "Help him, Osiyar."

"I don't know where he is." Osiyar pulled away from Alla's clutching hands. If these people would only go away and leave him in peace, he would be able to think clearly about what had just happened and might be able to make some sense of it.

Herne bustled in with a treatment rod. Alla rose and went to stand between Suria and Gaidar.

"This will put you right back to sleep," Herne told him. "Then the rest of us can get some sleep, too."

"No," Osiyar said, gathering his strength.

"Don't be ridiculous," Herne advised. "It's the best thing for you." He bent over, took Osiyar's arm and began to lift his sleeve.

"I said, *no*." Osiyar stopped the physician in mid-motion. Herne froze, unable to move from his bent posture or to speak, though his furious eyes said all that his immobilized tongue could not.

When they realized that Osiyar had asserted some kind of control over Herne, everyone in the room moved backward from his bed at least one step. Except Tarik. He came toward the bed.

"Release Herne," Tarik ordered.

"First forbid him to inject me," Osiyar said. "He can hear you."

"No injection, Herne," Tarik said in a loud voice.

Osiyar nodded and Herne straightened.

"By all the stars!" Herne raged. "You promised to harm no one here."

"Have I harmed you?" Osiyar asked. When Herne shook his head, unable to speak for sheer anger, Osiyar continued. "I have the right to protect myself, even from well-meant medical treatment. I do not wish to return to sleep. I need to think about the vision I just had."

"Can you help Reid?" Alla asked.

"I promise nothing," Osiyar told her. "I do not understand what I just saw and felt. Neither Reid nor Janina is an overt telepath, yet I received a message."

"You told us once that your High Priestess believed Reid might have latent powers," Tarik said.

"That is not true!" Alla cried, as she had protested on the previous occasion. "Reid is no telepath."

"Osiyar, if Reid were drowning," Tarik went on as though Alla had not made her outraged exclamation, "and he were crying out for help with every particle of his being, might you not sense his cry?"

"It is possible," Osiyar answered, "especially if I were deeply asleep and thus unguarded and open to such a cry."

"Then he is dead." Alla sagged, all protest gone. Beneath the bright overhead lights, her thin face looked pale and drawn. Gaidar put a brawny arm across her shoulders to support her, while Suria took her hand and pressed it tightly.

"I think it very likely he is dead," Osiyar responded. "I regret having to tell you that. It is amazing to me how deeply I feel your grief, Alla. I wish I had words to ease your pain."

"I know who can help us learn Reid's fate for certain," Tarik mused, "if they are willing to explore a part of the world far from their usual range, and if you will give them the information they will need."

"The Chon," Osiyar said softly, meeting Tarik's searching look with no evasion. His eagerness must have shown in his face, for Tarik's night-blue eyes were filled with curiosity.

"It is almost dawn," Tarik said. "The Chon will waken soon to begin fishing in the lake for their morning meal. Get up, Osiyar, and we will go out to meet them. Herne said you would be well enough to get out of bed later today. A few hours won't make much difference to your health."

"I'm not sure that's wise," Herne grumbled. "If he is well enough to do what he just did to me, then we ought to keep him under some kind of restraint and well sedated."

"It's you who ought to be restrained," Osiyar

said, swinging his feet to the floor. "Restrained from forcing unwanted treatments on patients who don't need them." He stood up, then promptly sat down again, shamed by the weakness in his legs.

"How do you expect to stand?" asked Herne crossly. "You've been in bed for days and your broken leg is still healing. You will have to help him, Tarik, and he'll need a crutch. Or perhaps Gaidar can carry him outside. I'm certainly not going to touch him again."

"There is no need for you or Gaidar to go along. Just bring him the crutch." Tarik turned to his wife. "Come with us, Narisa. You have a special afinity for the birds, so you may be able to help. The rest of you go back to bed or begin your day, as you wish, but stay inside the building for now. I don't want you to disturb the birds."

"Let me go with you, too," Alla begged, and after a moment's consideration, Tarik nodded his permission.

With Osiyar hobbling on the crutch Herne gave him, and Tarik helping him when necessary, the four of them walked to the beach on the side of the island nearest to the cliffs where the Chon lived. The sun was just rising.

Osiyar caught his breath at the beauty of the landscape before him. The island lay at one end of an immense lake. On the mainland to the left rose the cliffs where the birds lived, while to the right the forest ended in a white sandy beach. The warm season was waning, so trees and underbrush were tinged with gold and bronze and deep, glowing reds, all of which were reflected in the placid waters of the lake. In the far distance rose a single mountain capped with snow that, as the sun moved higher, changed color from pink to gold to pure, glistening white, shining against the purple-blue sky. Behind the little group on the beach lay the lush growth of the island, with the white headquarters building at its center.

Tarik had told Osiyar how he and Narisa had found the island on their first visit to the world they called Dulan's Planet, and how they had returned with their comrades to establish a small colony to monitor the activities of the Cetans. Tarik's wife Narisa had explained how the Chon had helped them on that earlier visit. Now Osiyar waited to meet the birds that had once been companions to his people, the birds the telepaths had long believed extinct through Cetan violence.

From openings in the cliffs high above them, graceful green or blue forms swooped, winging their way across the lake. Osiyar watched, touched beyond speech by the sight.

"They fish in the early morning and again at evening," Narisa said. In the softness of her voice, Osiyar sensed her understanding of his reverent mood.

"Will they come at your bidding?" he asked.

"Almost always. Do you want to try to call them?"

"You do it," Osiyar decided. "Let them grow

accustomed to me before I attempt to communicate with them."

Two birds came, a blue one with an old scar on its beak, and a green one. While Osiyar watched them, moved almost to tears by the appearance of beings from an ancient legend, they landed on the sand near Narisa. They were beautiful, with fine, richly colored feathers and long beaks, and they were tall. Standing, they were almost Narisa's size. She touched the green one, stroking its wing.

Osiyar could not make himself wait any longer. Filled with an excitement he had never known before, he put out his hands, palms up, and opened his mind. There was a confusing surge of impressions at first, then a steadying as the birds' inherited memories awakened and they allowed a portion of Osiyar's consciousness to touch a part of their awareness. It was not the same as the mind-linking he had experienced with Tamat and Sidra. Because of differences in their patterns of comprehension, complete linking with this other species would be difficult and dangerous for both man and bird. But these representatives of the Chon did understand that he was a descendant of their telepathic friends of long ago, and for a time he stood bathed in their joy at his presence.

After a while, Osiyar let them know that two humans were lost and in danger. He tried to envision the far northern country, to show the birds where Reid and Janina might be, but, never having been there, he could not form a picture in his mind. He sensed the birds' fear at what lay on the eastern side of the continent, and he understood that to protect their reduced numbers from possible future Cetan violence they had restricted their range to the area between the lake and the far side of the prairie.

All at once Osiyar felt another presence intruding on the communion he had established with the Chon. With a shock, he recognized Alla. Her desperate fear for Reid was communicating itself to the birds. Her love and concern for her cousin, memories of Reid as a small boy, and her pride in his accomplishments poured out of Alla in a flood of emotion that Osiyar found painful to bear. He wondered how the birds could tolerate it. And he wished there had been someone in his life who cared for him so much.

Unable to fight off the emotional battering of Alla's hopes and fears for Reid, Osiyar closed his mind again, breaking off contact with the birds. He had not really been well enough yet for the sustained effort of contact with another species. A wave of weakness washed over him. He shook his head, staggering, and came to himself to find Tarik holding him upright. He was about to scold Alla for her foolish and uncontrolled interference, when she turned to him, her face alight.

"You've done it," she said. "They will help."

"Is this true?" Tarik asked.

"Of course it is." Alla answered for Osiyar. "They will search this side of the grey mountains, to the end of the land, where all is ice and cold. And they will search the sea beyond, for as far as they can fly. Thank you, Osiyar. I knew you wouldn't fail us."

Osiyar said nothing to that. Instead, he admitted to the fatigue he felt so they would ask him no questions. After they had seen him safely back to his bed to rest, he began to wonder about Alla and how she had known what the birds were planning to do. As he thought about her, he remembered how she had told him shortly after he was rescued that she was absolutely certain Reid was still alive. Had some telepathic connection between them convinced her of that improbable fact?

Tamat had believed Reid possessed some latent portion of the Gift. Alla was Reid's first cousin, with much of the same genetic material. Might she also have some part of the Gift? If so, Osiyar doubted that she was consciously aware of it. She would have denied it in any case, because in the Jurisdiction, her native part of the galaxy, telepathy was forbidden. But if she did possess a portion of the Gift, she could pass her unsuspected abilities on to future generations.

Osiyar wondered with growing excitement if it might be possible to begin anew, to breed a new population of his people, trained to use the Gift for the good of all and linked in co-operation and affection with the Chon. He would have to lead them, for there was no one else who had the experience and the training necessary to accomplish such a purpose. So far as he knew, he and Janina, who under certain circumstances was capable of prophecy, were now the only descendants left of the original colony of telepaths. Reid and Janina, if they were alive, would willingly provide the new genetic material Tamat had wanted, for they were lovers bound together more completely than even they realized.

As for Alla, that slender, difficult, oddly attractive creature who seemed to care for no one but Reid—might Alla, if properly approached, consent to be Osiyar's mate? Did he want her if she would agree? It was a possibility that ought to be carefully considered.

From that morning, Osiyar began to watch the tall, dark young woman with a very special interest.

CHAPTER 17

When Janina regained consciousness, she was lying on a narrow, stony beach. Towering grey rocks piled on all sides blocked any possibility of escape from her forbidding refuge, and an icy wind was blowing, making her shiver in spite of sunshine and blue sky. She was half frozen, and she felt nauseated and dizzy.

She was completely alone. There was no sign of Reid or of their boat. She remembered falling overboard. She clearly recalled the sensation of plunging downward through endless ages of freezing water, knowing she would never breathe air again, yet wanting with all her heart to rise to the surface, to find Reid. And she remembered understanding that she would never see him or hold him in her arms again, that she would die in the sea.

How, then, had she come to this desolate beach? And where was Reid? Was he, perhaps, lying injured on the other side of that broken pile of foam-speckled rocks to her right? Or had his broken body been tossed by the waves onto the more level outcropping on her left? She had to know. If Reid was anywhere in her vicinity, she would find him.

That decision made, she quickly scrambled to her feet, only to double up when a fresh wave of nausea overcame her. She went to her knees, coughing up salty water. After she had finished, she stayed as she was for a while, with her head bent, waiting for the dizziness to pass. When she felt a little stronger, she got to her feet again and staggered across hard pebbles to the nearer pile of rocks on her right. She dragged herself slowly up the rocks, not wasting her energy in calling out Reid's name, thinking only of the task she had set for herself, forcing herself by sheer willpower to the top of that slippery heap. Waves smashed at her, soaking her badly chilled body with more cold and wet.

Reid was not on the rocks. Beyond the pile she had climbed there was only a second beach, stonier and narrower than the one on which she had wakened. Beyond it, the solid rocks plummeted straight into the water. Janina sat on the topmost rock of the pile she had climbed and hung her head in disappointment and suddenly renewed nausea.

A wave crashed over her, nearly dragging her into the sea as it receded. Janina clung to the rock, fighting the ocean's pull. When the wave had gone, she climbed back down as quickly as she could, and retreated above the waterline of the beach.

She would have to search the rocks on the other side. She stood wavering in her weakness, trying to collect enough strength for the effort.

"Chon. Chon-chon." The loud cry made her look upward. Two large birds flew above the beach, wheeling and dipping on the wind. They came closer and closer, until finally they lighted at the very edge of the sea. One was blue, the other green. More than a little frightened by their size, Janina watched them with apprehension. They appeared to be looking directly at her. She wondered if they would attack her, and how she would fight them off if they did.

From above her came a low-pitched humming noise that gathered strength until it blotted out the sound of the sea. Oddly, the birds did not fly away from that noise. Janina had the feeling that they were waiting for something to happen.

When she looked upward again, searching for the source of the humming sound, there appeared far above her a dark grey oval shape, pointed at one end, with a red stripe along its side. She stared at it in fascinated, immobilized shock as the shape descended until it settled on the beach. It was enormous, bigger than any fishing boat she had ever seen.

She was comforted to note that the birds did not move or display any fear of the object now resting on the beach in sudden silence. If the birds did not think it would harm them, perhaps it would not hurt her, either.

The grey object had barely stopped moving before a door slid open in the side and a woman stepped out. She was followed by three men. They were all dressed in brilliant orange suits like the one Reid had worn the day she met him.

Greatly relieved to recognize humans, and filled with renewed hope, Janina stepped forward. From their clothing she assumed these were Reid's friends. They must still be looking for him after all this time. If she was right about them, they would help her to find him.

The woman, who came toward her first, was tall and slender, with short dark hair. She looked angry. Or perhaps she was just worried about Reid. Janina hurried toward her, stumbling over loose stones, forgetting in her excitement how cold and miserable she was.

"Where is Reid?" the woman demanded. "What have you done with him?"

Janina stopped short. After an instant of surprise at the rude greeting, she thought she understood. The woman looked remarkably like Reid.

"You must be Alla, his kinswoman," Janina said, putting out her hand. "I am—"

"I know who you are," the woman snapped. "Where is Reid?"

Janina glanced at the men with Alla to see if they were as angry as she seemed to be. The man nearest to her was slim, with sharp features, black hair, and deep blue eyes. He looked serious but kind. The second man was large-boned and tall, and wore a sour expression on his face. The third man, who was leaning on a walking stick, was blond and incredibly handsome. Janina could not believe her eyes.

"Osiyar?" she exclaimed. "Osiyar, where are your bracelets? Is Tamat with you? Is she well? We saw the volcanoes—Osiyar, tell me Tamat is well."

"Tamat lives no more in this world," Osiyar said, confirming Janina's fears. "I will explain that later. I will tell you everything you wish to know."

A strong hand grabbed at her shoulder, pulling Janina around to face grey eyes blazing with anger.

"Answer me, you stupid little fool!" Alla raged, her face contorted with fury. "You are the cause of all my cousin's trouble. You are the reason he was cast adrift, the reason his life has been in danger. And look at you—skin and bones and not even as tall as my shoulder. You thought you were a fit mate for Reid? I'll see you torn in pieces first!"

"Alla, stop it." The dark man came forward and took Alla by the wrist. He had not raised his voice, nor did he appear to exert much manual pressure, yet Alla dropped her hand from Janina's shoulder at once. But he could not stop her tongue.

"Tarik, you know she is the reason Reid is missing. If she hadn't worked her wiles on him, he wouldn't have been set adrift."

"I believe," Osiyar said quietly, leaning heavily on his walking stick as he came forward, "that it was Reid who seduced Janina. But at Ruthlen it is—was—the custom to punish both parties on the rare occasion when a priestess is violated."

"Violated!" Alla screeched. "Reid would never—"

"Shall we forget our differences and try to find Reid?" Tarik suggested. "Janina, when did you last see him?"

"On the boat," she replied promptly, eager to do anything that might help Reid. "There was a terrible storm. We were nearly driven upon the rocks. Reid was trying to keep the boat afloat. When it heeled over, I fell into the sea. I am afraid for him," she ended on a choked sob.

"Where was that?" Tarik asked.

"I'm not certain. It was night, and I had been asleep until Reid called me. He said something about a whirlpool, or an eddy, that made him lose control of the boat."

"While you slept!" exclaimed Alla. "Not only did you cause all his problems, you were obviously no help to him, you useless piece of baggage."

"Alla," Tarik said in a quiet, deadly voice, "get into the shuttlecraft, take the navigator's seat, *and keep quiet.*"

Alla looked rebellious at first, then shrugged and did as she had been told.

"She is worried about Reid," Tarik explained to Janina. She saw the sympathy in his dark blue eyes and instinctively knew that while he would never say anything unkind about Alla, he would protect Janina against the woman's unreasonable anger.

No, not unreasonable. Alla loved Reid, too, and if in her fear for him she needed someone to blame, then Janina could understand and would accept the temporary abuse because they both had the same goal—Reid's safe return.

"This is Herne, our physician," Tarik said, indicating the larger man. "I suspect he is growing concerned about you."

"It's about time you remembered I'm here," Herne responded. "While we stand listening to Alla overrunning with undeserved anger toward her, this young woman is rapidly becoming a candidate for pneumonia and frostbite. Look at her. Her clothes, such as they are, are soaked, and she can't stop shivering."

"I will be all right as soon as we find Reid," Janina assured him. "He isn't there. I looked at those rocks, but I haven't climbed the flat rock on the other side of the beach yet."

"Do you mean you climbed all the way to the top, with the waves washing over you?" Herne asked. "Young woman—Janina, is it?—get into that shuttlecraft at once and let me examine you."

"I suggest you do as he commands," Osiyar told her. "Herne is a most determined man."

"And you stay away from her," Herne retorted. "She has enough to contend with. She doesn't need you to invade her mind."

"He can't do that without my permission," Janina told him.

"So you say," Herne replied with a snort. Taking Janina's elbow firmly in one hand, he began to steer her toward the shuttlecraft door. "But he doesn't need permission to stop you in mid-motion and hold you there until he's ready to release you."

At that, Janina looked at Osiyar, just in time to see him exchange an amused glance with Tarik. She had never seen a light-hearted Osiyar before, yet now Osiyar looked almost happy and he seemed to be on friendly terms with Tarik.

Considering the exterior size of the shuttlecraft, the cabin inside was unexpectedly small. That, Herne informed her, was in order to leave space for cargo, or, if necessary, for stretcher-beds to transport injured people who could not sit. He made Janina stand in the narrow aisle while he waved a silver rod around all of her body from head to toe. Then he read off the information provided by an oblong grey metal box fitted with an amazing array of dials and winking lights. She did not mind the rather impersonal examination. In spite of his gruffness, she sensed that Herne wanted to take care of her. Besides, the shuttlecraft cabin was warm and well protected from the bitter wind. The worst of her shivering had stopped.

"She appears to be in good condition," Herne said to Tarik, "except for some congestion in her lungs. That is probably from inhaling sea water. She has a low-grade infection of some kind, but no fever, so I won't worry about the infection until I can perform a better examination at headquarters. I suggest we put her into dry clothes and let her sleep a while."

"I can't sleep," Janina objected. "I have to help you find Reid."

"If you are like most women, you'll do whatever you want regardless of what I say," Herne responded. "At least put on dry clothing."

He found an extra orange suit for her, then turned his back, standing so his bulky frame blocked her from the view of anyone else in the cabin while she changed out of her sodden tunic and trousers. Janina was too uncomfortable in her wet clothes to worry about modesty, but she thanked Herne once she was dressed, and thanked him again when he helped her turn up the too-long sleeves and legs of her new suit.

"Better sit down," Herne said, pushing her into a padded seat and fastening an elastic strap across her shoulders.

"No, I have to get out," Janina objected. "We have to search for Reid."

"We have a faster way to do that than by climbing over wet rocks," Herne said, seating himself beside her and adjusting his own elastic strap. "Just watch the viewscreen."

Janina saw that Osiyar had limped into the shuttlecraft to take the seat behind hers. Tarik and Alla were in the first pair of seats. Tarik was doing something to a wide panel in front of him that had more knobs and blinking lights than Herne's grey box. When he pulled a lever, she felt vibrations shake the shuttlecraft, followed by the sensation that her body had been lifted into the air while her stomach remained on the ground.

"Watch there." Herne indicated a large blank square set into the wall of the shuttlecraft just above the panel where Tarik was working. A moment later the square was blank no longer. Janina could see the beach where she had been, and the rocks she had climbed. The beach grew smaller. The ocean appeared, and the high rocks backing the beach. She saw the two large birds flying along with them. Then, suddenly, she could see a long stretch of coastline.

"How is that done?" Janina cried.

"With machinery, not with the mind," came Osiyar's voice from the seat in back of her. "When I first saw it, I couldn't believe it, either."

"We can look for Reid this way," said Herne. "With all of us watching the screen, there is little chance we'll miss any sign of his presence. And the birds will help us, too. They directed us to you."

"First we are going to search the shore near where we found you," Tarik explained, speaking over his shoulder. "If he's not there, we'll try to find the whirlpool you mentioned."

He adjusted a dial, and instantly Janina felt as though she had moved much closer to the land, but she understood that this was some trick of the machinery. She knew they were flying through the air, yet she was not afraid. In fact, she was exhilarated by this new experience. If only Reid were there to share it with her!

By watching the screen, she could see when Tarik turned the shuttlecraft away from the coast and moved it out to sea, with the birds still accompanying them. At first she saw nothing except heaving waves, but then she noticed the water swirling into a gigantic circle with a depression at its center. Off to one side of the whirlpool a long spur of rock reared upward, and flung onto the rock, broken into pieces . . .

"That's it, that's the boat!" Were it not for the safety harness, Janina would have been out of her seat. "Tarik, that's the boat!" she repeated.

Tarik turned the knob he had used before and the rock appeared nearer. Another twist of the knob, a slight adjustment of focus. Janina held her breath. Below them, the birds circled the rock.

"There!" Alla cried. "There he is, next to the wreckage."

"Reid?" Janina could hardly speak, could barely breathe. The figure she saw on the rock looked so small and broken—and so very still.

"I'll go down," Herne said to Tarik.

"I'm going, too." Alla was out of her seat, reaching for a bulky, sleeveless garment. With a quick motion she pulled it over her treksuit and fastened it down the front. She tossed a similar garment to Herne.

"Let me go along," Janina begged.

"You don't belong there," Alla told her rudely. "You'd be in the way."

"Stay here, Janina," Herne said more kindly.

"You are weaker than you think, and that's a dangerous descent to a slippery surface. We don't want to have to rescue you a second time in one day. You can see everything that happens on the viewscreen, and you will be here waiting for Reid when we bring him up."

Enthralled, she watched the viewscreen as Herne and Alla were lowered from the shuttlecraft on what looked like heavy ropes, while Tarik kept the craft steady high above the rocks.

"Ordinarily, when they reach ground level, they would disconnect themselves from the lines," Tarik explained. "But not here. If they fall into the sea we want to be able to pull them back, and the vests they are wearing will keep them afloat until we do."

Osiyar asked a few questions about the machinery used to lower Herne and Alla, but Janina wasn't listening. All her attention was on the viewscreen. Alla had reached the rocks. Janina watched her fling herself onto Reid's body.

It should be me down there, Janina thought, and felt a surge of jealousy, until Herne's voice crackled through the shuttlecraft cabin.

"He's still alive," Herne reported. "Half drowned, badly injured, but alive."

Janina leaned back in her seat, tears of relief overflowing.

"Janina, Osiyar, I will need your help," Tarik said.

Janina wiped her cheeks. Osiyar had released his own safety harness and now helped Janina out of hers. Following Tarik's directions, they went through the hatch into the cargo hold. Janina clutched at Osiyar, nearly upsetting his precarious, one-legged balance, for there in the floor before her yawned the open hatch through which Herne and Alla had been lowered. The ropes holding them descended from what looked like a heavy beam that ran from end to end of the shuttlecraft.

"Just step around the opening." Osiyar showed her the row of handgrips in the wall to which she could cling as they made their way past the gaping hatch. They located a special mesh stretcher and the release for a third rope. At Tarik's command, they attached the stretcher to the rope, then sent both through the hatch and down to the rocks below. Watching the rope unreel, Janina saw that it was not the kind of plant-fiber rope she had always known, but was made of a combination of metal and some other flexible material.

Their next task was to unfold and set up a stretcher-bed, which they secured to the wall by special hooks, then padded with a thick heating blanket. Janina began to appreciate how cleverly the shuttlecraft had been designed. In a way it reminded her of the broken boat on the rocks below. Like the boat, the shuttlecraft had a compartment or a holder for every object in it, so that while it was in motion, nothing could roll around and cause damage or injury.

Herne came up from the rocks first, followed by the unconscious Reid, who was tightly strapped into the stretcher. Alla arrived last, but by that time Janina was not watching the hatch any more; she was helping Herne to secure the folding stretcher to the stretcher-bed. Herne refused to allow Reid to be moved any more than was absolutely necessary, so they cut off his saturated garments and covered him with another heating blanket.

"The one you put on the stretcher-bed will warm his back," Herne explained, adjusting the temperature gauge, "and this one will warm the other side of him. He's lost a lot of body heat. That sea water is too cold for a human to survive very long with the waves constantly washing over him."

Janina heard the concern in Herne's voice with a clutch at her heart. She knelt beside Reid, smoothing his hair back from his pale, cold face while Herne worked on him.

When Alla finally appeared through the hatch, it was Osiyar who reached out a hand to pull her over so she could stand, and Osiyar who pressed the button to close the hatch. Alla held on to him for just a moment, to steady herself. Then, with the hatch shut and latched, she removed her safety vest and went to Reid.

"Get away from him," she said, pushing Janina aside so she could kneel at the stretcher-bed. "You've done enough harm already. Don't do any more."

"She is assisting me, and she has been very helpful," Herne said in a loud voice. "You've had your moments alone with him, now it's Janina's turn."

"Alla, come forward, please, and make your report." That was Tarik's voice, heard through a speaker near Osiyar's head. Though she plainly did not want to leave Reid, Alla obeyed him, but not before sending a last angry look Janina's way.

"Did you open the communicator?" Herne glanced up from his patient to Osiyar. When Osiyar nodded and pushed the communicator button to closed position again, Herne said, "Thank you. That woman is too possessive of her cousin. I'm glad Tarik heard her. She will obey him."

"I think," Osiyar said, "that Alla ought to be induced to change her mind about certain matters."

"If you can make her change her mind about anything, the rest of us will be grateful to you. She's a difficult woman at the best of times, but since Reid has been missing she's been impossible."

"She was worried about him. I for one can't blame her for that." Janina was still tenderly stroking Reid's forehead while she closely watched everything Herne was doing. "Will he live?"

"I haven't finished my examination yet," Herne said, his voice rough. "Move away now, Janina, and give me more space. Go stand over there with Osiyar."

Herne pulled the heat blanket back and waved the silver instrument, which he had told Janina was a diagnostic rod, up and down over Reid's legs and feet.

"Where did he get these welts on his left ankle and right knee? I've never seen anything exactly like them before. You have the same kind of welt on your left wrist. What caused it?"

"Two sea monsters attacked us," Janina said, and heard Osiyar gasp. At Herne's insistence, she went on to explain what the monsters looked like and how she and Reid had fought them and won.

"You will have to tell Alla about this," Herne remarked absently, his attention mostly on the red marks on Reid's legs. "She's the specialist in interplanetary zoology. I wouldn't be at all surprised if she decides she wants to mount an expedition to capture one of your monsters so she can study it. Perhaps we ought to let her try."

Momentarily diverted from her concern over Reid, Janina smothered a giggle at Herne's dry tone of voice.

"No one," Osiyar said with awe deepening his voice, "has ever won a battle with a sea monster before."

"How could you know that?" Janina asked bitterly. "Except for my parents and one or two other unfortunates who were caught near the village, the only people who meet the monsters are those who are set adrift, and they are forbidden to return, aren't they?"

Herne refolded the heat blanket over Reid's

legs and straightened, looking grim.

"Will he live?" Janina asked again, almost afraid to hear the answer to her question.

"I'm not sure," Herne said, watching her face carefully. "Like yours, Reid's lungs are congested with inhaled sea water, and I have no doubt he swallowed a lot of it, too. He's suffering from severe exposure, his body temperature is well below normal, and he has several broken bones. He also has some kind of infection, though I don't know yet exactly what it is. It could be some toxic substance contracted from the sea monster through the punctures in those welts. As soon as we reach headquarters, I want to re-examine you, Janina, to find out if the infection you are suffering from is the same as Reid's."

"Why don't you put her in your hospital room along with Reid?" Osiyar suggested. "I am healthy enough now to move to an ordinary room. Janina will rest more easily knowing she is next to Reid, and you can watch over both of them. You will also be able to exert some control over Alla's concern for her cousin and prevent her from exhausting Janina with her accusations."

"That's a good idea," Herne replied, sending another sharp glance in Osiyar's direction. "You do need medical care, Janina. From what you have just said about your adventures, it's plain to me that you've both been through an ordeal that would have destroyed many people."

"Don't let it destroy Reid," Janina pleaded.

"He deserves to live, Herne. He fought so hard to be sure both of us would live. I would not have lasted one day without him."

When the shuttlecraft landed at the lake, Reid was still unconscious. Two of Tarik's colonists were waiting for them with a hoverbed, which Osiyar explained was propelled on a cushion of air. They laid Reid, still strapped to the foldable mesh stretcher in which he had been removed from the rocks, onto this floating bed and rushed him toward the headquarters building. Herne stayed with Reid every step of the way, monitoring his condition constantly. Alla ran with Herne. After rudely shouldering Janina aside, she kept one possessive hand on Reid's shoulder.

Feeling unable to face another confrontation with Alla, knowing she could be of no help to Herne, and certain he would tell her at once of any change in Reid's status, Janina followed more slowly, with a limping Osiyar as her guide. She stopped when she saw the building to which they were going.

"It looks just like the temple," she said.

"The designs are identical," Osiyar replied, resting for a minute on his walking stick before moving on again, "but this place is very different from Ruthlen, as you will see. I should say, as you will feel, for it differs most in the relationships among its inhabitants, who are remarkably diverse."

They were met at the entrance by a pretty, brown-haired woman with a warm smile.

"I'm Narisa, Tarik's wife," the woman said, showing Janina into the central room. "We have been in constant contact with Tarik, so I know your situation, and I am so glad he found you. You will want a hot bath and some food."

"I just want to be with Reid," Janina said, then stopped short at the sight of an obviously angry Alla.

"You aren't allowed in there," Alla said, indicating a closed door. "No one is, except Suria. Herne ordered me out of the room. If I can't be with him, you certainly can't."

"Alla, we both care about Reid," Janina responded. "We shouldn't quarrel when we want the same thing—Reid's quick recovery."

"If he dies," Alla spat at her, "it will be because of you."

"It is true," Janina said, "that if Reid and I hadn't loved each other, we never would have been set adrift. Instead, we would have remained at Ruthlen, to die when the volcano erupted. Would you have preferred that, Alla? At least Reid is still alive, and he is here, where Herne can help him."

Before Alla could answer that, Narisa spoke to her.

"Would you take over the computer-communicator for me? Gaidar has gone back to the *Kalina* to monitor a new volcanic eruption, so we need someone here to be in contact with him at all times."

"I would be most interested," Osiyar put in, speaking to Alla, "if you would explain your communications system to me. I would like to understand how you knew what was happening in Ruthlen."

"It's really very simple," Alla began, sparing one last baleful glance for Janina before turning toward the computer-communicator, taking Osiyar with her.

"Now," Narisa said with a smile, "let me show you our bathing room."

If she had not been so concerned for Reid, Janina would have enjoyed the next hour. The headquarters building was so like the temple at Ruthlen that she felt perfectly familiar with it. Yet, as Osiyar had said, there was a vital difference between the two. Where she had been accustomed to severity, and in some cases constant scorn, here she was treated with warm concern. After a hot bath that soaked the last of the ocean's chill from her bones, Narisa brought her a soft, pale green robe to wear, then fed her with vegetable stew and fresh, chewy bread. Tarik's wife spoke freely about the new colony, answered Janina's questions about the Chon, and explained how Osiyar had been found. Janina knew it was all an attempt to divert her from her fears for Reid. She was grateful, but nothing could dispell the knot in her stomach that tightened each time she looked at the closed door behind which her lover lay.

When the door finally opened, Herne stuck his head out, saw Janina, and put one finger on his lips, signaling silence. Alla had not seen the physician, since she was still at the computer-communicator with her back to the door while she spoke to Osiyar. Herne beckoned to Janina.

"Go on," whispered Narisa with a conspiratorial smile.

Janina slipped through the door as Herne closed it.

"He's conscious and lucid," Herne said, "but he is still very weak, and I can't get a diagnosis on that infection. He asked to see you. I think he wants to be certain you are really alive. You may have a few moments with him, and that's all." With that, Herne tactfully left them alone.

The door was hardly closed behind him before Janina was at Reid's side. Except for the spots of bright red on each cheek, Reid's face was pale, and his hand felt icy-cold when she clasped it in both of hers.

"You are here," he said in a weak voice. "I thought Herne was just saying that to make me feel better."

"We only have a moment or two," Janina began, intending to tell him how much she loved him. He interrupted her, and she let him speak, recognizing the great effort it was taking for him to get the words out, and knowing there must be something important he wanted to say.

"I felt you slip away," he whispered. "My hands were numb from the cold. I couldn't hold on to you any longer. When you were gone, I wanted to die, too." Janina saw tears in his eyes.

"Tarik says I must have fought my way out of the whirlpool and into a minor current that took me away and tossed me ashore," she told him.

"If Tarik hadn't found us, we would both surely have died. And if Osiyar hadn't had his vision of you drowning, they never would have looked for us where we were."

"Osiyar is here?"

Janina answered Reid's question with brief explanation.

"I cried out to Tamat," Reid said. "Do you suppose Osiyar heard me?"

"It is possible." Janina bent down to kiss him. Their tender moment was interrupted by a loud voice.

"You can't keep me out, Herne, so don't try."

The door to the sickroom opened and Alla appeared. Janina drew away from Reid. She would not upset him by quarreling with Alla in front of him. Behaving as though Janina was not in the room, Alla went to Reid and took his hand, smoothing his hair with her other hand as she kissed him.

"Herne says you will be better soon. Reid, I never stopped believing you were alive. I knew we would find you."

"Thank you, Alla," Reid said in a weak voice. "Have you met Janina?"

Alla's back went rigid. She glared at Janina.

"She," Alla stated hotly, "is the cause of all this. It's all her fault."

"I got lost," Reid told her, making an effort Janina could almost feel, "when I deliberately separated myself from you and Herne because the two of you were quarreling and I was sick of all the talk. I just wanted a few minutes of peace. But the forest was too thick, and I couldn't find you again."

"Are you trying to blame me?" Alla cried. "Reid, you are the closest thing to a brother I've ever known. I love you. I would never cause you harm!"

"Perhaps you love me too much," Reid whispered.

"*She* is the reason you were almost killed!"

"She saved my life. I love her," Reid said, closing his eyes in obvious weariness.

"Love her?" Alla gave a bitter laugh. "What about all the other women you've known? You never claimed to love any of them. Why this one?"

"Since the first day I met her," Reid said, forcing out the words, "there has been no one but Janina, nor ever will be. If she will have me, I'll marry her. I love you, too, Alla, and I want to be on good terms with you, but you will have to accept Janina."

"Never!"

"Alla," Janina said, seeing how ill and tired Reid was and wanting to spare him further argument, "face the thing you fear most, and fight it. That is what I had to do when we met the sea monsters. Let Reid go. You will be alone for a while, and I think that is what you fear most. But in time you will find a new center for your life."

"Don't you dare tell me what I ought to do!

Reid is my cousin, my only relative, my closest friend. I will *not* let him go."

"If you cling to him, he will pull away on his own and you will lose him. If you accept me, Reid will remain close to you, and in time we can all be friends."

"Reid, I will come back," Alla declared, "when you are alone and we can talk as we used to do."

"You will not be allowed back," Herne said, coming into the room. "I'll not have you two women fighting over my patient. Look at the man; you've drained what little strength he had. I want both of you out of here right now."

"Let Janina stay," Reid whispered.

"No," Janina said. "I want to be with you, you know that. But Herne is right. You need to rest."

She wanted to kiss him good-bye, but Herne had his silver diagnostic rod out and Alla was glaring at her, so she only smiled at Reid before she left him.

She was allowed to sleep in the hospital room that night, provided she did not try to talk to Reid. Herne stayed with them, periodically checking the lights and numbers on the panels behind the head of each bed. She slept better knowing he was there, keeping close watch over Reid.

Reid was still asleep when she rose in the morning. Though Herne, still in attendance, said nothing to her about his condition, she noticed that the lights and numbers behind his bed were very different from those behind her own bed, and the thought of what that might mean nagged at her.

When she had been to the bathing room and was dressed again in the pale green robe, she tried to re-enter the hospital room to see if Reid was awake yet. Narisa prevented her.

"You may not go in," Narisa said. "There has been a sudden deterioration in Reid's condition. Herne and Suria are with him. Herne said to tell you he will let you know soon just what is wrong. He ordered me to make certain you eat something in the meantime."

But Janina could not eat. She paced back and forth in the central room, all her thoughts on Reid. When Alla appeared, Narisa gave her the news about her cousin. With a grim face, Alla took her position at the computer-communicator, having said not one word to Janina.

Time passed with excruciating slowness until at last the door to Reid's room opened and a woman came out whom Janina had not seen before—a woman with flaming red hair and a beautiful face, set now in serious lines.

"I am Suria," the woman said to Janina. "Herne wants me to examine you and take tissue and blood specimens for analysis. Reid has developed a raging infection, and Herne thinks it may be the same infection he detected in you yesterday."

"Do you mean she's contagious?" Alla spoke from her seat at the computer-communicator across the room. "In addition to everything else she has done to Reid, she has also infected him with some unspeakable disease? Is that what Herne thinks?"

"What Herne thinks," Janina answered her, "is that the infection may have entered Reid's body during our battle with the sea monsters. Because I only have a small welt on my wrist, I may have a lesser infection. That is what he told me on our way here."

"So of course poor Reid must suffer, after fighting to save you," Alla cried, rising to come toward Janina. "Let me see this so-called welt."

"I am the one who fought off the monster when it would have eaten Reid," Janina said quietly, holding out her left arm.

She calmly faced a searching look from grey eyes unnervingly similar to Reid's, before Alla turned her attention to Janina's wrist.

"Look here, Suria." Alla pressed a slightly swollen spot, then bent closer to inspect a second area of darker red marks. "I'll take a tissue sample here, and extract what fluid I can from this area of induration. I'll analyze it at once. I may be able to make an antitoxin."

"Alla, Herne warned me to keep you away from Reid," Suria said gently. "You are too involved emotionally to be a rational nurse."

"I'm not going to nurse him. I have to admit Herne is right about that," Alla said. "But I am the one best qualified to investigate an injury caused by an animal. I'm the zoologist here. You do the examination and take the blood specimen; I'll worry about these welts. Janina, will you give me permission to remove some tissue?"

"If it will help Reid," Janina replied, looking right into Alla's eyes, "you may take my entire arm."

"Don't tempt her," Suria warned.

"If I refused," Janina said wryly, "she would probably hit me over the head and amputate my arm anyway, if she needed it. Wouldn't you, Alla?"

"Yes, I would." With that matter-of-fact statement, Alla swung around. "Narisa, can you monitor the computer-communicator for a while?"

"I am already here," Narisa replied. She had taken Alla's seat at the table in the center of the room. "Do everything you can for Reid. You are relieved of all other duties for now."

The two women took Janina to a small room that served as a laboratory. There Suria examined her with the silver diagnostic rod and took a series of specimens. Then Alla made Janina lay her arm on a sterile cloth while she removed from her wrist the fluid and tissue she needed to analyze the infection. Alla was not gentle about it, but Janina did not care. She could endure anything if it would help Reid.

"It has been several days since we were attacked," Janina said in answer to one of Alla's many probing questions about the sea monsters. "I'm not sure exactly how long ago it was. I soaked my arm in cold sea water shortly afterward. It seemed to help."

"Salt water." Alla pursed her lips. "What

about Reid? Did he soak his legs?"

"He was asleep. He was so tired, I guess he just ignored his injuries. It wasn't until the next day that he got into the water, when we repaired the rudder. Do you think that is why I'm not sick and he is?"

"I will know the answer to that question after I've analyzed these. That's all, Janina. I'm finished with you." Alla turned away, holding the tray with the specimens she had taken.

"Thank you, Janina," Suria said, smiling at her. "Why don't you try to sleep now? Herne suggested that you return to the second bed in the hospital room so he can check on you regularly. And I'm sure you would like to be with Reid."

Alla said nothing. She was busy at a nearby counter, working on the specimens.

CHAPTER 18

Janina slept all that day, waking in early evening.

"There is no change," Herne told her when she sat up on the edge of her bed to see Reid better. He was unconscious. There were so many tubes and machines surrounding him that she was unable even to take his hand. She choked back a sob.

"Osiyar is waiting for you in the central room," Herne said, sounding annoyed. "Go talk to him. You can't do anything here except get in my way."

She did as he suggested, knowing instinctively that Herne's harsh manner concealed a depth of concern for Reid and for her. Tamat had sometimes treated her in the same way when she was worried about her.

She found Osiyar just outside the hospital room door.

"Herne suggested I take you for a walk," he informed her. "I will introduce you to the Chon."

"I think we've met before," Janina said, recalling the large birds that had preceded Tarik's rescue crew. "Reid spoke about them to Tamat. I would like to see them again."

They walked on the soft white sand, watching the birds at their evening fishing while the sun sank into pink-gold glory, its last rays setting fire to the burnished late-season leaves of nearby trees. Osiyar went to the water's edge, where he stood silently for a while, until a large green bird lighted next to him.

"You may touch it," he said. "Open your mind, then put your hand on its wing."

"My mind will not open as yours does, Osiyar." Nevertheless, Janina followed the mental ritual she had used over and over again at Tamat's command. The bird stood watching her. Nothing happened except that Janina had an impression of patient politeness. She reached out to make contact with the stiff feathers of one wing. The bird let her touch it, then let her stroke the wing a few times, before it turned its attention to Osiyar. Janina saw Osiyar's face go smooth and still, and she sensed that the two were communicating. Then Osiyar smiled, nodding, and the bird flew away.

"I am in communion with them every day," Osiyar said, his expression and his voice filled with wonder. "It is a privilege beyond anything I ever dreamed of in Ruthlen. This is a place unequaled in my poor experience, Janina. Here, for the first time in my life, I feel free. Here I sense wonderful opportunities waiting."

Janina bowed her head, understanding what Osiyar meant. She felt much the same way about Tarik's colony. But there was a matter she could not let pass without discussion. She broke into the peaceful evening mood in order to obtain the answers she needed to know.

"Explain to me what happened in Ruthlen," she commanded boldly, knowing there would never be a better time than this to have the truth from Osiyar. "I have speculated frequently about Sidra—and about your relationship to her."

"Sidra was to blame for much of your unhappiness at the temple," Osiyar said. "She not only criticized you directly, but also in private, to the other priests and priestesses, to me, and even to Tamat. She wanted you eliminated from our ranks because she knew that Tamat loved you. She was jealous of that love. After Reid arrived in Ruthlen, Sidra understood that you were more truly bound to him than you could ever be bound as a priestess. She feared the power of your love for each other, feared it would change Ruthlen and imperil her own plans. She believed Reid had guessed her decision to destroy both of you as soon as Tamat was dead, and she intended to make certain that Tamat died once she had completed the Sacred Mind-Linking with Sidra. Whatever Tamat's true condition at the end of that linking, Sidra would make it appear that the strain had killed her, so Sidra would never be blamed. In her own strange way, she loved Tamat, but after so many years as Tamat's assistant she had grown impatient to assume what she believed was her rightful position. That impatience, coupled with her jealousy of you, led her to devise her evil plan."

"Was it your plan, too, Osiyar?" Janina silently vowed that if he had caused or even intended any harm to Tamat, she would see him punished.

"Sidra slowly drew me into her schemes," Osiyar admitted, "and then held me fast by the visions of forbidden ecstasy which she planted in my mind. But I never wanted you or Reid to be harmed. I agreed with Tamat that Reid was capable of bringing new vitality to the next generation. And eventually I came to understand that however carefully Sidra had cultivated her portion of the Gift, she was unfit to be High Priestess. Tamat knew it too, at the end, thanks to Reid's willingness to open his mind to her. It was only then that I at last knew the full extent of Sidra's plans."

Osiyar fell silent. Janina did not interrupt his thoughts, and after a while he began to speak again.

"In her deepest heart, Sidra had nothing but scorn for the restrictions of the Chosen Way. Once she was High Priestess, she intended to use the Gift in forbidden ways to gain absolute control over Ruthlen. After the Sacred Mind-Linking was completed and she had the ancestral memories, Sidra would have been stronger than any telepath in our history. She would have been unstoppable by any of the rest of us. Tamat knew that."

"Tell me about Tamat's end," Janina said.

"I was linked with her at the moment of her death, until the final instant, when she broke free so that she would not take me with her," Osiyar revealed. "She wanted me to live. She forgave me for my foolish involvement with Sidra, and forgave Sidra, too, though she would not relent in the imposition of Sidra's required punishment. Tamat's last thoughts were of you. She loved you, Janina, and had done everything she could do to help you escape safely."

The quiet sincerity of his explanation drove out of Janina's thoughts any idea that Osiyar might have harmed Tamat. She had been wrong to imagine such a thing for even a moment. Whatever his faults, Osiyar had always been loyal to Tamat, and to the Gift they both revered.

"Where is Sidra now?" Janina asked.

"Dead," Osiyar told her. "The entire village and the temple were destroyed. Herne and Alla were with Tarik when I was found. They will tell you I speak the truth."

"Then you and Reid and I are the only survivors?"

"We are, unless someone escaped without our knowing," Osiyar said, adding, "I am going to remain with Tarik's people. I want to begin a new life."

"So do I." Janina smiled at him, forgiving any part he had played in what had been done to herself and Reid. "I have changed, Osiyar. There is much to be said for setting people adrift and letting them find their own way."

"You will not be my enemy?"

"No. Tamat was fond of you, and I value her judgment. She said you were lost."

"Lost?" Osiyar gave a short, bitter laugh. "Adrift? Yes, I was. Now, perhaps I can find my way, too."

The shuttlecraft landed on the beach as Janina and Osiyar approached the headquarters building.

"Tarik has been to the spaceship *Kalina* to exchange personnel," Osiyar said, watching the hatch slide open. "Come and meet Gaidar."

A tall, burly man with yellow hair and a short, neat beard jumped onto the sand behind Tarik. His handsome face was punctuated by a nose that looked as though it had been broken several times, and a wide grin that reminded Janina of a naughty little boy.

"So, you are the rescued heroine?" he rumbled in a deep voice. Janina's extended hand disappeared into his. "Tarik tells me you saved Reid. Alla will be jealous of you." Even white teeth flashed as he laughed. He had golden eyes. With a frightening chill, Janina recalled what golden eyes meant. This man could only be—.

"Gaidar is a Cetan," Osiyar told her, watching her closely to observe her reaction when he confirmed her fear.

Janina began to tremble. She stared at the man before her, not understanding why he was with Tarik, or how apparently civilized people could permit a rapacious, violent barbarian to live among them. Gaidar tightened his grip on her hand, not letting her withdraw it. His smile certainly did not look evil. In fact, it conveyed warmth and friendliness.

"He's perfectly safe," Tarik said, having noticed the expression on Janina's face.

"No one is perfect," Gaidar noted. "Least of all me. But I promise I will not harm you, little Janina, and Suria is not at all afraid of me, so you needn't be, either."

"Suria?" Janina spoke in a weak, cracked voice, not quite believing what she was hearing and seeing.

"My mate, soon to be my permanent wife. You have met her, I think." Gaidar dropped Janina's hand to put one huge arm around her shoulders and hug her. The embrace stopped just short of crushing every bone in her upper body. "Welcome to headquarters," he said.

When Gaidar released her, he and Tarik started toward the building in the center of the island. Janina and Osiyar followed them.

"A Cetan lives here," Janina murmured, still unable to believe it. "He lives in peace and friendship with these good people."

"I had the same reaction when I first met him," Osiyar confided. "But I like him now, and I believe him when he says the Cetans will abide by their new treaty to wage war among the planets no longer."

"We in Ruthlen expended so much energy guarding against Cetans. For six hundred years, every day and every night the priestesses kept the blanking shield in place. They might have used the Gift for so many other things. And all those virgin lives, wasted."

"The shield was necessary when first it was begun," Osiyar replied. "Now is a different time from then. Ruthlen's great fault was that nothing ever changed there except the seasons. Tarik tells me it was the same in the Jurisdiction until recently. I have changed, too, Janina. I have learned that non-telepaths can be my friends, and that not all Cetans are barbaric marauders."

"And so you thought it amusing to introduce me to Gaidar without warning me." She shook her head, realizing that she was not the least bit angry with him for the trick. "You have developed a sense of humor, Osiyar."

"I never had anything to laugh about before," he said.

Janina and Osiyar, Narisa and Tarik, along with Suria and Gaidar were all sitting around a large table eating their evening meal when Herne came out of the hospital room with a grim face that told Janina the news was not good. At the same time, Alla appeared from the laboratory to join him.

"Come with me, Janina," Herne ordered abruptly. "Suria, I will need you, too."

"Of course." Suria rose, starting toward the hospital room door.

"What is it?" Tarik pushed aside his plate and stood too. "You may as well tell the rest of us, Herne. We are all Reid's friends and we're concerned about him."

"My guess was right," Herne said. "Alla's tests have confirmed it. Reid is suffering from an infection contracted during his battle with the sea monster."

"I fought the monsters, too, but I'm not sick," Janina said, unwilling to dwell on the possible meaning of Herne's somber expression.

"Yes, you are, you just don't know it yet," Alla told her. "But you will before much longer if you don't have treatment."

"Unfortunately, she is right," Herne said. "The welt on your arm is much smaller than either of those on Reid's legs, and the ice-cold sea water you soaked your arm in helped to cleanse your wound. By your account, Reid did not put his wounds into water until the following day. You do have the same infection he has, though in a milder form. Untreated, you will probably be miserably sick for a few days, after which, barring any unforeseen complications, you ought to recover. Reid will very likely die."

Janina could say nothing. She looked from Herne to Alla, seeing in Alla's grey eyes bitter confirmation of Herne's words, and a world of blame. In that instant Janina knew if Reid died, she did not want to go on living. He was her true mate. Without him life had no purpose.

Oddly, it was Gaidar the Cetan who seemed to understand what she was feeling. He came to her, and with a rough gentleness that touched her deeply, put one arm around her. She leaned against him in gratitude, trying desperately not to cry. Then she straightened and Gaidar let her go, again apparently understanding how she felt. She could not give way to tears or weakness. She had to be strong and ready to do whatever Herne might require of her. She would do anything necessary to help him save her love.

"Herne, what do you propose to do for Reid?" That was Tarik, cutting through all discussion and fearful emotion to reach the vital question.

"Alla has concocted a potion she insists is the antitoxin for this infection," Herne said. "I will have to trust her when she tells me it will work, because there's no time to test the stuff. I must admit her data seem accurate enough. We will give a small dose to Janina, to be certain she doesn't become as sick as Reid is, then give the rest to Reid and hope it doesn't kill him at once. After that, I want to put him into total suspension for twenty days. It's the only chance he has to live long enough for the antitoxin to work and his body to heal completely."

"No!" Alla took a menacing step toward Herne. "You never mentioned total suspension to me. It's too dangerous. I won't allow it."

"Do you want him to die?" asked Herne.

"My antitoxin is enough. It will work," she insisted.

"Reid's condition is so critical he won't survive the antitoxin," Herne asserted.

"What is this total suspension?" Janina asked.

"It slows all the body's functions," Herne explained. "It will give the antitoxin time to work and lessen any side-effects the medicine might have. It is Reid's only chance."

"You are going to kill him!" Alla shouted.

"Suria," Tarik ordered, "give us your opinion."

"Personal or professional?" Suria asked dryly, looking from Alla to Herne before meeting Tarik's serious gaze. "Alla would never do anything to harm Reid, so the antitoxin must be safe to use. And in spite of his sour personality, Herne is the best physician I have ever met. But I think we should also ask Janina's opinion. Reid is her mate."

"She has no right to say anything about Reid!" cried Alla.

"She has every right," Tarik responded. "Your remarks are out of order, Alla. Janina, tell us what you think."

"Herne, you are the doctor here. Do whatever must be done to help Reid live," Janina said. "Alla, if you need another specimen from my arm, take it. If draining all my blood and using it will help, do it. But please believe that I would rather die than see any harm come to Reid."

"I take it that means you vote for suspension," Herne said. "I'll get started at once. Suria, come help me."

"Just a moment." Osiyar stepped forward. "Is Reid conscious?"

"Not really," Herne answered. "He's semi-conscious every now and then. He does seem to know me."

"I have some training in healing," Osiyar said. "Let me help you ease Reid into this suspended state you propose for him, and later ease him out of it. If I can touch his mind and thus take away some of his fear and confusion, he will heal faster."

"Tarik?" Herne looked at his commander. "I won't allow this without your express permission. If I were in the Jurisdiction and let a telepath near a patient of mine, I'd be forbidden to practice medicine any more. However, I believe Osiyar just might be able to give Reid an extra chance to live."

"Permission granted." Tarik spoke without an instant's hesitation. "Thank you, Osiyar."

"Janina?" Herne's eyes were on her. "Will you agree to this?"

"Yes," she said. "I trust Osiyar. And I trust you."

"Alla?" Herne asked.

"No." Alla looked defiantly into Osiyar's eyes for a long moment. "Oh, all right. Yes, do it. But if Reid dies because of you, I will personally slit your throat, Osiyar."

"You may try," Osiyar said calmly.

"Come to the hospital room, Janina," Herne ordered. "I want to connect you to the life monitor, just in case you have an adverse reaction to Alla's magic potion."

Reid was breathing through a long green tube attached to a machine. His face was so waxy-white that she would have thought he had died while they argued over his treatment, were it not for the panel on the wall behind his bed, where lights blinked and numbers constantly changed. This was not the Reid she knew, not the tough, determined man who had sailed into dangerous and uncharted waters without flinching, nor the passionate, generous lover, either. She wanted to throw herself on his inert body and beg him to come back to her, but she feared that if she did, she might disconnect some of the tubes and harm him. She turned resolutely away from his bed, leaving him to the healing skills of Herne and Osiyar.

"Lie down here." Suria led her to the other bed in the room, the one Janina had been sleeping in each night.

"Let Alla give me the antitoxin," Janina said.

Suria looked surprised, but nodded. Alla looked even more surprised. Janina saw her frown a little, then shake her head, and she knew Osiyar had touched Alla's thoughts without seeking her permission because this was an emergency.

"She may dislike me, but she won't kill me," Janina said to Osiyar, who now stood with Herne beside Reid's bed.

"No, she won't," Osiyar agreed.

Alla held a short cylindrical object against Janina's upper arm. When she pressed a button at the top, the skin beneath the cylinder stung, then went numb.

"How do you feel?" Suria asked.

"Strange. Nauseated," Janina whispered. She began to choke and struggled to gasp out her next words. "Suria, I . . . can't . . . breathe." From a great distance she heard Herne's voice.

"She's having a severe reaction to the antitoxin! Suria, give me—"

Herne's urgent order faded into a loud roaring noise. Janina's head was spinning. The room went black. She was whirling through a lightless, soundless vortex where she could not breathe, or see, or hear anyone speaking to her. There was no pain, only blackness and a never-ending loneliness. She was swept deeper and deeper into the vortex. She knew it was useless to try to break out of it. She would never get out, never see Reid again, never be held in his arms, never tell him—what?

There was something she had to tell him, something urgent. She felt a small flutter inside her mind, a faint recognition of waiting life that Reid needed to know about. Another flutter and it was gone and nearly forgotten. Now she sank still deeper into blackness . . . emptiness . . .

nothingness. . . .

Janina. Love.

Reid?

Stay with me.

Reid, where are you?

Beloved . . .

Beloved. My only love . . .

Never leave me, beloved.

Reid!

Something caught her, held her mind, while the vortex spun downward and moved around her. She fought the new entity at first, because it was not Reid. Or was it? She sensed his presence, but now he was joined to another. And he was weak, even weaker than she. She wanted to cling to Reid, but he was separated from her by that other presence.

Osiyar! He was holding her, preventing her from falling further into the vortex. She felt the cool precision of his mind, and his calm assessment of the situation. He was holding Reid as well as Janina, keeping them from falling to the uttermost depths of that lightless black *thing*, and the effort was draining him. It would not be much longer before all three of them began to sink, and when they did, they would never return to the outer world.

Help me, Janina. Use your Gift, or Reid will surely die.

I have no portion of the Gift.

Tamat believed it was buried deep. The whisper in her mind faded. Osiyar was growing weaker.

She felt herself beginning to sink into the vortex again. Reid and Osiyar would fall with her unless she did something to stop what was happening.

Janina . . .

Reid?

Try, love . . . try . . . open your mind . . . and your heart . . . help Osiyar . . .

Reid, I don't want to lose you. I won't lose you. She tried. She fought with her own mind until suddenly what she sought came to her—a golden, singing power that pushed the black walls of the vortex away and filled her with joy at its unfolding.

She knew how to use it; she remembered the rules Tamat had drilled into her for useless years of unproductive hope. Now Tamat's hopes were fulfilled. This time, at last, Janina would not fail her.

Janina felt Osiyar's presence again, felt him growing stronger when they wove their minds together to protect Reid. Reid was so weak, so terribly weak, and he needed all the strength of both of them to support him, to keep him alive.

She had no sense of time. She and Osiyar held Reid away from the vortex with their linked minds, keeping him safe until she sensed a lightening of Reid's weight and felt him drifting away from her. Then she knew Herne had him in suspension and she and Osiyar could let him go.

Even as she knew it, she felt Osiyar begin to separate his mind from hers. It was as though he took her hand and led her out of the widening vortex, which now was filled with golden light.

Rest, Janina. Osiyar's thoughts removed themselves from hers and set her free.

A pearly-grey mist drifted through her mind, a soft, opalescent mist. When it faded, she knew nothing more. . . .

CHAPTER 19

*She was walking through a meadow, hand-in-*hand with Reid. Yellow and white and purple flowers starred the long grass, while blue butterflies skimmed from blossom to blossom, sipping the sweet nectar they offered. The purple-blue sky arched cloudless overhead, and a gentle breeze blew. A short distance away the rippling river flowed, with their boat rocking lightly at anchor in the cove.

Janina wore a long white gown and flowers in her silver-gold hair. Reid was in his orange treksuit. He had left it open at the neck, so she could see the beginning of the dark hair on his chest.

She knew that when their walk ended at the beach beside the cove, they would lie down upon the vines that covered the gravel and there they would make love. But first she had something to tell him, a surprise to delight him and turn his fierce grey eyes soft with tenderness and joy. She had never been so happy. She would wait no longer. She would tell him now.

She stopped walking and caught his other hand in hers, turning him to face her. They stood among the flowers and the blue butterflies, hands linked, a tall, dark man with broad shoulders, and a small, slender woman whose pale hair streamed down her back.

"I love you," he whispered, and began to fade.

"Don't go," she pleaded. "I have to tell you . . ."

He was gone. He had disappeared and yet he was everywhere, in her and around her, filling her heart and mind, her very soul.

The beautiful landscape faded away as Reid had, leaving Janina in a white-walled hospital room where Reid's body lay encased in an oblong, pale blue bubble.

Had her walk with him been a dream, or had their minds in some mysterious way linked again to return to the place where she had first experienced freedom and joy with him? Certainly he was gone from her now. Through the translucent material surrounding him, she could just barely make out his profile. There was no movement at all within the bubble, and no sound. The lights on the panel behind his bed no longer blinked; they just stayed lit, and the flashing numbers did not change.

What the outcome of the suspension treatment would be she could not guess, but she was certain that Reid was, for the time being at least, safe under Herne's care. She had been with Reid, she had touched his mind, and he knew how much she loved him and wanted him to come back to her. Now she would have to be patient and wait.

She turned her head a little and saw Osiyar lying on a hoverbed with his eyes closed.

"He is sleeping," Suria said, moving into Janina's line of vision. "How do you feel?"

"I'm not sure. I'm light-headed. My thoughts are still fuzzy."

"That was to be expected. You had a severe allergic reaction to the antitoxin," Suria said.

"Did Reid?" Janina asked at once.

"No. We were afraid he might, after what happened to you, but Herne said we had no choice, we had to give him the injection. Reid had no adverse reaction at all. After the injection, Osiyar helped him into the suspended state, which is why Osiyar is sleeping now. He was completely worn out after finishing with Reid."

"Yes, I remember." Seeing Suria's curious look, Janina shook her head, realizing that her new friend could not understand all that had happened while Osiyar's mind was linked to Reid's.

"If you want, I will bring you something to eat," Suria offered.

Janina was ravenously hungry. She quickly ate everything Suria gave her, before falling asleep again. She wakened to find Reid's condition unchanged, but Osiyar and the hoverbed were gone.

"He's by the lake, with the Chon," Herne said in answer to Janina's question. "You may get up if you want. You are perfectly healthy now, though you will probably feel weak for a day or two. Go on, the fresh air will be good for you. There is nothing new to report about Reid, so for the moment think of your own health."

She found Osiyar in communion with the Chon. She was tempted to try to communicate with them as he did, but when she would have opened her mind to them, she suddenly felt sick and dizzy. By the time she had recovered, Osiyar was standing before her, looking worried.

"I thought if I could touch them," she said, "then I might be able to reach Reid, too."

"Do not even think of it," he commanded. "You cannot wake your portion of the Gift by the ordinary discipline most telepaths use. You are different.

"Janina," he said with a quiet confidence that reminded her that he had once been a High Priest, "after my experience with you and Reid, I am convinced that your portion of the Gift is buried so deep within you that it can only be released by artificial means. It was released the first time after Tamat prepared the potion for your Testing. The second time was when you received the antitoxin Alla made. Perhaps the two mixtures were similar in some way. But let the Gift rest where it is. Reid will not think any less of you, nor will anyone here, including me, if you cannot function as a telepath."

Janina nodded agreement, knowing he was right. Nor would he have accepted thanks for what he had done for her and for Reid. His help had been only what was expected of a High Priest of Ruthlen, and her thanks would have been as insulting as an offer to pay him.

But whatever Osiyar or the others might think of Janina, there was one on that island who did not like her at all. When she and Osiyar turned to walk back to the headquarters building, Alla stood blocking their way.

"I see you are fully restored to health," Alla said in a provocative tone of voice. "While poor Reid lies immobilized, you are free to go wherever you want."

"I wish with all my heart that I were in suspension, and Reid was standing here on the beach," Janina cried.

"Of course you do," Alla said in the same tone.

"Alla, there is an important fact that you should know," Osiyar told the angry woman before them. "When you and Herne were lost in the forest near Ruthlen, it was Janina who finally convinced Tamat to let Tarik know where you were so you could be rescued. She saved your lives, Alla."

"How generous of her," Alla sneered. "Yet she kept Reid in Ruthlen for herself, didn't she?"

"She begged Tamat to let him go. Janina loves Reid enough to want to see him freed from a situation that was making him unhappy, even though his leaving would have broken her heart.

It was not Janina, but Tamat, who told me this," Osiyar said, when Alla would have interrupted again. "That is love, Alla—to be willing to sacrifice what you want for the good of the loved one. Perhaps you ought to think seriously about Janina's example."

"I thought you knew nothing about love," said Alla, and then fell silent. Osiyar motioned for her to walk ahead of him and Janina. The three of them took the path to the center of the island.

"Tell me," said Osiyar, one foot on the first step leading to the great double doors, "have you opened the safe stone yet?"

"What stone?" Alla asked.

"Tell her, Janina," commanded Osiyar with what Janina considered an astonishingly mischievous smile. Though Alla stood puzzled and frowning by the doors, Janina knew what Osiyar meant. She answered his command promptly, wondering as she did so just what he was planning.

"If this building is like the temple at Ruthlen and like the pavilion in our sacred grove," Janina said, "the stone just behind the third step as you walk to the entrance will open. It is traditionally a safe place to hide the most important documents, those that must never be lost. Under both stones at Ruthlen, there were medical supplies for any emergency, along with a map showing the way to Tathan, the old city. Tamat used to tell us there was a map beneath the safe stone of every building the original settlers erected."

"The only information we found here was on the computer-communicator the telepaths had left behind," Alla said. "There are rather cryptic directions to the old city, but no map, and we have been unable to locate the city using the directions."

"Have you looked beneath the stone?" asked Osiyar.

"How could we?" Alla snapped. "We didn't know about it."

"Janina, will you ask Tarik to join us?" said Osiyar. As Janina disappeared into the building, he knelt to push hard at the end of one of the smooth white stones at Alla's feet. "Alla, help me. It has been six hundred years since this stone was last moved."

Alla was on her knees beside him, pushing on the stone with him when Janina returned with Tarik. Tarik got down on the steps with Alla and Osiyar, to grab at the slightly raised edge opposite the spot where the other two were pushing. After a good deal of straining, the stone finally swung open. Within the space now revealed lay a packet wrapped with smooth, shiny fabric. Tarik lifted it out.

"We will open it inside," he said, his face alight with excitement.

After he had unwrapped the document inside the packet, he carefully unfolded it, spreading it out on the table where they usually took their meals.

"There," Osiyar said, one finger hovering just above a line of delicate writing on the aged, cracked piece of fibrous material. "That is where Tathan lies. Shall we visit the city of my ancestors, Tarik? As you can see, it is near the equator. The coming cold won't matter there. If we leave quickly enough, the expedition members can escape the worst of the winter storms and will have no difficulty traveling."

"Using a shuttlecraft and this map, it wouldn't take long to reach," Tarik agreed. "Yes, I will consider it."

"So close to this planet's equator, there will be new varieties of tropical plant and animal life to discover," Alla mused, her eyes on the map.

Janina saw Osiyar's humorous glance resting on Alla. Later, after Tarik had refolded the map and stored it in a safe place, and after Alla had gone into her laboratory, Janina drew Osiyar away from the other people now in the central room.

"Thank you for diverting Alla and giving her something else to think about besides Reid and how much she dislikes me," she said.

"I plan an even longer diversion for Alla," Osiyar told her. "It will not be difficult to make certain she goes on that expedition."

The venture to Tathan was proposed to the assembled colonists that evening and was enthusiastically agreed upon. Within a day, preparations were under way, though no participants had yet been chosen.

The autumn days passed slowly. Janina recovered completely from her ordeal on the sea and from the adverse reaction to the antitoxin, but she continued to suffer occasional bouts of nausea. Finally, during one of the frequent examinations Herne insisted upon, she mentioned her problem to Suria.

"Most pregnant women experience some nausea in the beginning," Suria said. "It will disappear in time."

"Pregnant?" Janina, watching Suria's expression change from amusement to shock, thought she must have looked equally shocked. "Pregnant," she said again.

"I thought you knew," Suria cried. "I detected it the first time I examined you, but it is such a private thing I never mentioned it to you or anyone else until you were ready to speak of it. I thought you didn't want to talk about it because you and Reid have no permanent arrangement and because of the Jurisdiction regulations about childbearing. I just assumed that Herne knew and was advising you, but I haven't had a chance to discuss all of my medical findings with him because most of his time is taken up with Reid, and we have been dealing only with immediate problems. Oh, Janina, I am sorry I was overly discreet! But of course, if you were trained as a virgin priestess, you probably never considered the possibility, did you? Nor thought of ways to prevent it."

"I wouldn't have wanted to prevent it. The child is part of Reid, and therefore precious to me. Suria, I think I did know. When I was so sick, when Osiyar—" she stopped, recalling the tiny flutter she had felt when she and Reid and

Osiyar were caught in that terrible black vortex. She had sensed another presence there, an entity not yet fully formed. And there had been the wonderful secret she had been about to share with Reid when they walked in the meadow. Yes, she had known. "Could the antitoxin have hurt the baby in any way?" she asked, suddenly frightened for the new life within her.

"That is a good question, and one I did not ask earlier because your life was in danger and there was no doubt you needed the antitoxin. Let me do a more complete examination on this child of yours." Suria took up the diagnostic rod and adjusted it. A few minutes later she reported, "All is well, Janina. There is nothing to worry about."

"A baby." Janina put her hands on her still-flat abdomen. "What a wonderful thing to tell Reid when he wakes up. He will wake up, won't he, Suria?"

"We can hope for the best," Suria said evasively. Then, taking Janina's hand, she went on. "I want you to know that I am a midwife. Herne and I both will be available to you when your time comes. Your child will be born safely."

In the current atmosphere of hushed concern for Reid that pervaded Tarik's headquarters, Janina's happy face brought puzzled looks until she revealed her good news to Narisa, and then to everyone else.

"That's wonderful," Narisa said, hugging her.

"If you were living in Jurisdiction territory," Alla informed her coldly, "you would be severely punished for conceiving a child without permission."

"She is not in the Jurisdiction, she's under my command." Tarik came to Janina's defense. "If she and Reid want a child, that is their concern, not yours."

"Reid is unable to say whether he wants this child or not," Alla cried. "Who's to say it really is Reid's? Who knows what happened at Ruthlen, or what kind of life she led there?"

"I am here to say that Janina was never touched by any man until Reid came to Ruthlen," Osiyar declared.

"Of course you will take her side," Alla said spitefully.

"Come with me, Alla." Osiyar's voice was soft. "I would speak with you in private."

Alla looked rebellious, but she followed Osiyar outside the building. Behind them, Tarik looked at Janina with raised brows.

"Is he controlling her?" Tarik asked.

"Not in the way you mean," Janina replied, adding, "He would never harm her."

"Perhaps it's Osiyar's safety that ought to concern us," Tarik said with a laugh, and turned back to his work.

When they came to his favorite spot on the beach, Osiyar stopped, facing Alla. Behind him rose the cliffs, with the Chon flying in and out of their homes in the rock.

"This behavior is unworthy of you," Osiyar said with blunt sternness. "Your childish jealousy is evident to everyone who hears you attack Janina. Leave her alone. She and Reid have been bound together since she foretold his coming to Ruthlen."

"What nonsense! Reid was my cousin first, before ever he met that fool of a girl," Alla stated with a stubborn forward thrust of her lower lip. "But now she is having his child. It will never again be the same as it was between Reid and me. She has won, and I have lost him."

"You speak as though you owned him. No one can own another person," Osiyar told her. "What you need is someone to fulfill your desires, including the desires you are not aware you have."

He was pleased when she did not pretend to misunderstand him.

"There is no one among the colonists that I would be interested in," Alla responded with a lift of her proud chin.

"Do you know what I'm thinking?" Osiyar asked.

"Of course not. I'm not a telepath," she said with some sharpness.

"I'm thinking that I am not one of the colonists," Osiyar said. "I'm thinking that you are a beautiful woman. And a lonely woman. As I am alone."

"Is this a declaration of love?" Alla scoffed.

"I have never loved." Osiyar smiled a little. "But lately I have known friendship—for Reid and Janina, for Tarik, and even for Gaidar. I can offer you friendship."

"Only friendship?"

"Don't laugh at friendship. It is a rare and unusual thing." Osiyar took a deep breath before he went on. "My old life is gone. All the vows and expectations that bound me while I was in Ruthlen are dissolved now. It is time for me to make a new beginning. It is time to take a mate."

She was silent, looking away from him, watching the birds fly across the lake to fish. When she spoke again, he knew her brilliant mind had leapt to the important issue behind his unemotional proposal.

"Will your children be telepaths?" she asked, still not looking at him.

"If I chose the right mother for them," he replied.

"Such children would be difficult to raise."

"Not if both parents take part in the raising."

"What you suggest is, in fact, an experiment," she said, sounding interested in the possibility.

"In interplanetary zoology," he added with apparent seriousness. "It is your specialty, is it not?"

"That, and botany." She did look at him then, right into his eyes with fearless curiosity. "What happens when you mate? Do you invade your partner's mind?"

"Not at first. Not until you are ready for the stronger bonding. I would instruct you, so you would know what to expect. It is not a thing to fear, Alla."

"I'm not afraid." She sounded almost defiant. "I was only asking a question."

"Beyond your justifiable concern," he said, "lies a deeper intimacy than you have ever known, and delicious, unimaginable pleasure."

"Intimacy?"

"Do you fear it?"

"I always have," she responded honestly.

"Except for Reid, who is your close kin, and therefore forbidden to you. And therefore safe to love, for you will never be disappointed in something you cannot have."

"Have you read my mind already, Osiyar?"

"No. And it is not a 'reading,' it is a knowing. There is a difference."

"You would know me, but I could never know your mind."

"Ah, but you could. There is more to you than you realize." He saw that her stubborn lower lip was trembling. To his own surprise, he felt an urgent desire to kiss that hard yet vulnerable mouth. He put out his right hand and laid it on her shoulder. She did not move away. "Will you take the first step with me, Alla?"

"Yes," she said, "I will. But you understand, I do it only in the interests of scientific research."

"Of course," he said, drawing her into his arms. "And so do I, my lovely experiment. So do I."

"Narisa, if I am to go to Tathan, then you, as my second in command, will have to remain behind," Tarik told his wife.

"I refuse to obey that order," Narisa declared. "Gaidar and Suria can manage very well, and we have an excellent second communications officer to take Reid's place. If there should be an emergency here, we can return within a few hours, and if we are needed aboard the *Kalina*, we can reach orbit as easily from Tathan as from here. You and I will go, along with Osiyar and Alla."

It took three more days of discussion, but at last Tarik accepted Narisa's argument.

"I cannot leave until Reid is well," Alla insisted. "I am not certain I should go at all." Day after day she continued to waver, until Osiyar, understanding the conflict she felt, spoke to Tarik, and Tarik commanded her to join the expedition whether Reid recovered or not.

On the night before they were to leave for Tathan, Herne and Osiyar closed themselves into Reid's hospital room while Osiyar linked his mind with Reid's once more, this time to ease him out of suspension.

"He will waken in a day or two, perhaps sooner," Herne announced hours later. "He will recover, Alla. You may leave tomorrow without any worry for him."

The next morning, after all the good-byes had been said and the shuttlecraft was just about to lift off from the beach, Herne arrived, beckoning to Janina, who had walked to the beach with Osiyar.

"He's awake," Herne said. "You may see him now."

Janina started to run up the beach—and stopped just as she reached the trees. Spinning around, she raced back to the shuttlecraft, where Osiyar was sliding the hatch shut.

"Wait!" she cried, waving both arms. "You have to wait. Osiyar, let me inside. Alla! Alla, Reid is awake. Go to him."

Without a word to Janina, Alla tumbled through the hatch and ran for the headquarters building.

"So much for generosity," Herne said to Janina. "She didn't even thank you."

"I will have Reid for all of my life," Janina replied. "Alla must give him up, and she has to do it now, this morning. Reid will tell her so."

But Alla stopped before she reached the path through the trees. Turning, she retraced her steps until she stood before Janina.

"You would have let me see him first," she said. "Why?"

"You love him," Janina responded. "And he loves you. You are his only blood kin. Go on, Alla. Tarik will wait for you."

"No." Alla tried to smile, but could not. Janina saw the quickly-banished tears, and the loss in Alla's face, before Alla set her features into a hard mask.

"You are not the only one who can give up your love for his own good," Alla said in a tight, cold voice. "You carry his child inside you. Reid's child makes us kin, Janina, whether I like it or not. He needs to know about the baby. Go tell him. And tell him—say I love him but I have important work to do. Tell him I said good-bye."

Janina put out both hands, wanting to touch

Alla, to let her know how much her sacrifice meant, for it was a great sacrifice on Alla's part. Alla brushed her hands aside, turning toward the shuttlecraft where Osiyar waited in the hatchway.

"Good-bye," Janina called after her. "Good luck."

With no last look but only a quick backward wave of one hand, Alla disappeared into the hatch. Osiyar closed the door and a moment later the shuttlecraft roared into the sky.

Reid looked remarkably well for someone who had been so sick for so long. Sitting on the side of his bed, Janina put her arms around him.

"I felt you with me," he murmured. "You and Osiyar. My love and my friend."

"Hush," Janina whispered, wanting him to rest. "I'll tell you all about it later. We are safe now, Reid. Our long journey is over. I'm only sorry I was such a coward about so many things along the way."

"You are no coward at all," Reid said. "You are the bravest woman I have ever known, and the most intelligent. You saved my life twice."

She considered his words, realizing that she no longer thought of herself as weak or stupid. Still . . .

"I was terrified every moment," she said.

"So was I," Reid admitted.

"You?" She stared at him in wonder. "You are no coward."

"It's not absence of fear that keeps a person

from being a coward," he said, "but the determination to fight through the fear to do the thing that must be done. You certainly accomplished that."

"Face the thing you fear," she murmured softly.

"What did you say?"

"Nothing," she replied, smiling to herself with sudden confidence. "Nothing at all."

She snuggled closer to him, tucking her head under his chin. His lips repeatedly brushed her forehead, until she lifted her face and their mouths met. His arms tightened around her.

"You are supposed to be convalescing," she scolded when she could speak again.

"I believe a little gentle exercise is beneficial to those who have been ill," he responded solemnly, pulling her against him once more.

"Herne may come in at any moment."

"Herne will leave us alone."

"Then Suria—" She could not finish what she meant to say, for his mouth stopped her words.

It was not the vigorous loving she had known with Reid in the past. He was still too weak for that, but Janina understood that it was vitally important to him to claim her once more for his own. He wooed her with gentle caresses, while she kissed and fondled and nibbled in return, and finally slid beneath him to pull him down on top of her. And when she felt him deep within her at last, she knew that she had needed this lovemaking, too, had needed her own affirmation of his love for her.

When they were both completely satisfied, she lay with her head on his shoulder and her hand at his waist while his fingers laced through hers.

"How do you like Alla?" he asked.

"She doesn't approve of me," Janina murmured.

"She has never approved of any woman I've known," Reid said with a chuckle. "I'm surprised she didn't get to my room before you did. Or didn't anyone tell her I was awake?"

"I told her," Janina replied, and delivered Alla's message to him.

"She has gone away?" Reid asked, incredulous. "I can't believe this."

"She will be back soon. It's only a ten-day preliminary expedition," Janina said, laughing a little. "She went with Osiyar. She has spent a lot of time with him recently."

"With Osiyar? Alla and Osiyar?" Reid began to laugh. Janina joined him. They made so much noise that Herne slid the hospital room door open a little to see if anything was wrong. When he spied Janina's green robe on the floor, and two forms beneath the blue hospital blanket, he quietly closed the door again and went away, leaving them to their love.